SUPERNATURAL.
THE USUAL SACRIFICES

ALSO AVAILABLE FROM TITAN BOOKS:

SUPERNATURAL™
THE USUAL SACRIFICES

YVONNE NAVARRO

SUPERNATURAL created by Eric Kripke

TITAN BOOKS

Supernatural: The Usual Sacrifices
Print edition ISBN: 9781783298563
E-book edition ISBN: 9781783298570

Published by Titan Books
A division of Titan Publishing Group Ltd
144 Southwark St, London SE1 0UP

First edition: June 2017
10 9 8 7 6 5 4 3 2 1

This one's for Alex, who's grown up in the most spectacular way.

HISTORIAN'S NOTE
This novel takes place during season ten, between
"The Hunter Games" and "Halt & Catch Fire."

PROLOGUE

He'd come in here on a self-appointed mission, to see if he could end, once and for all, the hellish secret that was finally tearing the town apart. Too many people had died over too many years. Everyone knew what was going on yet no one would admit it, much less bring it out in the open and figure out how to end the problem. Well, it was high time somebody stepped up. No pre-planning but that was okay—no one knew this area better than he did, no one could. He'd been born in this county and had spent decades exploring, only to be here, right now—

Running for his life.

A rock bounced onto the path somewhere behind him. He spun, then froze, trying to hear if there was more movement. He couldn't tell above the noise his own body was making; no matter how he tried to suppress it, his breathing whooshed in and out of his thin chest, sounding like a bellows being pumped in front of a fireplace. His heart was pounding so hard both temples pulsed, and each beat sent a jagged, thin flash of lightning at the edges of his vision, a sign that his blood pressure was way too high. That was the least of his worries, and the best he could hope for was to not get a sudden angina attack.

Three more rocks—closer to the size of small boulders— rolled onto the path, far enough away that he could barely see them at the edge of the weak cone of light given off by his flashlight. These were followed by a pattering of small pebbles, the sort of sounds made by someone perhaps scuffing their feet across the ground… actually, several someones, although nothing showed on the path behind him except dull, gray rock.

He knew this route, had traveled it many times, although never while being hunted like this—something had altered, a shift in the ground had opened up a new path where one should never have been. Be that as it may, there was a fork in the passage not too far ahead. On the right was a wide, clear path, on the left a small offshoot that, if he could get to it in time, he could scramble up and might be too narrow for them to follow. He hadn't moved this fast in years, but he thought he might just have a chance of making it. Of course, those same years had made him older, his bones more brittle, his joints more painful.

Body, don't fail me now, he thought as he swung the flashlight back to light his way, then clawed himself along, following the dull swaying beam. His breathing was harsher now, each exhalation exploding from his chest with a cough, each inhalation a strained wheeze. He was too old to be in here, his frame made too frail by age, his old man knees unstable. No, he was not too old. He would not give in, splay himself across the dirt like some gristly old sacrifice. Stubbornness kept him going even though he scraped his hands on the walls right through his gloves and felt jagged rock gouge into his shoulder despite the heavy denim of his shirt.

He skidded to a stop at the fork, then lurched left and pulled himself up, the palms of his hands burning as he pawed at the rock walls and sent loose stones downward, searching for places that would hold his weight. The stringy muscles in his thin arms quivered, but in the end they held; the tunnel was small and nothing followed, and he climbed, up and up, toward the safety of a distant, small circle of light he knew was somewhere overhead.

All the while imagining he could feel their hot and hungry breath at his ankles.

ONE

"Find something interesting?"

Dean Winchester looked up as Sam, his younger brother, came up behind him and looked over Dean's shoulder at the computer screen. "I might be getting an itch," he said.

Sam grinned. "Maybe you've got bugs."

"Funny," Dean muttered. "Check this out." He pushed his chair aside so that Sam could get close enough to read.

Brownsdale, KY—April 4: The Edwardson County Sheriff's Department issued an AMBER Alert for twin thirteen-year-old girls Marley and Fallon Dietz when they failed to return to their cousin's home the previous day. Both girls are described as being five-feet tall and slender, with blue eyes and brown hair. No foul play has yet been proven and the sheriff's department believes there is a possibility that the girls may have run away. Photos and more information is available on the county website.

Sam frowned as he got to the end of the paragraph, then his gaze caught his brother's.

"Pretty interesting, am I right?" Dean poked at the screen to emphasize his words.

Sam nodded. "Is that all there is?"

"For this incident, yeah." Dean tapped a few more keys, then hit the Enter key hard enough to make the keyboard bounce. "But then there are these." The screen filled with images of news clippings. "They date back… well, a long way."

"What the hell?" Sam pushed his hair off his forehead. "Are those what I think they are?"

"You win the prize, little brother." Dean used the mouse to scroll down, faster than either of them could read. "Disappearances."

Sam stared at him. "You're kidding. From the same town?"

Dean shook his head. "No, but definitely from the same county—there are a dozen or more towns around there ranging in size from almost no one to seven or eight thousand people. It looks like most of them were 'invisible.' You know, homeless kids, hitchhikers, transients, drunks. People no one cares about."

Dean got up and went around the table so Sam could sit in front of the computer. Sam knew exactly what Dean was talking about. In a way, wasn't that what they were… invisible? Sure, they interacted with people all the time, not to mention those of the non-human variety. And yeah, maybe he and Dean were memorable, but not to… normal folks. And normalcy, let's face it, constituted most of the world. Although they had a badass reputation in the realm of the weird, when he and Dean were finished with a case, had figured out a way to get rid of whatever Big Bad was trying to claw its way through, who in the ordinary world remembered them?

That was probably just as well.

He blinked and realized Dean was looking at him, one eyebrow arched. "You have something to say?"

"If they're people no one misses, how do you know they're missing to begin with?"

"Call it a hunch." Sam's fingers did a quick staccato over the keyboard. "Let's check the math." He waited as his data search was completed, then nodded. "Yeah. The numbers are there, at regular intervals—they aren't that hard to spot. I think the local law just doesn't want to see it." Over the last few hours Sam had pulled a fair number of old record books down, and now he slid one across the wood tabletop.

Dean picked it up and read the spine: *The Untold History of Kentucky*. "Seriously? You're quoting statistics from a book that's…" He flipped the cover open, barely keeping the pieces together when the front and the first few pages tried to break away from the battered spine. "From 1949? How is that going to help?" He dropped that one, then reached for an even older book. "*Hunters of Kentucky: A Narrative History of America's First Far West, 1750–1792*," he read. "Published in—" he rolled his eyes—"1853. Are you looking for a case or taking a history lesson?"

"It's a matter of combining the old and the new to come up with an up-to-date educational calculation."

"Ah," Dean said. "A wag."

"What?"

"Wild-ass guess."

TWO

Most—okay, almost all—of the time when they were driving to the next case, it seemed to be raining and in the dark. Or maybe that was just the way Dean felt, like a character in a cartoon who had a little black thundercloud floating over his head all the time, complete with raindrops and zaps of lightning. Except in his version, the zaps were shaped like the Mark of Cain and did crap like melt your face off if they hit the right spot. But Baby, his beloved Impala, was here for them all the time, slipping down the highways like a grumbling black shadow, and if nothing else came through for them she had their backs, keeping them warm, dry, and protected on their travels.

No rain this time, though. As usual, Dean had driven straight through the night, and by the time he and Sam rolled into the town of Brownsdale, Kentucky a brilliant sunrise was a couple of hours behind them. As they cruised down the main thoroughfare Sam and Dean rolled down the windows, getting a dose of the clean-smelling air as it warmed up. The street was like something out of a Grant Wood painting of rural America, all vintage red brick buildings with colorful signs displaying old-fashioned lettering. There were wrought iron and wooden benches next to the doorways of some of the shops, and pots brimming with purple, white and scarlet petunias next to others. No traffic yet, but—

"Is that birdsong?" Sam asked. His tone sounded doubtful as he stuck his face out the window. "I can't remember the last time we heard that. It's—"

"Creepy," Dean said. "Yeah, I know." He scanned the street but it was too early to be especially busy.

"This place kind of reminds me of that movie where robots replace the women and make everything perfect," Sam said.

"*Stepford Wives*," Dean put in.

Sam frowned at him. "I thought you only watched porn."

Dean shrugged. "It had its moments."

Sam rolled his eyes then turned his attention back to the street. "Look up there on the right. There's life in this place after all."

"Setting up for something," Dean said. "Let's check it out." He pulled the car to the curb and cut off the engine, then sat there for a moment, studying Main Street. They were a quarter block from a T-intersection where yellow and red tents, three in all, had been set up on the sidewalk across from where a smaller street turned off the main one. A few people were puttering around at tables that had been set up under the tents, but from this distance Sam and Dean couldn't figure out what they were doing. After a couple of minutes two women stepped out and hung a sign that ran the length of all three tents.

"Brownsdale Car Show and Arts and Crafts Festival," Sam read aloud. "Seems safe enough, plus it might be a good chance to talk to the locals."

"Let's go," Dean said. They got out of the car and walked down the street to where it split at Green Street. The main drag had been empty, but now they saw where everyone had gone. An assortment of vehicles were parked on both sides for a good three blocks down, with another line of cars end to end in the center of the wide street. There was everything from Corvettes and pickups to gorgeous muscle cars from the fifties and sixties. Here and there in the lines were true relics, heavy pick-up trucks and low-slung sedans from the forties, even a couple of Model Ts. The polished colors looked painfully bright in the strong morning sunlight, the abundant chrome and mirrors making starburst glare patterns. Nice stuff to look at, although Dean thought Baby was way above the crowd in this motor show.

Set behind many of the cars were lawn chairs, side tables and smaller canopies meant to provide shade. The majority of the chairs were empty, with the car owners still working to get their vehicles just right, polishing chrome, using hand vacuums on the floorboards, carefully wiping dust from the dashboards and shining up the windows. Most of the men and women ignored Sam and Dean as they walked down the blocks, still deep in the process of getting ready for the show. It was a small town but there was a pretty good turnout— maybe there was more going on here than bragging rights, like a cash prize.

When they paused to admire a lime-green 1967 Camaro

SS with black racing stripes, a middle-aged woman smiled at them from a chair behind it. "How y'all doing this morning?" she asked. "Looking like it'll be a nice day for the show."

"We're good," Sam answered. "You?"

"Just fine." Her southern accent was strong enough to make the words sound like Jus' faihn. "This baby's for sale, if you're interested. Completely restored, and the engine has all genuine parts."

"Bet that took a while," Dean said. "Thanks, but we're set."

She perked up. "Yeah? Got something good, I take it?"

Dean smiled slightly. "Oh, yeah. An Impala, same year as yours."

"Nice," she said. She looked at them speculatively. "My name's Lucy. You boys aren't from here, are you?"

Sam smiled at her. "What tipped you off?"

"Yankee accents," she declared. "Not that I have any problem with the northerners," she hastened to add. "Don't make no never mind to me where people come from. I just—"

"So you're from town, Lucy?" Dean stepped in smoothly.

She blinked. "Me? Oh, no. I'm from Tennessee. Gallatin, to be exact. Drove up yesterday afternoon, just for this show. My husband's set on selling the Camaro this year. Thinks he'll get enough to buy him a fishing cabin somewhere." She shrugged and glanced at the cars to her right before looking back at them. "He's crazy, if you ask me. I mean, it's a pretty car, sure, but ain't nobody in this town got that kind of cash. And even if they did, you'd never know it."

Sam glanced at his brother. "Why is that?" he asked.

Lucy smoothed the front of her floral blouse and leaned

forward, as if trying to make sure no one overheard them even though no one else was within earshot. "Well, people in this place aren't exactly models of southern hospitality, you know?"

Dean frowned. "I don't follow."

"Where I grew up, you were friendly with folks, especially if you'd invited them in the first place." The woman looked smug, as though she had imparted some particularly juicy secret. When the brothers looked blank, she didn't hesitate to elaborate. "This is the south," she said emphatically. "They put on this car show every year, but all they do is take the entry fee and give out a cheap silver-looking cup three days later. They ain't friendly—they won't even make polite conversation with you. Why, I know a bunch of people here from the car show circuit, and the only reason they come to Brownsdale at all is to get together with their old car friends."

"Like going to a crappy bar for a good pal's birthday," Dean said.

"Exactly." Lucy looked triumphant. "You won't make new friends here, that's for sure."

"Thanks for the info," Sam said.

"Absolutely." She smiled widely, then focused hard on Dean and winked. "Let me know if you change your mind."

He gave her a smile that was obviously fake, then almost dragged his brother away.

Sam smirked. "Was she talking about buying her car or—"

"Bite me," Dean said. "Let's go find something to eat."

Back at the car Sam pulled up a map of the surrounding area on his phone. "If you turn around and just keep following Main, it curves and keeps going. There's a place called Linda's Hilltop Restaurant. Seems to be the local place for decent food."

Dean swung the Impala in a U-turn and scanned the street as he drove. "Kind of funny to have everything closed when you have an event going on," he remarked.

"Yeah," Sam said. "But it wouldn't be the first time the locals didn't like tourists."

"Not much else going on here to boost the economy."

"There is that," Sam said, and pointed at a faded, oversized billboard that read Big Mike Welcomes You to Mammoth Cave.

"Yeah," Dean agreed. "But you'd think they'd be a little more enthusiastic."

"Seen a bunch of signs."

"And all in the same beat-up shape," Dean said. He sat up a little straighter. "There's a grocery store with cars in the parking lot."

Sam's eyebrows rose. "At last, signs of life."

Dean was going to keep driving, then he saw a woman in her thirties come out of the store, a couple of plastic bags swinging from her hands. She was heading toward a blue Toyota and Dean impulsively pulled into the lot, stopping the Impala between her and the small car. Sam put on his best smile and leaned his head out of the window. "Good morning, ma'am. Can I ask you a question?"

The woman ran.

Dean and Sam were so surprised that they just sat there and stared. She held onto her bags—barely—and sprinted around the back of their car. As she passed the driver's door she almost looked like the human version of the roadrunner in that cartoon, running away from the coyote.

Dean opened the door and started to get out. "Wait, we're not—"

The woman, an attractive brunette wearing a T-shirt and jeans, slammed against the door of her car, pressing her key fob frantically. "Go away!" she screamed as she yanked open the door. "I don't talk to strangers!"

Dean snapped his mouth shut and froze with one foot on the pavement and the other still in the Impala. The woman threw herself and her bags into the driver's seat and slammed the door so hard the car rocked. An instant later the locks engaged, the engine started, and she hit the accelerator hard enough to make the tires squeal as she drove out of the lot.

"What the hell was that?" Dean asked.

"I'd like to make a joke but that was really crazy." Sam twisted around in the passenger seat so he could watch the Toyota as it hightailed out of sight back toward the main part of town.

"I was just trying to make conversation," Sam complained. "Like Lucy said—southern hospitality."

Dean snickered. "Looks like she didn't find you so hospitable." He settled back into the driver's seat and pulled back onto Main Street.

"Maybe we'll have better luck at the restaurant," Sam said.

Dean started to slow the car. "Hey, that sign says there's a fast food restau—"

"I'm not eating a cheeseburger at nine in the morning," Sam said. "Keep going."

Dean made a disgruntled noise but picked up speed again.

The day was still full of sunlight and they passed tidy little houses with lawns so green they could have been spray-painted by leprechauns. There were longer stretches where there were no houses and the ground cover, grass or weeds or whatever, wasn't quite up to that lush color. A brown sign flashed by on the right that announced Mammoth Cave National Park was five miles down a road to their left. A little farther on, the restaurant came up on the left side.

Linda's Hilltop Restaurant was in a long, single-story building that would have looked like a strip mall store except it had been fancied up with copper metal roofing and log siding; a rustic front porch with a railing made of the same kind of logs stretched the width of the building and sported log rocking chairs below signs offering log headboards for sale. When they pulled into a parking space in front, they could also see tables and benches for sale on the porch, and that the rocking chairs had signs on them advertising wood furniture. Timber was definitely the going theme.

The inside was more of the same, thick wood tables and chairs cast in the golden glow of paneling, and more crowded than they expected. When they walked in, they both caught a softening of the noise level, the kind that happens when people stop talking around you. Sam grabbed a couple of random touristy brochures from a rack by the door then found a table and sat, acting like nothing was out of the ordinary. When he looked down, he was holding advertisements for trail riding, a horse farm, and a vineyard.

Dean eyed the ads. "A horse farm? Seriously?"

Sam glanced around. "I don't see you doing better."

Before Dean could respond, a gangly-looking young man came up, holding up two cups and a pot. "Coffee?"

"Absolutely," Dean said.

"Mindy is your waitress. She'll be right with you."

They watched him leave, then bent back over the brochures as though they were studying them. It didn't take long for the conversation level in the room to get back to normal, especially after Mindy stopped by and took their orders. Mindy turned out to be a tall, slender redhead of indeterminate age and who wore just enough makeup to make her look like she'd recently come off a beach. Her brown eyes were friendly and warm, especially when they focused on Dean. Dean's gaze followed her when she headed back to the kitchen, until Sam's sharp kick under the table finally got him refocused.

Certain words and phrases seemed to catch in their ears, maybe because of their instincts.

Just babies—

Hell of a thing, them disappearing—

Sheriff's all up in arms—

Parents are flying in—

Going on the third day—

Never find 'em alive now—

Mindy's honey-sweet voice slid into their ears. "Here you go, boys." She set a plate of bacon and eggs in front of Sam, then a plate of... something in front of Dean. She tapped the ketchup bottle with one finger. "Y'all let me know if you need anything else." Dean's gaze paused on her again for one long second, then he turned back to his plate and grinned.

"What the hell is that?" Sam demanded.

Dean glanced at him. "The number eight special," he answered. "Didn't you see it on the menu?"

"No," Sam retorted. "I think my eyes blacked it out, trying to protect my body."

Dean got both hands around a mass of food at least three inches thick and lifted it to his mouth. "This," he said, "is a Big Cave Country Breakfast Sandwich. It's a half-pound burger topped with not one, but two fried eggs and six slices of bacon. It comes with a large order of hash browns." He opened his mouth, then stopped to add, "No rabbit food, but I did tell Mindy to double the cheese."

Sam watched—how could he not?—as his brother somehow opened his mouth wide enough to get it around the sandwich. Dean bit down and cooked egg yolk squirted out both sides and onto his face, dripping down his fingers.

"Mmmmmm," Dean said happily. "Thooo gooth." He managed to keep his mouth mostly closed while he chewed, but yellow goo slid down his chin, making Dean look like some kind of human mustard dispenser.

Sam looked down at his bacon and eggs, concentrating on their simplicity. Two of each, plus a side of home fries, wheat toast with butter and homemade jam. An honest and all-American breakfast not designed to flow straight into his arteries and thicken up like wallpaper paste. He took a bite, then another, chewing and enjoying it as long as he didn't look up at Dean.

"Looks like you need some more napkins, sugar."

Sam still managed not to look up as Mindy put an inch-thick wad of napkins in front of Dean. He was hungry, damn it, and he was not going to let the sight of his big brother eating like a starving rugaru obliterate his appetite. Anyway, he might be a little disgusted at the sounds coming from across the table, but the truth was he couldn't truly be ticked off at Dean for enjoying the meal so much. After everything Dean had been through, and all the things Dean had done for him, if all it took in life to make his brother happy was meat and cheese, Sam wished he could give him a lifetime's worth right now.

The thought made Sam smile to himself and he dug in, risking a glance across the table now and then. The napkins had done the trick and his brother was no longer bathing in egg yolk. While he ate, Sam checked out the other patrons; it was a typical small-town breakfast crowd, not a whole lot to get excited about… except, perhaps, for the guy at the two-top in the back by the restrooms. He was an old timer with a slightly proprietary expression as he watched everyone else in the room. That more than anything said he was a regular, as did the way his brows came together just a fraction when his gaze passed over Sam and Dean. Was that a look reserved for tourists in general, was he on to them, or was he suspicious of new people in town because he had something to hide? All good questions, and Sam was just the person to dig up the answer, especially when the older man couldn't seem to stop glancing their way.

Amazingly Sam finished his breakfast at about the same time Dean chewed his way through the monstrous sandwich. They sat in silence, sipping coffee refills and surreptitiously studying everyone else. Out of the corner of his eye, Dean saw the old man get up and head for the men's room. He waited until the door closed, then casually got up and headed over; when he tried the knob it was locked, so he leaned against the wall and faked poking at his phone. The instant he heard the click of the lock releasing he spun and opened the door just enough to force his way inside.

The man gaped at him but Dean held up a badge before he could open his mouth to yell. "FBI," Dean snapped. "What's your name?" The restroom was barely large enough to be called handicapped accessible, so they were only a few feet apart. Up close, Dean realized the other guy wasn't as old as he'd thought. A life spent on a farm or working outside had aged his skin, and he was maybe in his late thirties, early forties at the outside. The nearly shaven hair beneath the sides of a dark-green John Deere cap was the same dirty blond as his eyebrows, and there were a couple of extra chins hanging below his round, surprised face.

"T-Travis," he sputtered. "Travis Miller." He tried to take a step backward but the sink got in the way. In a gray T-shirt and denim overalls, Travis was the picture of down-home country. Despite the first impression, he wasn't that much overweight—the arms poking out of his shirt sleeves weren't lean but they still showed plenty of decent muscle.

Dean flipped the badge closed and shoved it into his pocket. "You've been watching my partner and I ever since we came in," he said. "Why?"

Travis blinked and tried to pull back, but there was nowhere to go; he looked a bit like a turtle trying to pull its head back into its shell. "No real reason. Y'all ain't from around here."

Dean glowered at him. "Do I have 'stupid' written on my forehead? How many people come and go in Brownsdale on a weekend there's a car show?" When Travis shrugged uncomfortably, he poked him in the shoulder, hard. "So I'll ask you again. Why were you watching us?"

The other man shrugged. "There's just something about you that don't fit. Folks around here is on edge these past couple of days anyways."

"Why's that?"

Travis shrugged again, and this time his gaze flicked away for a second. "Local goings on, nothing—"

"To do with the two girls who have gone missing, right?" Dean finished for him. When Travis didn't respond, he again pulled out his FBI badge and waved it under the man's nose. "That's why we're here, Mr. Miller. It would be appreciated if you'd cooperate." When the guy still wouldn't say anything, Dean decided to sweeten the pot. "This disappearance matches several open cases over in Louisville," he said. "It would be a terrible thing if anyone else went missing when you could have helped prevent that."

Travis Miller's eyes almost bulged. "Me? I don't know anything. Sure, I've seen those girls around, only once mind you, but I never even met them." His gaze jumped sideways again.

"But?" Dean prompted. "What aren't you telling me?"

"Well," Travis said reluctantly, "it's just that, you know, people go missing all the time around here." The incredulous look on Dean's face made the hefty man shift his weight from one leg to the other. "It's a passing-through thing," he offered. "We've gotten to where we expect it—one day there's a guy shows up, maybe a backpacker or something, after a day or three he's gone. Everybody in town knows they never intended to stay to begin with, and the cave takes its share, too." His cheeks had taken on the pink color of anxiety. "New folks come in to check it out because it's homey, then they realize there ain't no jobs. Homeless people, hitchhikers, druggies—you get all kinds coming through here, especially in the summer. They're here, and then they're gone."

Dean folded his arms, staying in place so Miller couldn't push past him and out of the restroom. "What did you mean by 'the cave takes its share?'"

This time Travis shoved his hands deep into his overalls and wouldn't meet his eyes. "Can't explain, really. That's just what everybody always says. That's the way it's always been. Since I was a kid I've heard that expression. It's probably just crazy talk. Old folks making up crap to scare the kids into behaving."

Dean stared hard at him but he had a feeling he'd gotten as much as he was going to out of Travis Miller.

"Can I go now, mister?"

"Agent," Dean reminded him.

"Agent," Travis corrected. "If one of us doesn't come out of this bathroom, people are gonna start wondering."

"Young girls disappearing seems a little more important," Dean said.

"Right," the other man agreed hastily, but he looked longingly at the door.

Dean yanked it open. "Go."

Travis didn't need a second invitation, and by the time Dean stepped out himself, the only sign of the other man was a glimpse of the front door closing behind him.

"Well?" Sam said as Dean came back to the table.

"Not exactly the local encyclopedia," Dean told him. "But he did say one thing that was interesting." He told his brother what Travis had mentioned about the cave.

Sam sat back, frowning. "Trying to wrap my head around how a cave could 'take' anything," he said. "You mean like a sacrifice?"

"I think so," Dean shrugged. " Could be the goddess Pele and a volcano type of thing? Damned long trip from Hawaii to here though."

Sam held up one of a new stack of brochures. "No volcanic activity, either."

"Let's go find a room first and we'll go from there," Dean said.

Sam nodded and stood, tossing some money on the table. "Is that enough to pay for your big mouth sandwich?"

"Big Cave sandwich," Dean said, eyeing the bills next to the plate. "And no."

Sam's mouth fell open. "Seriously?"

"Nope." Dean grinned at him. "That wasn't fast food, brother. That was divine."

THREE

They rented a room at a place called, predictably, the Cave Country Inn. All of the bigger rooms at the place were already booked, courtesy of the car show, but what they got covered the basics: two double beds, a bathroom, desk, a couple of chairs and, of course, a wireless connection. A few plastic-framed pictures of Mammoth Cave's more colorful caverns were arranged on the wall between the bedroom and the bath, while behind the bed was a floor-to-ceiling mural of the cave's hundreds, maybe thousands, of stalactites and stalagmites in a multitude of sizes. The shades on the bedside lamps were thick and translucent, the same color of so much of the stone in the cave. With the lamps lit, the mural cast a muted golden glow on the brown and gold bedspreads as well as everything else in the room. The desk was a sort of large shadow box with a quarter-inch slab of permanently affixed Plexiglas as its top; below the glass, looking a little grimy after who knew how many years, were chunks of minerals presumably harvested from Mammoth Cave itself: calcite in varying colors, gypsum, crystals, a number of beautiful geodes as well as unfamiliar rocks that were labeled with names neither brother could pronounce.

Sam set up his laptop on the desk and tried to get an Internet connection while Dean poked around the room, checking out information about the local sights. Finally, Sam made a frustrated sound and shut the laptop. "I'm thinking the claim of 'free wireless' was false advertising," he said. "Can't bring up a thing. Maybe we should head out."

"Where to?"

"The local library." A corner of Sam's mouth turned up. "Next best thing to the favorite coffee shop for the lowdown on a small town."

The Edwardson County Public Library on Matthew Street was a small, modern building made of pinkish bricks under a white metal roof. It was standard low-budget government, a sprawling single-story box with metal-trimmed windows and gray block letters in a semi-circle over the entrance. Inside it was roomy and overly bright thanks to evenly spaced squares of fluorescent lights set into the low ceiling. A lot of the furniture was trimmed in faux wood laminate that was too light and hard on the eyes, almost orange, and somehow made the gray-patterned industrial carpeting look mottled in pink.

Sam had been disappointed when they pulled into the parking lot, and he felt even more let down when they walked inside. Brownsdale was a small historical town with a lot of great vintage buildings, and he'd expected the library would be the same: a two- or three-story work of old brick and building stones with an arched stone entryway at the top of a double-wide set of granite steps, maybe even have a peaked roof with carved stone decorations below the eaves. A building like that was where historical information should be stored and would have reminded him of the bunker, a place you could sit back and soak up the knowledge. This had gone so far to the modern that there weren't even pictures on the walls. The computer room was nothing but long lines of computer stations against a blank wall; it looked like a setup waiting for a couple dozen androids to mindlessly input data.

The brothers wandered around a bit, hoping to find an area that held old newspaper archives or microfiche files. On their second trip past the front desk, a young man came out of a door off to the side and saw them. He was tall and young, with choppy brown hair and a short, neatly trimmed moustache and beard; the bright red sweater he wore over a white collared shirt made him look like the only walking spot of color in the place.

"Hi," he said. "I'm Owen Meyer, the librarian. May I help you find something?"

"Yeah," Dean answered. "We'd like to check out the history of the town. Old newspapers, crime reports, stuff like that."

Meyer blinked. "Crime reports?"

Sam met his gaze steadily. "I'm writing a book."

"Right." Owen's return smile was off somehow, a strange combination of grimace and nervousness that made Sam wonder if the pleasant-looking young man had something to hide. Now that Sam studied him, the guy just looked wrong—too pale, stiff in the way people get when they've stayed up too late or had a really rotten night's sleep.

Before Sam could say anything else, Owen motioned at them. "Follow me, please." He led them to a door at the far end then pulled a key ring from his pocket. "We keep the microfiches and official history records in another room. Brownsdale has a history going back several hundred years, so there are some rare items in storage. Just to be safe, we keep track of who's in here." He unlocked the door and flipped a switch, then lifted a small notebook from the top of a file cabinet and offered it to them along with a pen. "If you would sign in, gentlemen?"

"Of course." Sam took it and wrote down the name that matched his FBI-of-the-day badge, then handed the book to Dean, who did the same.

Owen took back the book and glanced at it, then jerked. He glared at them. "What's the deal?" he demanded suddenly. "If you have questions for me, then just ask. You don't have to try and sneak in and spy on me. I'll answer anything I can."

"Whoa," Dean said. "Down, boy. Kind of jumpy, aren't you?"

"It's been that kind of day," Owen shot back.

Sam eyed the librarian. "What do you mean, 'spy on you?' Are we supposed to know who you are?"

Owen's return gaze didn't waver. "You're FBI. I know you're here about my cousins."

Sam and Dean exchanged glances, then it clicked in Sam's mind. "Marley and Fallon."

Owen's chin lifted a little. "I suppose it's reasonable

that I'm first on the list of suspects. But I've already been interviewed by the sheriff and I also don't know where they went, so it would be a lot more productive to channel your energy toward searching for them."

Dean lifted an eyebrow. "And their parents are…"

A pained expression flashed across the young man's face and his hand went through his hair, making it stand up in more places than it already was. "On a rafting trip down the Colorado River," he answered. "No cell phone service at the bottom of the Grand Canyon and no way to pinpoint their exact location at any one time. Their group pulls out of the river sometime tomorrow morning and gets lifted back to their starting point by helicopter." His voice shook as he said the next words. "When they land, the local sheriff will be waiting to tell them the girls are missing."

"Ouch," Sam muttered under his breath.

"Let's just say we're not here to go all TV crime drama on you," Dean said, "but we are looking into finding out what happened to the girls. Any other disappearances on the books?"

Owen frowned. "Well…"

Sam stared hard at him. "What aren't you telling us?"

When Owen still hesitated, Dean scowled and took a step forward that put him nose to nose with the librarian. Owen was almost as tall as Dean, but a lot thinner—the difference in bulk made the leaner man seem to shrink. "Are you really up for an interrogation?"

Owen let out a breath neither of the brothers had realized he was holding. "This town is soaked in superstition, right down the family trees of every person in it. Disappearances are kind of a way of life around here—hardly anyone notices."

Dean's mouth dropped open. "Say what?"

"This is a small town," Sam countered. "You're telling us the townspeople, who are probably all distant relatives of each other, don't care when someone goes missing?"

Owen held out his hands. "That's just it—the folks who disappear are never from Brownsdale. It's usually drifters, unemployed folks looking for work. People passing through or who stay for a few days, a week at most. When they're gone…" He shrugged. "They're gone. Who's to say they weren't leaving to begin with? And if they leave belongings behind— backpacks, a few clothes, whatever—it's just assumed the stuff was so ratty they didn't want to take it with them."

"Seriously?" Dean demanded. "You just don't care?"

"Hey," Owen said, offended. "I didn't say I personally felt that way. Most head librarian positions require a decade or more of experience and I'd only had my degree for a year. When this job opened up I applied for it on a whim; when they offered me the position, I moved here to take it about eight months ago. I don't mind the small-town location—I don't like crowded cities—but the local attitude is definitely not mine. And trust me, it'll be another twenty years before the people in Brownsdale don't consider me to be an outsider."

"Let's all have a seat," Sam said. "I think we'd like to hear more about Brownsdale."

"Yeah," Dean agreed. "Especially what you called the 'local attitude.'"

Owen nodded. "All right. But first I want to hook you up with the local history, old and more recent."

* * *

By the time the library closed at noon, both brothers felt like their heads had been stuffed with enough dates, statistics, and local history to make their brains bulge. And no wonder: the town itself had been founded in 1826, but the Edwardson County and Kentucky state records went a lot farther back, all the way to 1727, most of which had never been uploaded. They weren't that interested in the records of births and deaths, and that was a good thing; those started getting recorded in 1852 but the archives were sketchy at best, with large chunks of information missing between 1852 and 1911, and it wasn't until the laws were rewritten several times that the counties started trying to comply. By 1920, finally, births and deaths were routinely recorded. They delved into it with Owen mainly to get an idea of Brownsdale's residents and how long families had been here.

Archives of the newspapers were a different story. Between the three of them they went through microfiches, files of old newsprint, and clippings dating back to 1916, when the earliest newspaper had been published in Brownsdale. They wrote page after page of notes and dates, and when they finally put it all together, the data didn't lie: the number of disappearances was more than six times the national average. They had to wonder why these people had never been recorded or noticed.

Owen locked the front door and shut off the lights, then pulled the brothers into his office. The room was small to begin with and even when they settled onto the two chairs available on the front side of Owen's desk, Sam and Dean made the space feel almost claustrophobic. There wasn't much to the room beyond the same kind of laminated modern furniture that was out in the main library. A couple of requisite bookcases filled with reference materials stood behind the desk, a small window with no curtains was set high in the wall to the side. There was a poster of the United States, unframed, tacked to one wall and on the other was a poster of the Mammoth Cave system.

On Owen's desk were two framed five-by-seven photographs. One was of an older couple; Sam assumed these were Owen's parents. He picked up the other photo and looked at it long enough to try and commit it to memory. It was a color family portrait showing two smiling girls, obviously Marley and Fallon, next to a man and woman. The girls were young and pretty, identical twins sporting the same outfit. Only their earrings were different; the one on the left was wearing heart-shaped silver studs, while tiny four-leaf clovers in enameled green dangled from the other girl's ears. The woman looked a lot like the older woman in the first photograph.

Owen sat heavily on the chair behind the desk. "I don't know what I'm going to tell their mom and dad." His voice was wooden, empty. "I was supposed to take care of them. It was my idea to bring the girls out here while my aunt and uncle went on that rafting trip."

"So what happened?" asked Dean. "When exactly did they go missing?"

"They were gone when I got home from work the day before yesterday," Owen answered. "They didn't tell me anything when I saw them in the morning. Nothing about what they were going to do other than the typical answer of 'hang out.' And no note, either." He looked absolutely miserable. "I was going crazy just sitting at home and waiting. They didn't want me hanging around the sheriff's office, so I came in here."

"Could the girls have run away?" Sam asked.

Owen didn't hesitate to meet Sam's eyes. "I can't imagine why they would, seriously. I was getting along with them really well, I always have. There are no issues with their parents and they were looking forward to coming out here. They wanted to explore the cave but I told them they couldn't do that on their own. I promised them we'd get a guided tour this weekend, the longest one they have. It's called the Wild Cave Tour and they only do it on weekends. Five miles long, and it takes six hours."

"Wait," Sam said, "they wanted to explore the cave?"

Owen shrugged. "Sure. Everyone does. It's one of the main reasons they wanted to come out here." He leaned forward. "Think about it. This is just a Podunk little town. There isn't much for a couple of teenage girls to do. They weren't going to be here that long and I told them that it might be boring during the days while I was at work, but I promised to take a couple of days off. I was going to do that Monday and Tuesday so their parents would have a little time to recover from the rafting trip, a couple of days to themselves."

Sam lifted an eyebrow. "Any chance they went exploring by themselves?"

Owen stared at his desk. "Probably."

Sam shifted. "Is it really that dangerous for them to go alone?"

Owen nodded. "The cave system is immense," he said. "And there's also an entrance to Crystal Cave, a bit farther out. If I was a kid and wanted to go exploring without a bunch of adults around to stop me, that would be the place I'd pick. But that's been closed off for several years. I guess they could still get in, but I thought it was pretty well blocked. They've done some searches in there already, plus in the main system, but they've come up with nothing." His expression was bleak. "I really don't think they're going to try all that hard."

"Really?" Sam was surprised. "Two young girls disappear and no one wants to look for them?"

Owen rubbed at his temples. "I told you. It's this damned town," he said. "A bunch of superstitious old people and their ancient beliefs."

Dean leaned forward. "Run it by me again what that means."

"I mean they think that in order for the town to be prosperous, the cave has to take its own."

Sam frowned. "Take what, exactly?"

"That's what they think happens to all these people: the drifters, the hitchhikers, the homeless, the drug addicts. The people who are… what would you call them? Impermanent. They think the cave takes them as some sort of sacrifice. That's why the police never look for the people who disappear. They just claim they were 'passing through' or something like that—that those folks never meant to stay."

"And everyone accepts this?" Dean looked at his brother. "And they don't care?"

Owen's shoulders slumped. "Well, no. The cave has never

'taken' anyone local before, at least not to my knowledge. But like I said, I'm an outsider and they don't talk much to me. I'm getting some odd looks from the townsfolk. It's like they're afraid the cave has decided to up the ante or something."

Sam cleared his throat. "And exactly what does the cave do to these people it takes?"

Owen frowned. The skin beneath his eyes looked bruised from lack of sleep. "I don't know," he answered after a moment of consideration. "Nobody will talk about it, but when you live here you hear people whispering. The general belief is they 'go to sleep' somehow, that nothing worse than that happens. They go to sleep and… just fade away inside the cave. If that's true—and no one's ever seen or recovered a body to prove it—then it would be something crazy like a pocket of toxic gas somewhere in the cave system. But it would be awfully strange that all these people somehow found that same pocket of gas."

Dean looked doubtful. "And it sure would be a big pile of bodies in one spot, wouldn't it?"

Owen nodded. "I suppose there could be multiple pockets, but…" His voice faded, then picked up. "God, what if it's all true? What if there really is something to the stories and the girls went in there and died, all because I didn't believe what I thought were a bunch of stupid old stories?"

Neither Sam nor Dean could think of anything to say that was truthful, and when they kept silent, Owen scrubbed at his face with his hands. "I wish I could search myself," Owen said. Frustration had replaced the bleakness on his face. "But I don't know the cave at all and there's nothing here in the library that's good enough to use in exploring it. I've only gone on a tour one time, way back when I first moved here. Everything I tell people who come in and ask comes from books and pamphlets I get from the park itself, and if I don't know the answer I send them to the hiking shop down on Main. The guy who runs it is supposed to be an expert on the cave. Like I told you, I went on one of the park service tours, but the word is that hiking shop guy gives personalized tours on his own. He has some kind of license and he knows the cave better than anyone."

Sam and Dean looked at each other. "I guess that's where we're headed now," Dean said.

FOUR

Owen let the two FBI agents out the front door of the library and relocked it behind them. He started to turn away, then saw the silver sheriff's car pull up and block the agents' car in their parking space. He stepped to the side of the window and watched them, seeing the sheriff talk his talk and watching the way the agents answered. Something told him the officer wouldn't exactly cooperate with these two men—they were the standard outsiders, not privy to the goings-on in Brownsdale or understanding of the way small-town minds worked. He thought about going out there but there was really no point; even though he knew they were probably talking about Marley and Fallon, and Owen himself. All three men would still, in a way that made no sense to Owen at all, consider it none of his business. Owen had gone his rounds in the verbal ring with Sheriff Thompson earlier, and although he hadn't lost, he hadn't exactly won either, if "winning" meant he was in the clear. He knew he was still a suspect and Owen supposed that only made sense.

He waited patiently, staring out the window at them but not really seeing anything. Instead his mind was replaying the scene the last morning the girls had been with him. They'd been sitting at his small breakfast table, an opened box of Multi-Grain Cheerios in front of them. The three of them had decimated the contents, with Fallon overfilling her bowl because the box had almost been empty and she thought leaving a half inch of cereal in it was stupid.

"You're really going to eat all that?" Owen had asked.

"Absolutely," Fallon replied. "Waste not, want not." Before Owen could point out how worn out that phrase was, his niece had launched into a lecture about the environment and corporate greed that had left him more than a little stunned at how well-informed she was. Marley and Fallon were identical twins and had grown up tight, like most twins do. Just stepping into their teens had made their self-images veer a little and they were starting to show personal preferences for colors and clothes as each girl's individualism began to expand. Personality-wise they were still close and happy, lacking the sarcasm that so often crept into tweens because of peer pressure and television. He hoped the passion he saw in them for the world in which they lived was strong enough to survive the crazy teenage years.

There had been a lot of laughter and joking in the Meyer household that morning, a lot of the poking at cell phone screens that had invaded everyone's lives in what Owen thought of as an electronic equivalent of a pandemic. He had his own but refused to engage with any social media on it, refused to be tethered to it like the kids were nowadays. He remembered, even if it was just barely, a time before the smartphones, when you went to class and actually read a book, looked at the teacher instead of a small black screen.

"Phones off during meals," he'd told them. He'd gotten some predictable grumbling but they'd still been in good spirits—let's face it, Owen was headed to work soon and then they could wile away the entire day texting and Facebooking and playing games, if that's what they wanted.

Only they hadn't.

They'd headed out to... do what?

Walk around, hang out, make the long walk into town and do some shopping? Not that; according to Sheriff Thompson, not a soul had seen them the day they'd disappeared. He'd sent deputies around, put out an AMBER Alert, slapped it on the front page of the newspaper, and even hung posters all over town. The response had been zip. And nothing from the girls' cell phones; either they were turned off or, more likely, the batteries had gone dead.

What then? Marley and Fallon must've gone hiking, wandering the paths in the forest that made up Mammoth Cave National Park. You could get to the edge of the park if you wandered across the fields—and no one would care if you did. But the paths in the park were well maintained and clearly marked; following those would have ultimately led them back to trail heads bearing directions on how to get back to where they needed to be.

So the final what. The hard one.

They'd gone exploring in the cave system.

Owen's stomach clenched and for a moment he tasted bile. He swallowed and concentrated on keeping the taste down— he hadn't eaten since lunch yesterday, forgetting about dinner last night and breakfast this morning when faced with the fact that...

That...

My God, he thought, Marley and Fallon are missing. They're MISSING.

Sudden heat ran up his neck and circled his skull, messing with his balance. The room went gray around him and Owen dropped to his knees, not feeling the floor slam into his bony kneecaps. He sat back on his heels, wobbling, then his hands splayed out to either side and the cool linoleum pressed against his palms. He let himself lean forward until his ribcage pressed against the tops of his thighs, stretching his arms forward and pressing his forehead against the floor in a child's yoga pose.

Finally his head cleared and he pulled himself back to his feet, then walked, still unsteady, back toward his office. At that last moment Owen veered and went back to the archive room and let himself in. The agents had left their selection of books and papers on the table—as with any library, only the librarians were authorized to re-shelve books and replace file materials. No one ever came back here but Owen, and he'd decided to deal with it later.

Now it all made sense.

Those agents, their investigating, their questions, hadn't been... normal? No, that wasn't the right word. They hadn't been conservative. In fact, they had been downright out there, almost crazy, in the paths their logic seemed to take.

Except...

This wasn't a normal town, was it?

No, not at all. Owen knew it, Sheriff Thompson knew it, the people who lived here knew it, and now Owen was pretty sure those two agents did, too. There was something underneath Brownsdale, something that... wanted. Owen didn't know what it was, but he suspected that this nameless thing had a way of taking what it desired via the people who had come and gone and never been heard from again.

And now Marley and Fallon were among them.

This town was a monster, and that monster had his cousins. He had to find a way to track them, find them, get them back. The girls were his family, damn it, his flesh and blood. Maybe the rest of the people here could turn their backs on the missing—those hitchhikers and drifters and homeless— but Owen would not stand by while they ignored the twins. And if—no, when—he found them, he would find some way to end all this, to see that no one ever disappeared in Brownsdale again.

Owen pulled the door to the old files room shut behind him, then locked it. He passed his office and stopped to make a quick call before tossing the key ring for the inside doors in the center drawer. Then he stood for a second, just listening. The building was silent around him, not even a ticking clock since the switch last month to digital satellite clocks. There were a lot of things he could do here—there were always books to re-shelve, new arrivals to catalog—but he felt like he'd given enough of himself to the county today.

He started to go out the front and saw the sheriff's vehicle was still there, the lawman still talking to the agents, so he went out the side exit instead. He'd wait here a while until the sheriff and the agents left, listening to the breeze blow the heavily leafed trees above a street that was almost deserted thanks to the car show. Or maybe he'd putter around the archives room again, just for the hell of it.

And under the town, Owen thought, something unspeakable waited.

FIVE

"First let's put on our suits, then head to the sheriff's office," Sam said as they walked out of the library and started to climb into the car. "See if they have any other details, find out exactly what they're doing to locate the girls. Maybe by showing up we can put some pressure on them to get off their asses."

"I don't think we have to go to them," Dean said. "It looks like the sheriff is coming to us." He inclined his head toward the other end of the parking lot, where a sleek silver sedan with black and gold lettering had just turned in. It glided to a stop across the front of the Impala, blocking them in. The man who climbed out was anything but the stereotype of a portly, laid-back small-town sheriff. He was in his fifties and tall and lean, his uniform sharply pressed and absolutely perfect. He shut the car door behind him and put a hat on his head, then walked up to them. The expression on his face was perfect small-town suspicion.

"Help you boys?" he asked. "Haven't seen you around here before."

The gold name tag on his shirt read Thompson. Sam gave the man a polite nod as he pulled out an FBI badge. "I'm Agent May and this is my partner, Agent Taylor," he said. "We're looking into the disappearance of the Dietz girls."

"Sheriff Thompson, though around here people just call me Michael." The lawman lifted his chin. "I guess you've been in there talking to Owen," he said. Dean nodded. The sheriff's eyes were a sharp, clear green. "You think he's involved in this?"

The brothers glanced at each other. "No," Sam said. "He seems pretty broken up about it."

Sheriff Thompson looked back at them, expressionless. "It wouldn't be the first time a man did something unexpected."

"True, but he doesn't seem the type," Dean said.

"Thought we'd come by and take a look at your files," Sam put in before they could get into some standard cop-type discussion about profiling. "See what's going on in your search."

The sheriff crossed his arms in an unconsciously protective gesture. "Not much progress, I'm afraid. If they've gone into the cave, it's not likely we'll ever find them. They could also be runaways, or they could've been snatched by some pervert."

"I suppose that's possible," Sam said. "But my partner and I have done a little research and we do see that Brownsdale has a history of disappearances."

The sheriff adjusted his hat, then adjusted his crossed arms tighter over his chest. "If you're talking about hobos and such, you're making a whole lot out of nothing. We get a bunch of people passing through here just because it is what it is—Mammoth Cave. It's one of the most beautiful caves in the world. Lots of young people think they can run scams and such on the tourists, but we let 'em know right off the bat that we don't put up with that kind of nonsense. People come, check it out, they leave. As far as going missing, there's no proof of these disappearances you're talking about."

"Right," Sam said. "No proof."

The three men stared at each other for a long moment, then Sheriff Thompson turned back to his car. "Well, you boys stop by anytime you like. Files are open to you, of course. Always want to help the FBI." There was an undertone of something in his voice, a coldness that indicated his statement was as far from the truth as it could be.

The sheriff climbed into his car and shut the door. He sat there, looking down, but it wasn't clear if he was looking at a phone or taking notes. Maybe both. Or maybe he was inputting their license plate number into a computer. "That was interesting," Dean said as they watched him finally pull away. The big cruiser made no noise, just slid away like a slick silver snake.

"Yeah," Sam said. "I guess he's one of the superstitious old people Owen was talking about."

"How so?"

"Like that biblical river," Sam said. "In denial."

"You still want to go by?"

"Maybe later," Sam answered. "If nothing else, we can look at the maps, see if they really have sent anyone at all out to look for the girls. Right now I say we head on over to the hiking shop."

* * *

In his rearview mirror, Michael Thompson watched with a sour expression on his face as the two agents pulled out of the library. For a couple of lawmen, they were driving one hell of a car, a black Impala that looked like it had just rolled off the factory line. Dark as oil and not a ding on her. 1967, if Thompson had his year right—and he damned sure did, since his daddy had worked at a car repair shop until the day the old man's heart had seized up and dropped him in his tracks in 2001. A car like that had a good-sized trunk, Thompson mused, so it was probably something impounded from a drug runner, or maybe a murderer—fit more than a few bodies in a trunk like that. Nice undercover vehicle, that's for sure. He wondered what Owen Meyer had told them about the town and its history; the young guy was smart and he had access to all the historical stuff. If those FBI guys put two and two together…

Stop it, Thompson told himself. There's nothing going on in this town, damn it.

At least nothing they'll ever know about.

Still, a couple of blocks later, when he was sure they were gone on their way, Thompson pulled the cruiser to the side of the road and put it in park, tapping a finger on the steering wheel with one hand while his other hand rubbed at a sudden spike of pain between his eyebrows. How had he let two family members of someone who lived in town go missing? It wasn't supposed to be that way; he had lived in Brownsdale all his life and it had never been that way.

You know how it happened.

Thompson inhaled deeply and let his head fall back against

the headrest as he stared at the ceiling of the car. Locals didn't disappear, but the girls weren't locals, were they? Owen Meyer hadn't lived in this town long enough for the cave to… what? Know him? Somehow register that he and his should be left alone? They had been in town for only a couple of days, and there had been no way Thompson could've known they were related to Owen Meyer.

Old rumors and bedtime stories to make the kids behave, Thompson thought. That's all anyone has to believe. That's all.

His shook his head and his hands curled around the steering wheel hard enough to make his knuckles go white. Brownsdale wasn't the tiny country town it had been when he was a boy and dreaming about being a cop when he grew up. Back then people had minded their own business and outsiders had left them alone. Now it was the age of technology and communication—that these two FBI agents were here at all was a testament to that. Three decades ago it would've taken time, telephone calls, written forms, even person-to-person visits that involved half-day drives, to exchange all the details on a case. Now it wasn't a matter of weeks, or even days—organizations, especially government ones, shared information almost instantly. Other agencies were picking up on the disappearances in this area, noticing the numbers, wanting answers. Denial on his part wasn't ignorance on the part of others, and sooner or later the truth would come out.

And that was what, exactly?

Nothing more than what I let them know.

But Sheriff Thompson wasn't precisely sure about that.

He'd spent thirty-some years, his entire career, perfecting the art of hiding his head in the sand, and now that he was finally pulling it out, he had no idea what he was facing.

But he knew one thing, all right. It was going to be damned ugly.

The hiking shop Owen sent them to was called Go Cave Wild. It looked small on the outside, a glass and metal door flanked by a couple of large, clean windows full of the stuff needed for hiking and bird-watching. But when they stepped inside, the brothers realized the shop went back the full depth of the building. It was in a dark, vintage structure on the main street, but the proprietor was smart—he had the inside well lit so his customers could see everything he had to offer, which was a lot. There were things in here that neither brother had ever known existed. Of course, they had never been on a true spelunking trip or climbed Mount Everest, either.

"Good afternoon." The voice was gravelly but cheerful, friendly. "You looking for something in particular?" The shopkeeper was an older man, perhaps even in his seventies. He had badly cut iron-gray hair and brown eyes set in a face leathered by exposure to the elements. "I'm Beau Pyle, owner of this fine establishment."

He stuck his hand out and Sam shook it, noting that the skin on Pyle's fingers and palm was scraped and raw. "Yeah," Sam answered. "We'd like a couple of maps of the cave. We're mostly interested in the part called Crystal Cave."

"Ah," Pyle said. "Seems like everyone wants to see it now

that it's closed off. I don't blame 'em—it was one of the prettiest parts of the cave. Let me see what I can dig up."

"You don't keep that stuff out?" Dean asked, looking around.

"No." The man went behind the counter and started pulling out drawers set into the wall. "Not since it's been closed off. Plus refolding a map is an art form that not many people have truly mastered. Folks always screw it up."

The old man ran his finger down a line of labeled folders. "The boy up at the library gave me a call, said you might be by. Said you were FBI and asked if I could help as much as possible. Told him of course I would. Damned shame about his cousins. Sweet young girls like that."

"Did you know them?" Sam asked. "Maybe they came in here?"

"No." The old man shook his head to emphasize his answer. "Damned shame," he repeated. He looked up at them. "You know, I could take you in there myself. There'd be a fee, of course, but it wouldn't be much. And it would be a much better tour than any of the ones those park service people give. My family dates back to the earliest settlers around, like caretakers. No one knows the cave like me."

Sam looked at Dean. "We'll think about it," he said. "We want to do some checking around first, talk to a few people. In the meantime, we'll get some stuff and take a look at the maps."

"All righty then, you just let me know if you change your mind." The old man pulled some papers out, then turned and spread three or four complicated maps in front of them. Although the labeling stated all three of them were of the same Crystal Cave area, each looked completely different; the fourth and largest was a map of the overall system.

"It's a lot bigger than I thought," Dean said.

"Oh yeah," Pyle said. "It's part of Mammoth Cave, which is the longest cave system in the world; over four hundred miles of passageways, with more being added every year. Obviously that's the reason it's called 'mammoth.' I'm telling you, you don't want to go in there and get lost. You won't ever find your way out. Best bet is one of the park tours, or let me take you."

"Like I said, we'll think about it," Dean said. "In the meantime, what else would we need to go spelunking? The beginner's version, not the expert."

Pyle looked at him doubtfully, then sighed. "Well, you'll need to start with helmets and headlamps, of course. A spare headlamp, a good flashlight and extra batteries, protective clothing, plus knee pads and gloves." He showed Sam and Dean how beat up his hands were, covered with scrapes and blue-black bruises. "Rocks are unforgiving, plus it's cold in the cave, especially if—when—you get wet and muddy, so you'll want the right kind of clothing. Boots, duct tape, food and water."

Pyle looked like he had more to add, but Dean interrupted. "Round it up. We'll take it all to go."

The shopkeeper nodded and the brothers watched as he began to collect the items. After a few moments, Dean's gaze wandered across the array of things displayed on the counter. There were Velcro key holders, carabiners in gaudy colors, mini-knives that were too flimsy to be useful, the usual touristy stuff. Small, colorful stacks of pamphlets and business cards stuck out here and there. Because it lacked color, one of the cards caught Dean's attention and he grabbed it and held it up. "What's this?"

The old man glanced over, then stopped and looked at them steadily as he eyed the prim-looking white card in Dean's fingers. "Well," he said slowly, "this is going to sound kind of funny and not usually what agencies like yours get involved in, but we have this woman in town named Cinnamon Ellison. Lives over on B Street, and that's her card. She's one of those psychic reader people. I wouldn't normally believe in stuff like that, but she's my sister-in-law and I've seen her come up with some pretty amazing things. Never heard of her finding any missing people, mind you, but I don't know that she's tried. That might not be her forte and she doesn't share a lot of her personal business with me anyway. But she is pretty good at giving some folks a little glimpse of the future. You ought to stop by, see if she has something to say, before you go poking around the cave. Just my opinion, of course."

"We might just do that," Sam said as they gathered up their purchases. Dean slipped the card into his pocket.

"Yeah," he said as he watched them go. But he didn't sound like he believed them.

Outside the shop, Sam looked at his watch. "It's too late to do the cave thing today."

Dean scowled at him. "You want to leave those girls out there for another night?"

"First of all," Sam said in his most reasonable voice, "we don't know that they're actually in the cave." Before Dean could argue, he added, "And secondly, we have to figure out how to carry all this crap we just bought."

"Your point?"

"Is that there's no point wasting time in the cave if they didn't actually go there. And even if we did know for sure we still have to find the entrance to Crystal Cave—assuming that they even went in that way—and then figure out how to get inside. Bottom line is we don't have enough daylight left to get that far."

Dean looked like he wanted to argue, then glanced at the mellowing sunlight and changed his mind. "Fine. Let's head back to the room. But I'm just saying, tomorrow would be a rocking day to go caving."

Sam started to pull open the passenger door, then winced. "Did you really just say that?"

Dean grinned at him from the other side of the car. "Pretty good, huh?"

"Dude, that was terrible."

Dean gave him a dismissive wave. "If we're going to be spelunkers, you gotta get with the cave humor, bro."

Sam rolled his eyes and wondered if the best thing Mammoth Cave could do for his brother was give him a good knock on the head.

Six

Finally Owen decided to just head home. The drive was short, taking a little over ten minutes in total, a straight shot down two-lane roads that had little traffic. When he'd first come to town he'd stayed in a motel while he searched for a place; his agent had pointed him toward the very affordable house out on Beaver Dam Church Road but Owen had considered the place too far from the library. In actuality, it was only about five miles, but a couple of years at graduate school in Illinois had acclimated him to a much shorter commute. Those first few weeks in Brownsdale it had seemed to take forever; now the idea of even calling his drive home a "commute" was laughable.

Owen pulled into the carport of his small white house and sat there for a few minutes, trying to clear his head. It was all muddled up with thoughts of when the girls had first arrived at his place to now, when they were suddenly just… gone. He finally shut off the engine and went inside, and of course the first thing he checked was their room. The tidy house was a three-bedroom split plan, with the biggest bedroom his, the next one down his office, and the third a guest room. Like the larger room he used for his office, this one had built-in bookshelves, although not as many. He hadn't done anything with the room since he'd moved in, but when the girls' visit was finalized he'd moved out the boxes and crap he'd been storing in there and painted the walls a neutral beige. After shampooing the tan carpet, he went out and bought twin beds and mattresses before trying to decorate the room in something he thought a couple of thirteen-year-old girls would appreciate. Not too frilly and goofy, definitely not an overload on pink. He'd seen the girls at the last family holiday and they were growing up fast, caught between teenagers and tomboys. They were petite with matching shoulder-length brown hair and pretty smiles that came out often. Still kids, sure, but in the shape of their faces Owen could see the beautiful women they would someday be, the bright blue eyes that would knock all the boys on their asses.

If they got to grow up to be young women.

With a struggle, he pushed the thought away and looked around the room. There was a little pink in it, but only as an accent color. He'd chosen thick light-green comforters with matching plaid pillow shams, then loaded the beds up with three more pillows each. Between the beds was a white nightstand that was really a low chest of drawers Owen had picked up at an antique store and painted; it was wide enough to have a small reading lamp on each side. For the overhead light, he'd chosen one of those art deco chandeliers to light up the entire room. A matching green Roman shade hung at the window and he'd put a long wooden table between the built-in bookshelves as a desk for whatever projects his cousins might want to work on. There were books on the shelves, of course—he was a librarian, right?—but not too many. He'd cleaned out the ones he knew they wouldn't be interested in, reference books and such, and put in some of the best ones he'd checked out of the YA section at the library. The desk table was covered with a tablecloth in a green plaid that matched the pillow shams on the bed, and a couple of chairs finished it off.

So much care and detail had gone into this room. He'd wanted to make it comfortable and inviting, a place where the girls would want to come back often. And it seemed to have worked—now there was stuff thrown everywhere, in the sort of hot mess that only two teenage girls could create. Clothes and shoes they'd brought with them, even silly little skull bunny plush toys and stickers.

And it was okay that it was chaos, because wasn't that what teenagers did? When Marley and Fallon had arrived they'd brought with them enough luggage to stay for months, or at least that's what it had seemed like at the time. Overweight suitcases, backpacks, purses—Owen had never known that much luggage could be carried on an airplane. They'd landed at the Louisville airport and he'd driven up to get them on the previous Sunday.

He stood in the doorway and studied the room. There was no sign of the luggage, but that was stored in the front hallway closet, which was way bigger than the one in here. Now he walked over to the room's small closet—the house had been built seventy years ago—and pulled open the door. Yep, there they were, the small carry-on suitcases, a few shopping bags.

He shut the closet and went back to stand in the doorway, folding his arms and staring at the floor. What was missing? Something wasn't there. He had very little idea how teenagers' minds worked, especially those of teenage girls. He had no sisters or brothers and his only contact with teens these days was through the library programs. But something—

Purses.

Backpacks.

Owen's fingers tightened on his biceps. Could they really have run away? No, damn it—no. Like he'd told those FBI agents, there was no indication of it. But... was there ever? He just couldn't believe it. They had to have gone hiking, taken their backpacks and probably stuffed their purses into them, plus other stuff—snacks, MP3 players, their smartphones, whatever. Even though both phones were going straight to voice mail and the sheriff's office was maintaining there were no signals to track, it made sense that they would have them. No teenage girl would go anywhere, even into a cave or something outdoorsy like that, without her phone.

But if they had gone to the cave, the Mammoth entrance or, God forbid, the closed Crystal Cave one, how had they gotten there? The main entrance to Mammoth Cave Park was walkable, especially given the nice weather they'd been having. But surely someone had seen them on the side of the road? Finding their way to Crystal Cave would've been more of a challenge—it was almost twenty miles away.

Had someone given them a ride? If so, that person wasn't coming forward.

And Owen didn't want to think about what might've happened if whoever had picked them up decided not to go to the cave at all.

SEVEN

"The psychic?" Dean asked as he steered the car toward Cinnamon Ellison's house.

Sam shrugged. "It's not like we're going to get any help from the more respectable sources in this town. I'm up for trying every angle here."

Dean scratched his head. "I guess we'll find out if she's legit soon enough. Never met a psychic named after a spice before. Strippers, yes, but no psychics."

They pulled up in front of a small house with a green peaked roof and matching green trim around the windows. Bright orange and red roses were planted in neat flower boxes hung below the windows, and stuck amidst the flowers in each box was a small American flag that waved gently in the breeze. Like many of the houses in town it had a front porch, although this one was small and didn't extend the width of the building. A white rocking chair sat to the right of a front door that was painted green to match the roof and window trim. Next to it was a small yellow table sporting a large chunk of crystal, probably a souvenir from the cave. A tidy-looking deep-blue Prius was parked in the driveway, flanked on both sides by small expanses of well-tended grass. The walkway up to the house wasn't concrete, but cobblestone, an overload of cuteness. The look was accentuated by the ornate white picket fence that ran across the front and sides of the yard. They could see homey lace curtains framing the windows, pulled back in classic 'Let's Play House' fashion. Little sparkles of light shone from teardrop-shaped crystals hung inside on nearly invisible string. The whole effect was a little nauseating. The final touch was the sudden appearance of two cats twining around each other on the windowsill closest to the door, a silver one and a black one.

Sam and Dean got out of the car. At the house they climbed the single stair to the porch carefully, vaguely suspicious of this model of one hundred percent small-town America. Could anything really be this perfect?

As cats will do, the two in the window glared at them, then disappeared. "Here goes," Dean said, and gave the doorbell a sharp push. One of the windows was open an inch or two and they heard the first two bars of "The Star-Spangled Banner" chime delicately inside the house.

"You gotta be kidding," Dean said. "What if—"

He broke off as footsteps sounded on the other side of the door, then it was pulled open. The older woman who stood there looked nothing like a psychic or a witch, although both brothers knew there was no true stereotype; she was thin and only about five feet tall. Her eyes were bright blue and inquisitive in a make-up free, heart-shaped face below snow-colored hair pulled back from her face. She wore a long-sleeved navy blue dress with white dots—the dots must have been a thing for her, because wrapped around her neck was a wide purple scarf with smaller dots on it. The mismatched outfit didn't really fit with the neat, carefully coordinated colors and country charm of the outside of the house. She didn't look at all surprised to see them.

"Hello," she said in a pleasant voice. "May I help you?"

Dean stepped forward and offered his FBI identification at the same time Sam pulled his from his pocket. "FBI," he said. "Mr. Pyle from the hiking store recommended we talk to you. You're Cinnamon Ellison?"

The woman didn't bother to look at their identification, but she didn't move to let them inside, either. "Beau Pyle is my ex-brother-in-law," she said. "I'm sure he told you that." When they didn't answer, she pressed her lips together. "Or at least something approximating that. I assume he also told you I'm somewhat psychic."

Dean glanced at Sam, then back at her. "Yes."

"And you believed him?"

Dean's mouth worked but nothing came out. She'd surprised him. "I…"

"What he means to say is that we're open to exploring all possibilities," Sam said quickly.

She drew herself up, straight as a ruler, and somehow made herself seem a foot taller. "You are not FBI agents."

It was Sam's turn to be caught off guard. "Of course we are."

"No, you're not." Cinnamon Ellison put her hands on her hips defiantly. "And you are not coming into my house until you tell me the truth." When Dean held out his identification wallet again, she batted it away. "That's nonsense and you know it. I know it." Her mouth turned down at the edges. "I knew it the second you stepped onto my porch." She tapped the side of her head. "In here."

Dean shoved his ID case back into his pocket. "If you're so smart, why don't you tell us who we are?"

"I'm a psychic, not a facial recognition program," she snapped. "I never forget a face, but I have to see it for the first time to remember it."

"So you've had FBI agents here before?" Sam asked.

"Don't try to change the subject." Ellison reached out and poked him in the shoulder hard enough to make him take a half-step backward. "You're not FBI, so I want to know what you're doing in Brownsdale and why you're so intent on finding those two girls that went missing."

Dean raised one eyebrow. "Isn't everyone?"

"Perhaps, but you're not everyone. You don't even live in this town." She tilted her head, as if she were remembering something… or was perhaps thinking about it for the first time. "In fact, you aren't even police. You two are some kind of…" Her eyes squeezed shut momentarily. "Monster killers? No, that makes no sense."

The brothers glanced at each other, then without warning Dean took two fast steps forward, pushing the psychic back through the door and into her house; without questioning him, Sam followed and pulled the door closed. A quick turn, and he'd locked it.

"What are you doing?" Ellison's voice climbed quickly,

heading toward a scream—not that anyone out here would hear it. Still, that would be bad business and something neither of them wanted.

"Please," Sam said. He held out his hands to show they were empty, palm up like he would do to a scared dog. "I swear, we aren't here to hurt you. We have the best of intentions—"

"Like hell you do," she spat. "I know all about that road, young mister! I bet you have ropes and duct tape and all kinds of nefarious weapons out there in the trunk of your car."

"Nefarious?" Sam repeated.

"She's pegged us about the weapons," Dean said. "Look, ma'am, we just want to—"

The woman spun, snatched something off an end table covered by a crocheted doily, and flung it at Sam's head. Before it could connect, Dean lunged sideways and plucked the object, the heavy glass orb of a snow globe, out of midair. He held it up and sent an admonishing look toward Ellison.

"What the hell?" Sam gawked at the snow globe, then turned and glared at her. "You could have really hurt me with that thing."

Ellison looked around again, but before she could focus on anything else to throw, Dean was in front of her and blocking her reach. "Stop it," he said sternly. Inside the snow globe a Christmas village scene spun and glittered with false snow as he set the orb back on its base. He wrapped one hand around her upper arm and steered her to a chair. "Sit. The only person flipping out and trying to hurt anyone here is you."

Reluctantly Ellison obeyed, settling lightly onto a wingback chair upholstered in a colorful vintage floral pattern. Not surprisingly, she didn't seem to fit in with the chair or the rest of the sitting room. "Fine," she said, sounding like a prim little librarian. "What do you want with me?"

"It's not you we're particularly interested in," Sam answered. "But you're right about us wanting to find out what happened to the Dietz girls." He glanced around the room, then walked over to a yellow striped couch and pushed a couple of frilly pillows aside. "I'm going to sit, okay? Please don't throw anything else at me."

"Fine," Ellison said again, but something seemed to have softened slightly in her tone. She turned her gaze on Dean. "You sit, too. I don't like you looming over me."

"Uh... okay." Dean chose another chair, this one a round-backed rocker with a dainty embroidered pattern on the seat and back. He looked absurd when he settled onto it, like a lumberjack trying to relax in his great-grandmother's parlor.

For a few moments, no one said anything. Then Ellison sighed and folded her hands. "That phrase—monster hunters—keeps rolling around in my head. It popped into my thoughts a few seconds after I first saw you two and got stronger every time either of you touched me. Now it won't go away. So what does it mean?"

Sam pulled in a breath. "Exactly that. It's not symbolism or some kind of riddle. We hunt monsters."

"And demons and vampires and all kinds of things—"

"That go bump in the night," she interrupted. "Cute."

"Not at all," Dean responded. "Most of them are pretty damned ugly, as well as vicious and deadly. They'd kill you—us—if they had any chance at all, just for fun."

The woman peered at them, her blue eyes clear and sharp. "You're saying some kind of monster got those girls?"

"We're not saying that at all," Sam said. "We don't know anything... yet." He glanced at his brother. "But we're hoping, at least based on what Beau Pyle said, you might be able to help us."

Oddly, Ellison didn't seem to find their claims at all strange. Then she waved her hand dismissively. "Beau doesn't know a thing about me. He tells everyone we're in-laws but the truth is my sister divorced him forty years ago and then moved off to Louisville. He's been putting the moves on me ever since, like I'd date my sister's leavings. I've got more taste than that, I'll tell you."

Sam smiled a little as he leaned forward and clasped his hands between his knees. "You might not think much of him, but he did recommend you."

The older woman rolled her eyes. "Only because he thinks it'll soften me up. He's never believed I could do a damned thing, not really."

Sam studied her. "What do you mean 'not really?'"

She shrugged. "I've helped people out in this town over the years, a few now and then who were in a pretty bad way. Folks around here tell themselves they don't believe, and maybe they don't... but they don't forget, either."

Dean cleared his throat. "And how exactly did you help these people?"

Ellison looked at her ring-less fingers. The nails were unpainted and not very long, carefully filed to round tips. Unassuming, like she was, if you discounted the purple and the polka dots. She wasn't even wearing earrings. "I've seen a few things that were... coming," she answered in a low voice. "Like the time one of the oxygen tanks in the storage room at the nursing home was leaking. I called the head nurse but she didn't believe me, said I was off my rocker. So I called the sheriff's office, but they didn't believe me either."

"What happened?" Sam asked.

Ellison lifted her chin, giving them a glimpse of how stubborn she could be. "I'd seen in my head what would happen so I wasn't about to give up. I don't have a whole lot of friends in this town, seeing as how they all think I'm crazy, but I have a few. So I started calling around and asking who had loved ones in that home, parents or—God forbid—disabled children. There are two I know of. Brownsdale doesn't have its own hospital, but we get folks from up Bowling Green way because things are a lot less expensive here.

"Anyway, half a dozen phone calls later I found someone who knew a friend of a friend of a friend sort of thing. When that person got wind of it, there was no stopping him. He drove over and marched right up to the front desk, demanded someone personally take him down to the storage room. Said he wasn't going to let them stand by while his father blew up with the rest of the building. It was a fine mess, but by the time the police came he'd already forced a janitor to take him to the basement. They found the leak, evacuated the building, and got the fire department to take care of that tank."

"What about after the fact?" Dean asked her.

"What do you mean?"

"Events that have already occurred."

Ellison's fingers tightened momentarily. "You mean like solving crimes or something?"

"Yeah, that."

"I was the... what do you call it? Whistleblower, that's it, the whistleblower on that whole mess where three people at the nursing home were abusing the residents. I knew what they were doing—this time, the feelings of agony coming out of that place were almost unbearable—but again, neither the home nor the law in town believed me. What that means was that they really didn't want to do anything about it. So I went to the state police."

Sam tilted his head. "And they believed you?"

"No." Her gaze flicked away momentarily, then steadied. "Actually I knew they wouldn't before I even made the call, so I lied. I told him I was an anonymous witness, placed the call from a pay phone in town." She gave a chuckle that had an edge of embarrassment to it. "I even made sure I wore a hat big enough to hide my face. Anyway, they did a big investigation and ended up arresting those three people." She inhaled and her chin lifted in another small gesture, this time of annoyance. "I've offered my services to the sheriff's department on several occasions since then, but they've been very clear about not being interested. I guess they want to keep things the way they are."

Dean frowned. "The way they are?"

Ellison stood suddenly, making Sam jump and automatically assess anything that could be thrown in his direction. But she just paced, back and forth, as she told them more.

"Like every police facility, the sheriff's department has an evidence locker," she said. "Locked, of course, everything inventoried all nice and neat." She paused and it occurred to Sam that there was something odd about her voice; it had dropped in volume and every time she paused there was an eerie and unmistakable echo to her words. Sam and Dean glanced at each other, then looked back at her. Ellison was still walking back and forth, but her eyes had gone glassy and faraway. It was the same gaze they'd seen on many of the patients in the psych ward they'd once been admitted to, like they were lost in another world from which they couldn't—or wouldn't—escape. This woman, however, was different. Sam didn't think there was anything wrong with her mental faculties and she had, at least for them, recited a decent history of proven psychic ability. She seemed more like she was in a trance than having visions. Maybe both.

"So what is it about the evidence locker?" Sam prompted when she still said nothing. He kept his voice modulated, not wanting to break her focus.

Ellison looked up at the ceiling, as if she were scanning something they couldn't see. "There's a special section in the back and it's full," she said in that same, strange tone. "It's like a big wire cage and it has… things in it. Purses, sleeping bags, tents, backpacks, stuff like that. So many." Her voice fell to a whisper. "So very many."

Dean started to ask a question but abruptly she blinked and rubbed her eyes. "It's locked, and they keep a tarp over the whole thing. The deputies call it 'the black hole,' where they dump stuff that belongs to people no one can find." Her gaze met Dean's. "Not that they try."

"And do you know why they don't try?" Dean came back.

Ellison frowned and went back to the chair to sit. "No. I can't figure that out. Maybe…" She hesitated.

"What?" Sam asked.

She shook her head. "No, I'm just speculating. There's no proof."

"Tell us anyway," Dean said.

Ellison pressed her lips together. "Maybe they're afraid," she said finally. "I feel like they think that next time—any time—it could be them who goes missing, or maybe someone they love."

"But I thought that doesn't happen," Dean said. "The guy at the library told us that no one local ever goes missing."

She nodded. "Owen, right. Nice young man. Big mistake inviting family here to visit. He hasn't been here long enough to be considered a 'local.'"

Dean looked at his brother. "Maybe that's why his cousins were taken."

Ellison squinted at them, as if she hadn't heard properly. "Taken? By what?"

Dean leaned back and folded his arms. "Why don't you tell us?"

"So that's why you came to me." The older woman pushed an errant lock of white hair off her forehead. "I wish I could, but when I try all I get is blackness."

"The black hole," Sam murmured.

"Yes," she agreed. "Like that." She sent Dean a look that was almost sly. "Now if I could get my hands on something from that evidence room…" She let the statement go unfinished.

"That would help you find them?"

"I don't know," she admitted. "Sometimes touching things tells me nothing, sometimes everything. Sometimes just enough." She gave them a sudden, bright smile and nodded at Sam; it lit up her face and momentarily wiped away the strain that had been on it ever since they forced their way through the door. "Like when I tossed that snow globe at you, I knew your brother would catch it before it beaned you in the skull."

Sam had to laugh, but his grin quickly faded. "You think there's something in that evidence locker that'll help you find the Dietz twins?"

"I don't know," she repeated. "It depends whether or not something of theirs was tossed in there. If the same thing happened to them as all the others..." Ellison seemed to choke a little. "Then maybe I could at least find out what."

Sam rubbed his face. "You keep talking in the past tense. Like it's too late."

Ellison fixed her blue eyes on him. "Oh, it's definitely too late."

EIGHT

"What do you think?" Sam asked as he and Dean headed back to the Impala.

"She's legit," Dean answered.

"I know that. About the evidence thing. You think they're covering something up?"

"I think it's time to go formal on the sheriff and his cronies." Dean opened the door and settled behind the wheel. "They don't have the abilities that telepathy lady has, so our FBI creds will fly just fine with them. All we need to do is get in uniform."

The ride back to the motel didn't take long. Even though the day had slipped into late afternoon, it was still warm outside, the temperature high enough to make them sweat even with the windows down. Their room at the Cave Country Inn was muggy and dark, overly warm. Dean cranked up the air conditioning and they took turns taking quick showers, rinsing away the clammy perspiration and the pervasive feeling of sluggishness that came with the high humidity. When they were dressed and ready to go, both men felt a lot more able to deal with the barriers between them and what they needed to know.

Neither talked on the drive to the sheriff's department. There was no plan—as happened with so many of their cases, they would wing it, go with the flow and hope the stream took them in the right direction. Not that they didn't sometimes orchestrate things in advance, but mostly... no. After all these years they'd gotten used to the spontaneity of the job, of somehow pulling it all together at the end even if they weren't always seeing eye to eye. It was the Winchester way of things.

"Ready for this?" Dean asked as he turned the Impala into a diagonal parking spot across the street from the sheriff's office.

"As ever," Sam replied. He got out and closed the passenger-side door, then looked around. The brilliant blue sky of earlier was now spotted with afternoon clouds; every time one of them rolled across the sun the temperature seemed to drop by ten degrees. A few cars were parked here and there but mostly the street seemed deserted. "I guess most of the people around here are still at the car show."

Dean shrugged and patted the Impala's roof. "Got the best car in town right here. Let's go."

The sheriff's office was in a small brick building with a concrete and glass front. The door opened to a small reception room, big enough to hold a desk, a couple of chairs for visitors, and a double filing cabinet against the wall on the left. A few feet behind the desk was a wall sporting a locked steel door to the right of a few framed pictures and commendations.

A deputy, middle-aged with thick, short hair above a double chin and a generous belly pushing at his gray uniform, was sitting in front of a computer. He looked up. "Help you?"

They pulled out their FBI credentials but the deputy barely glanced at them. "We're looking into the disappearance of the Dietz twins, Deputy Sloane," Sam told him, using the name sewn onto the other man's shirt. "We need to take a look at your evidence locker."

Deputy Sloane dropped his gaze back to the computer screen. "Sorry," he said. "Only Sheriff Thompson can authorize that."

"We spoke with him this morning," Dean said. "He—"

"We keep the evidence in a room in the basement," Sloane interrupted. "Sheriff Thompson is the only one with the key."

Dean frowned. "In the entire department? That's kind of strange."

Sloane looked back at the brothers and his eyes darkened. "You calling me a liar?"

"Of course not," Sam said hastily. "Don't mind my partner. No filter."

Sloane's gaze stayed on Dean for a few seconds but Dean didn't flinch. Finally Sloane looked back at Sam. "The sheriff's gone for the day but he'll be in tomorrow."

"Any progress on the search for the girls?" Sam asked.

The deputy shrugged. "None that I know about."

Dean felt his jaw clench. There was a serious I don't give a crap attitude around here that was really pissing him off. "You have people out looking now? Anyone at all? Because you don't look that busy."

Sloane's eyes, dark brown and expressionless, met Dean's again. "I'm not at liberty to discuss the details of an ongoing investigation."

Dean stepped closer to the desk. "Listen, pal, we're the good guys, remember? A little cooperation goes a long way."

Deputy Sloane stood suddenly and leaned over the desk to face Dean. He was a big man, as tall as Sam, and his face was like stone. He clearly wasn't intimidated. "I don't know you and I don't answer to you. You want information, talk to the sheriff. He calls the shots around here—all the shots, and he hasn't mentioned you two at all. I don't take orders from anyone but him. You might be FBI but you still don't belong in this town."

Dean's scowl melted into amazement. "What? I—"

"We'll come back tomorrow," Sam cut in. He took his brother by the arm and pulled him away from the desk. "When the sheriff's here. I think that'll be better."

"Yeah," said Sloane. He was still focused on Dean, like he was daring him to start something. "That'll be better."

"What the hell was that?" Dean demanded outside.

"Hometown resistance," Sam answered. "Come on." The brothers walked back to the car and climbed in before Sam continued. "The only way we'll see what they have in that basement is through the sheriff."

"Yeah, because Deputy Dog in there won't do anything without his master's command. I really wanted to punch his lights out," Dean said, slamming the driver's-side door. "Now what?"

"I know." Sam glanced up at the cloud-studded sky, then

checked his watch. "Unless we can find the sheriff and convince him to go back to work tonight, we're stuck. And somehow I'm thinking that's a no go."

Watching in the side mirror, Dean saw the lights switch on in the sheriff's office. "How can these people not even care?" he asked incredulously. "Two girls, just kids, are out there somewhere and these people are sitting on their asses and doing nothing."

"I'm guessing once their parents find out tomorrow morning things are going to heat up fast around here. At least, I hope they do. Right now let's head back to the motel and hit the Internet, see if we can find anything else out about Brownsdale's history, or maybe the cave. It's all pretty and small-town America on the surface, but there's something really nasty underneath.

"We just have to figure out what it is."

NINE

Cinnamon Ellison put all thoughts of those two fake FBI agents out of her mind and made herself a cup of chamomile tea after she was ready for bed. This was her favorite time of day, or technically, time of night. Everything that was on her chores list had usually been accomplished and she had taken her evening shower. Now she was relaxed and as stress-free as she could be, almost ready to climb into bed and let sleep refuel her mind and body. While she drank her tea she made a conscious effort to empty her mind, like tossing out the trash. There were already too many complicated things in her life that she could dwell on, and the truth was she thought about them plenty during the day. But at night, every night, she would let them go.

When the last of her tea was gone, Cinnamon rinsed the cup and put it in the dishwasher, then headed to her bedroom. She loved this area of the house; it was a sanctuary of pale blue and cream, just the right colors to relax the mind. She pulled back the chenille bed spread and top sheet and crawled beneath the sheets with a contented sigh. The cats appeared, right on schedule, and settled themselves on the comforter over her feet. For just a moment she reveled in the clean, cool feel of the sheets against her skin, the warm weight of the cats on her ankles, then she reached up and shut off the bedside lamp.

Sleep overcame her quickly, as it usually did. Most nights she didn't dream. On those she did, they were usually fragmented, pleasant, or nonsensical mini-films that she barely, if at all, remembered the next morning.

Tonight would be very different.

She knew she was dreaming, she knew it, but she was helpless to make her eyes open and return her to the real world. Stranded within her own mind, she was in some kind of underground apartment, equipped with all manner of things she didn't understand: a library, austere kitchen facilities, bedrooms, some kind of weapons room, and a huge garage containing all sorts of vehicles. It wasn't quite dark; she could make out shapes and her basic surroundings—walls, ceilings, the floor, the furniture—but nothing with the crystal clarity to satisfy her natural inquisitiveness.

There was also a pervasive feeling of fear, as though at any moment she might turn down a corridor or open a door and find creatures, the existence of which she could never have imagined. Occasionally she would catch a glimpse of these monstrosities. These beings were less clear than her surroundings, almost nebulous but no less horrifying. She was far too terrified to open any door or pull aside any curtain to see what might be behind it, but they appeared anyway. There were faces with teeth, long and sharp, a flash of huge black wings at the far end of a fog-filled room. At other times thick, snake-like forms writhed on the carpeting beneath her feet and she stumbled as she tried to move away, doubly terrified that she would fall into their midst. Occasionally things flew past her head or she would feel the hard brush of something like bristly fur as it skimmed past her hip. Nothing was distinctively evil, but nothing was ever friendly either. This strange place seemed to go on and on and on, each room leading to another that in turn led nowhere.

And so it went, far into the night hours.

Cinnamon Ellison woke with a start. The weak light of dawn was bleeding through her gauzy curtains, but the comfort it brought into the room was false. Her teeth were clenched and her nerves were singing, and when she looked down at her hands she realized she had rolled her fingers into tight fists. The cats were gone, hiding because they'd probably sensed her mood. There would be no calm to the coming day.

She tried to think back over the dream, with its myriad changing scenes, the not-quite-faceless beings that had accompanied her through it. They were fading even as she struggled to recall them, but as it so often had recently, that one phrase popped into her thoughts:

Monster hunters.

On the heels of that, the image of those two fake FBI

agents flashed into her mind. She had no doubt the two were related. The obvious question was how.

But she wasn't sure she wanted to find out.

TEN

Owen Meyer was up way before dawn on Sunday morning, sitting at his kitchen table while the outside sky crawled from darkness to washed-out gray. There was a cup of coffee in front of him, but he'd made it out of habit alone; it had gone cold and he didn't want it anyway. He felt hollowed out, like someone had taken one of those pumpkin carving tools and ripped out his insides, scoop after painful scoop. What had been left behind was an empty, raw space that felt colder with every breath he took.

Where were the girls now? Somewhere in the cave, cold and shivering, terrified?

Or had they been taken by someone, a maniac or murderer, and subjected to things even more unspeakable?

Still he sat there, helpless, waiting as the seconds churned into minutes, the minutes dragged to hours, until his cell phone finally rang at just past eight-thirty. Owen looked at the screen and his heart did a sudden, painful slam in his chest. His mouth went dry at the same time an ulcer-like pain razored through his stomach. The phone's screen showed an image of Aunt Lena's smiling face. She looked so much like Owen's mother that for the first time he wondered what his dad would say if he knew Marley and Fallon were missing. A stupid thought, and he made himself refocus on Aunt Lena and Uncle Ray. He'd had this hope, which now seemed completely insane, that the girls would be found before their parents were through with their rafting trip, that he could tell them and the rest of the family about the entire thing as a sort of "listen to this scary but ultimately harmless thing that happened to us over the weekend."

But that had all gone into the garbage. Somewhere on the other end of the cell phone, on the shoreline of the Colorado River in the Grand Canyon, a local sheriff had given his aunt and uncle the news that their two thirteen-year-old daughters were gone. The two daughters they had left under Owen's care.

The phone rang again, making a sound much like a trickling stream. He'd picked that ringtone because he'd thought it represented his aunt—soft, warm, steady. He imagined that in a moment she would be more like a river slamming against its banks after a terrible flood.

Without him consciously willing it, his hand reached out and he hit the talk button as he lifted the phone to his ear. "Aunt Lena," he began. "I—"

"Oh my God, Owen. They're telling us the girls are gone! Is this true? Oh my God," she repeated. Her tone was high, her voice climbing in volume. "Is this true?"

"Yes," he said. "They disappeared—"

He didn't get a chance to finish before she began screaming in his ear. "What have you done? Oh my God, where are our daughters? You—"

Her voice was cut off suddenly, interrupted by Owen's Uncle Ray. For about three seconds it sounded like the man was going to stay calm, then his voice escalated to nothing short of a bellow. "What the hell happened?"

"Uncle Ray, I don't know!" Owen wailed. "I was at work and they left. I don't know where they went."

"You were supposed to take time off work and stay with them," his uncle said. If words over a telephone line could have a color, the older man's would have been red with fury. "That's the whole reason we let them come and stay with you, because you said you would take care of them."

"I know," Owen replied, "but I couldn't afford to take off the entire time they were here. I was going to take off tomorrow and Tuesday and drive them over to Mammoth Cave for a tour—"

His uncle's voice cut him off again. "Jesus, Owen—are they in the cave? Is that where they went?"

"I don't know," Owen repeated. "No one does."

"We'll be there as soon as we can get a flight," Uncle Ray said. "You'll find my girls, Owen. You'll find them before we get there."

The line went dead and Owen stood there for a long moment, the cell phone still pressed to his ear. Finally he lowered the phone and went back over to the kitchen table to sit. He hadn't even realized he'd stood when he first answered the phone, had been standing the entire time. His insides felt warped with the sensation of twisting fear you get when you know something's coming that's going to be horrible and you just can't stop it.

His thoughts flashed back to when he'd first proposed that the girls come and stay with him while Aunt Lena and Uncle Ray went on their rafting trip. Yes, it had been his idea. The visit had been in the works for six months, and although the girls had demonstrated mixed feelings about it at first, as the time drew closer they'd become more and more excited. Now he realized that among the things in their room that they had unpacked were a couple of books on cave exploring. It probably didn't help that Owen had stocked the bookcases in their room with at least half a dozen coffee-table books showing the beauty and splendor of many of the caverns that were part of the Mammoth Cave system.

Suddenly it didn't seem such a big mystery at all. They were lost in Mammoth Cave.

Sitting at the kitchen table, Owen let his head rest on his arms and cried.

Eleven

Church bells.

Clang—

Clang—

Clang—

Dean rolled over and groaned, trying to pull the flat hotel pillow over his head. For a moment he didn't know where he was or what was going on. Then he flipped onto his back and opened his eyes, staring at the old popcorn ceiling of the Cave Country Inn. Right, Brownsdale, Kentucky. Church bells—he'd never heard those in the bunker. When he turned his head to the right he saw his brother sitting up on the other bed.

Sam looked over at him. "Is that what I think it is?"

"Yeah," Dean answered. "Someone banging a big ass metal spoon against a hundred-gallon cook pot."

"That's what I thought," Sam said. He fell back with a groan and covered his ears.

Outside the room, the bells kept going. Just when the

brothers thought the noise would end, more joined in, apparently from another church. Like so many southern states, Kentucky had countless places of worship. In fact, their research had put the number of churches in the small town of Brownsdale at fifty-eight. Right now it sounded like they were all gearing up for some kind of holy symphony.

Another round joined in and Dean gave up and swung his legs over the side of the bed. "Might as well get up and find some breakfast," he said.

"Not a whole lot of choices in that regard," Sam said as he, too, climbed out of bed. "I think it's back to Linda's Hilltop."

"Oh, yeah!" Dean's grin was bright and wide, something rarely seen so early in the morning.

Sam shook his head. "Please don't tell me you need another one of those caveman-thing sandwiches."

His brother's smile never faltered.

Just for giggles they rode by the sheriff's office before heading to the restaurant, but they weren't surprised to find no one there, and no lights on, either. Apparently no one broke the law on Sunday mornings in this town. Maybe that was true—traffic on the streets was almost nonexistent. Occasionally they drove past a small church and saw that the parking lot was almost full. About the only other places open were convenience stores and gas stations. For a couple of anxious minutes, Dean was afraid the restaurant would be closed, but when he turned into the parking lot he was relieved to see it was crowded. Not so much so that there was a line, but it was clear that

Linda's was the spot for Sunday breakfast around here.

Sam snagged the Sunday paper from the machine outside and they headed toward a table on the left side, the only one that was empty. As they sat, a harried-looking busboy swiped a few crumbs off the tabletop and dropped napkins and silverware in front of them. "Y'all want coffee?" he asked. They both nodded.

At this time on a Sunday morning the place was filled more with old-timers than families or teenagers. It was almost a disappointment when no one so much as looked up when Sam and Dean came in. It took a while for the waitress to get to them, but when she did Sam ordered the same standard breakfast plate he'd had before. Dean chose another special off the menu, something Sam hadn't even noticed.

"What did you order?" Sam asked when the waitress had gone.

The corner of Dean's mouth turned up and his eyes gleamed. "Never you mind, little brother. You'll see it when it gets here."

"So it's going to be a mystery, huh?"

Dean shrugged. "Where's the fun in life if you can't have a surprise now and then?"

But surprise didn't quite cover it. When the waitress brought the food, the platter she set in front of Dean was immense, filled to overflowing with some kind of fried meat and eggs buried under layers of peppered gravy. Home fries cut with green peppers and onions ringed one side of the plate while two huge homemade biscuits balanced on the other edge. To top it off, she slid a side plate of pancakes next to Dean's coffee cup. Double globs of butter melted and ran down the edges of the pancakes.

"Yes yes yes," Dean said happily. "The Sunday chicken-fried steak and eggs with gravy special."

"I can't watch," Sam said. "Do you even realize how much of that is probably going into your arteries?"

Dean just raised his eyebrow and picked up his fork. "With all the crap we deal with in our lives good food is the last thing I worry about," he said. "In fact, I figure this is the thing least likely to kill me."

Miraculously, Dean was still able to walk out of the restaurant and get in his car. Sam slid into the passenger seat, then looked over to see his brother smiling contentedly.

"I could live here," he said happily.

That made Sam laugh. "Right. For about three days and then you'd run through everything on the menu." He gave his brother a sideways look. "And off the menu, too. Let's go."

Dean grunted and started the car. A few minutes later they were pulling into a spot across the street from the sheriff's office. They could see someone inside through the window, but from here they couldn't tell who it was. The silver patrol car that was parked around the side could have belonged to anyone in the department.

"Well," Sam said. "No time like the present."

They got out and walked across the street, and Sam groaned under his breath when they pulled open the door and realized Deputy Sloane was behind the desk. "Good morning," Sam said with fake cheerfulness.

"Same to you," Sloane said. "You boys back again about getting into the evidence room?"

"Yeah," Dean said. It was clear from the tone of his voice that he wasn't happy about even having to talk to Sloane.

Sloane motioned to the two chairs across from the desk. "Y'all take a seat," he said. "The sheriff will be here after church, like he always is." Sloane glanced at his watch. "Maybe a half-hour, not much longer."

So they waited. Sam passed the time by gazing at the certificates and pictures that were hung on the walls in an apparent random display, while Dean openly glowered at the deputy. Sloane paid him absolutely no attention, as though he were used to people disliking him. Now and then Dean made a motion like he was going to get up and Sam grabbed him by the suit sleeve and pulled him back, shaking his head. They'd get nothing out of this department if they acted like jerks.

Almost forty minutes later, and at the end of their patience, the door opened and Sheriff Thompson walked in. He wasn't surprised to see them—of course, he would've seen the Impala parked across the street. The smile he gave them was just as fake as Sam's had been earlier.

"Deputy Sloane let me know that you two want to get into the evidence locker," he drawled.

"That's right," Sam said.

The sheriff gazed at them but when neither brother said anything, he looked resigned. "I don't have anything down there that belongs to the Dietz girls," Thompson said. "But you're welcome to take a look. Always want to be cooperative with the Federal Bureau of Investigation."

The sarcasm was almost undetectable but Dean still caught it. He scowled, but before he could retort, Sam said, "That's great. You lead the way."

The sheriff nodded and they followed him around the desk and to the metal door in the corner of the room. There he unsnapped a heavily loaded key ring at his belt, then selected a key and twisted it into the lock. "Follow me," he said in a brusque voice.

They obeyed and trudged down a hallway lit by overhead fluorescents. It wasn't that long but there were no certificates or photographs here. Instead, there were doors on both sides of the hall and the walls were covered with maps and posters of Brownsdale and Edwardson County, as well as topographical maps of the area and a few more of the cave system. At the end of this hall was another metal door, where the sheriff selected a different key to open it. He reached inside and flipped on a light switch. "Watch your step going down," he instructed. "The steps are kind of narrow."

More fluorescent lights, this time a little farther apart. They turned to the left and descended into a windowless basement filled with neatly labeled boxes and other items that were too big or oddly shaped to store on shelves. These were bagged or wrapped in plastic or canvas, again with neatly printed identifying labels attached on the front. The room stretched the length and width of the building. At the far end, the left corner had been sectioned off with metal grating that ran from floor to ceiling. While the sheriff selected yet another key from his ring, Sam and Dean scanned the basement for surveillance cameras and saw them set at regular intervals on the ceiling. The feed probably went to the computer in the upstairs front office.

"Here you go," the sheriff said in a too-loud voice.

Sam nodded his thanks. "We might be a while," he said. "You don't have to babysit us."

"It's not a problem," the sheriff responded, "but actually I do. Procedure says I have to stay with you. Sorry, boys. It's not personal."

"Right," Dean said. "Not personal at all."

Sheriff Thompson only leaned against the open door and crossed one ankle over the other, then loosely folded his arms, something he seemed to do often. His relaxed stance was a lie; his eyes were sharp, missing nothing. There was a wry little smile at the corner of his mouth.

The locker was wide and Sam and Dean moved slowly down the aisle that ran through the center of it. There was nowhere they could be out of Sheriff Thompson's careful gaze. The shelves were filled with boxes and bagged items, all carefully labeled in the same format: date, last and first name of the case, type of case, and a summary of the contents. Although Sam kept his mouth shut, he noted that a number of them were labeled "missing person."

"What's that stuff in the back?" Dean asked suddenly. Sam had been reading the label on yet another missing person's case; now he turned to look where his brother was indicating.

Sheriff Thompson didn't move. "Junk," he said flatly. "Crap we pick up from the side of the road with no way to identify the owner. We toss it in the back there, keep it for a while—"

"How long is a while?" Sam interrupted.

The sheriff lifted one shoulder in a clear I don't give a damn movement. "Six months, not much longer than that. There's no room for it. We figure if the owner hasn't come back to look for their belongings by then, they never will."

Surprised, the brothers looked at each other. Neither said it, but that didn't make a whole lot of sense. Finding something by the side of the road didn't mean it was always a simple case of lost and found. What if someone was murdered out in these woods, and their body wasn't discovered for a couple of years? Each and every item in that haphazard pile was probably some kind of evidence, but saying something would only build a bigger brick wall between them and the sheriff.

"So no one's ever come back for something a year or two out?" Dean asked anyway. "You know, like a family that left something here on their last vacation?"

"Damn it," Sam muttered. "My shoe's untied again." He dropped to one knee and struggled with the laces.

"Nope." The sheriff met Dean's gaze. "Never had that happen a single time."

Sam stood. "Well, I guess there's not much to see in here, Agent Taylor, so let's head out." He looked at the lawman. "I hope you don't mind if we come back if we think of something else?"

Sheriff Thompson unfolded his arms. "Of course not. Visit anytime."

"Don't tell me you're buying that bull about keeping stuff for only six months," Dean said to Sam as they climbed into the car.

"Not for a second," Sam replied, "but I didn't see anything that I could specifically tie to the Dietz girls. I figured he'd find some excuse to eighty-six us searching through everything in there."

"I didn't see matching backpacks," Dean said. "They're twins, right? Don't twins do that?"

"I suppose," Sam said. "But I did grab this." He held up a small round charm. It had a cute pink skull on a red background, with glittery fake pink rhinestones around the outside edge.

"What's that?" Dean asked.

"Part of a keychain, I think. I reached through the wire and pulled it off a backpack while I was tying my shoe. It was in front, like it was put there recently. Maybe this will give Cinnamon Ellison something to go on." Sam pocketed it then held up his cell phone. "I also got a couple of shots of that pile of stuff. I did it on the sly so they won't be great quality and the lighting in there sucked, but it's what we have."

"All right," Dean said. "Let's head over there now."

TWELVE

Beau Pyle sat placidly in the Pleasant Union United Baptist Church, midway up the aisle and precisely in the center of the pews on the right side. No one noticed him, no one paid him any attention. Oh sure, they knew he owned the Go Cave Wild store, but that was it.

Or so he told himself every day.

He had been attending this church for seven-plus decades, and his parents, grandparents, and great-grandparents were buried in the small cemetery outside. Sadly, it was not the memories of the great people who had come before him in his family that remained uppermost in the minds of his fellow townsfolk. Oh no, that place of honor had been hijacked by a wild young man who had run off with his girlfriend's little sister, a lively young hellion ten years his junior.

One mistake, and it had ruined his life.

The memory of Brenda Ellison, with her wild dark hair falling in curls around her shoulders and her flashing green eyes, still haunted him, but not in a good way. His brain back then had been ruled by hormones, out of control and typical of a foolish youngster who couldn't see the future beyond next Friday night. The hell of it was that the future had been right in front of him, on his own damned arm: Cinnamon. It would be a cliché to say she paled in comparison to her younger sister, and that wasn't quite true anyway. Brenda had made Cinnamon seem invisible when the two were together. She had blotted out Cinnamon's fragile, glowing light like a bonfire overwhelms the small red gleam of coals in a barbecue pit. But as with all things that seem to explode with brilliance, Brenda's light had flared out once they had taken off and gotten married. And in the depths of Beau's heart and his soul, Cinnamon's sweet glow remained.

Strong. Steady. Never-ending.

He and Brenda had come back to Brownsdale after a couple of years, heads held high and defiant. Who cared what the townsfolk thought? Who cared what his parents thought? They had forgiven him, of course, and in time, so had hers. But love had been nothing but lust, and lust is a fleeting feeling and a poor foundation upon which to base a lifetime. The cracks had started, spread, and the house had crumbled.

Now, some fifty years later, Beau sat in church and listened to the preacher. Only regret sat beside him. Not Brenda, with whom he'd had no children and no contact since their divorce over four decades previous. And certainly not Cinnamon, the woman he had recognized too late as the one, true love of his life. Oh, she was civil enough. He had even apologized, spilling his heart at her feet and admitting his terrible mistake. It had made no difference; she would, he knew, never trust him again. And if the people of Brownsdale still talked about them now, how much more monumental would the gossip be should they ever get back together?

Enough remained of the spark of his old self, of the twenty-five-year-old who had left town on the run, to not care. But that was not Cinnamon's way—she could never endure it. And thus had ended the line of the Pyle family, as well as that of the Ellison family. Neither of the Ellison girls had ever borne children and he had been the last remaining son in the Pyle family tree.

What did the townsfolk think of him? It wasn't hard to guess. They saw an old fool, someone who had let his future slip through his fingers and was now paying for it every day.

An old fool.

Beau could live with that. His opinion of himself was much harsher. Brenda had long ago moved away, so she didn't care; she would never see these people again. She didn't even visit her sister.

But Cinnamon…

He wasn't so old and doddering that he didn't see the looks the other women gave her, the How could you have been so stupid? glances. So many years had passed but the old biddies still laughed and talked about Cinnamon behind her back. Catty, bitchy old women, but they were what they were. And he, Beau Pyle, had given them their subject.

My God, what had he done?

Finally, the sermon was over and Beau slipped the Bible into the holder on the pew in front of him, then collected his hat. He didn't stick around to shake the preacher's hand or chit-chat with anyone else. People who did that were noticed, and that's the last thing he wanted to be. He didn't see her, but Beau knew Cinnamon was there, too. Their families had always gone to this church—in fact, that's how he and Cinnamon had met, early in school, fated to grow into a childhood romance that would ultimately end in disaster. She'd be at the back, maybe in the next to last pew, where she could slip out as soon as Go in peace, have a nice day came out of the preacher's mouth. In her car and out of the parking lot before the majority of attendees spilled from the church doors. As it always did, the thought made shame swell in his chest. Such a long time ago, still such a fresh pain in his heart. Would it never end?

The morning sunshine was gone and Beau squinted through the light drizzle that had taken its place. He trained his eyes on the sidewalk so he wouldn't meet anyone else's gaze. Someone called out to him, but the voice came from far enough away that he could pretend he didn't hear; he stepped up his pace to get to his car before it happened again. If they really needed to talk to him, his number was in the phone book.

Today he was also thinking about those twin girls. They should have never gone missing. They weren't locals, but they were as close as they could be to it, and now the FBI was poking around. What was Sheriff Thompson doing about the situation? This should have never happened, never. The drifters, hitchhikers, even the occasional estranged husband making off with a mistress—these made him feel guilty, yes, but nothing like what he felt because of those two kids. The guilt was always there, but he was helpless in the shadow of it—it was his burden to bear, just as it had been his father's, his grandfather's, on and up the family tree back to when the first settlers had come to Edwardson County, before the area had even been named. He lived with the shame and the sin because there was no other choice, no other way to keep the town and its people safe from the hunger that existed deep within the cave.

The mountain must be fed.

That phrase, as crazy as it was, had been written in antique script on the inside cover of the family Bible brought from England hundreds of years ago. He had no idea how it had first come to pass that the Pyles were chosen for this responsibility, but chosen they had been. They were the guardians and they would protect the townspeople, sacrifice a small few, strangers only, for the greater good. No, for the survival of the rest.

Somehow Beau had failed, and the mountain had taken Marley and Fallon instead.

And he had a terrifying feeling about it, that if he didn't find out how this had happened and stop it from occurring again, the mountain's appetite would change. It would no longer be satisfied with the unwanted of society.

It would want the freshest, youngest, and most tender meat it could get.

THIRTEEN

Yesterday's sunshine had given way to a sky filled with a mottled mixture of light and dark clouds. Although the sunlight had been nice, Dean felt more at home in the rain. His life was its own little dark cloud. And although it seemed ridiculous, even Baby seemed to handle better on wet pavement rather than dry. He headed to Cinnamon Ellison's house without discussing it with Sam, who sat in the passenger seat flipping through the newspaper he'd brought with him from the restaurant.

"Anything new?" Dean finally asked.

Sam shook his head. "Nothing. And not even a mention of the missing girls."

The bells had stopped and the parking lots of the churches they passed were now mostly empty. There was more traffic on the road, with the grocery store spaces filling up. The town was finally waking up, to do whatever sleepy little southern towns did on Sundays.

It didn't take long to get to the psychic's house, but when

they pulled up there was no blue Prius parked in the driveway. For a moment, neither brother said anything.

"Now what?" Sam asked.

Dean gave him a lopsided grin. "Well, we can sit here and wait. Or we can go back to the restaurant."

Sam groaned. "You can't tell me you're hungry again. We just finished eating."

Dean shrugged. "I'll never pass up the chance to stock up for later. You never know when we might miss a meal. Besides, maybe she went out for breakfast."

Sam folded the paper and tossed it on the backseat. He sighed. "Fine, let's go back to the restaurant. But no more food for you. That's not how we blend in."

Dean looked at him. "What do you mean, no more food?"

"We're supposed to be flying under the radar, remember?" Sam raised a hand to stop Dean's protest. "I distinctly remember the waitress saying she'd never seen anyone who could so completely clean a plate of their heart attack gravy special."

"I'm honored," Dean said.

"I can think of better things to be proud of," Sam said under his breath. "Like maybe not killing anyone this week."

"Depending on the circumstances, that could be either bad or good."

"Take it however you like. Let's go." Sam settled back in his seat and folded the paper.

"Back again already?"

Sam sent Dean a knowing look as the waitress who had served Dean that ridiculous breakfast sandwich slid two empty cups onto the counter in front of them. "Y'all want coffee?"

"Sure," Dean said. He gave her his best boyish grin. "And keep it coming."

"Absolutely, sugar."

Sam waited until she'd filled the cups and walked away before he spoke. "Sugar? Seriously?"

"It's how they talk in the country," Dean told him.

"I thought that was just on television."

"Clearly not." Dean put his elbows on the counter and made a show of studying all the handwritten specials and the soda fountain menu above the pass-through to the kitchen. The restaurant was quickly filling up with the post-church crowd, entire families clad in their Sunday best. Kids ran from one table to another to talk to their friends while teenagers gave waves that were supposed to look careless. Parents said hello to people at other tables over the heads of their kids and talked about the weather.

And of course, the missing girls. Unfortunately, despite an hour of over-caffeinating themselves, the brothers picked up nothing new. Cinnamon Ellison didn't show up, and perhaps that wasn't surprising considering her not quite bitter words about the Brownsdale townsfolk and what they thought of her.

"Let's get out of here and head to Cinnamon's house," Sam finally said. "If she went to church, maybe did a few errands, she's probably home by now."

"What if she's not there?"

His brother shrugged. "We'll figure that out if we have to. I think we can find better things to do than sit here and watch you moon over the specials board and the waitress."

FOURTEEN

Owen woke drenched in sweat, lying on Fallon's bed. For a dizzying second he couldn't recall how he'd gotten there, then it all slammed back into his brain—the girls being missing, that horrible, heart-shattering conversation with his aunt and uncle. He remembered first sobbing, then outright wailing, pounding his fists on the kitchen table hard enough to make the salt and pepper shakers bounce and fall over. He'd cried until he couldn't anymore, until he had squeezed out the last bit of sorrow and couldn't lift his head. Then, after sitting there for God knows how long, he'd forced himself to his feet with the intention of lying on the couch.

But the girls' room had drawn him. Instead of resisting, he had gone to the door and stared in. The sun wasn't out so the light was muted through the curtains, giving the room a soft, serene glow that made his heart ache all over again. It reminded him of… finality, like the supreme hush in a funeral parlor. He had a sudden vision, horrifically detailed, of just that: a viewing room hung with heavy red velvet curtains to block the daylight, rows of chairs filled with silent people all staring forward, their stunned gazes fixed on two fancy white coffins edged in gold. Three ornate, heavy gold handles were spaced on each side, and the lids were open, showing the thick, quilted white satin inside. Then the vision changed, expanded, and he was standing right in front of the twin coffins, looking down at the green stems and fragile white blooms of a dozen lilies in each.

No bodies to bury.

Because Marley and Fallon were still missing.

Owen's knees had given out. First he'd sat on the edge of Fallon's bed, then finally, out of exhaustion, slipped sideways. He'd pulled one of the decorative pillows under his head and hung his feet off the end so his shoes wouldn't get the spread dirty. He wanted to think that was because she'd be upset about it when she came back, but he couldn't—it was just habit; wipe your feet at the door, don't put your shoes on the furniture. It hit him then, the realization that most people, or at least many, who went through this never stopped believing that the missing person would be found.

He had never once believed they'd be found to begin with.

And he wasn't the only one, was he? That damned Sheriff Thompson—was he even looking? Owen didn't think so. Where were the people handing out flyers, the front page newspaper stories, the search parties, for God's sake? The only people who'd even asked about the twins were those two FBI agents. At least they were doing some research, and had even dug into Brownsdale's sketchy history before they'd arrived.

That was, Owen thought, about the time he'd drifted off, but he woke up thinking about the last thing in his head before he'd fallen asleep: Brownsdale.

He pulled himself to his feet, automatically turned and replaced the pillow, then smoothed the comforter. The room was still filled with that strange, unsettling quiet, as though it would never again be occupied. A complete absence of noise that crawled across his skin like a warm but unpleasant breeze.

Although he didn't know why, Owen backed out of the twins' room carefully, as though if he turned his back he would miss something. He pulled the door shut, then headed to his own bedroom, where he began digging in the closet, looking for some things that he hadn't used regularly in years, way before he'd moved to this hellish southern town. That one paltry tour in Mammoth Cave, he knew, didn't count for anything. He placed his findings on his bed.

Heavy denim jeans, winter weight.

Hiking boots, a little stiff from storage.

Canvas jacket.

Long-sleeved shirt.

Thick socks.

Satisfied, Owen went out to the storage shed in the backyard. There he came up with work gloves, a sturdy baseball cap, and a heavy flashlight—a big Maglite that took three D-size batteries. He tested it in the dark shed and the light was bright and strong; he'd bought it only a couple of months ago because the power sometimes went out during heavy thunderstorms. As he was stepping out of the shed, Owen spotted a can of white spray paint and picked that up, as well. As an indicator of how to find your way back to a starting point, it was a hell of a lot better than breadcrumbs. Highly illegal, but he didn't care.

Inside he changed his clothes and checked the clock before finding an old backpack to carry the flashlight and can of paint, plus a decent amount of water and a few snacks for energy. There was still plenty of time to get out there and do the job that damned Thompson wasn't willing to. And why wasn't he?

Because this damned town was cursed, that's why. Not in some silly supernatural way, oh no. It was people, pure and simple. Evil people. There was something indefinable that ran through the heart of this place. Owen didn't have a clue what that thing was, but it was there—that he believed right down to his soul.

He wasn't a religious man. His parents had been regular churchgoers and had dutifully hauled him to church every week and on the appropriate holidays, but Owen had never felt the connection they obviously did. Instead, he would sit between them and dream about whatever book or comic he was currently reading, going over the details of the story if it was a good one, rewriting it in his imagination if he felt it was lacking. He stood when they stood, knelt when they knelt, did the handshake and hug thing with the people around him when the time came. It didn't bother him, but it didn't inspire him, either. Books did that, the written word. He had been the bookworm as a kid, the nerd as a teen, and now he was the librarian as a grownup.

After those agents had left the library, Owen had taken

a few minutes to dig deeper into the files on his own. He hadn't been intentionally holding back anything, but the more research he did, the more he became convinced that the disappearances weren't accidental. The townsfolk—via the local newspaper and the preachers—and the law had always been stalwart in their public statements that it was nothing but coincidence, that all those people had just passed through and that was that.

Right.

That's why backpacks were found in the woods, small tents and supplies were abandoned at campsites, wallets and women's handbags—money still inside—ended up in public trashcans, where townspeople found them and brought them to the sheriff's office.

Coincidence.

What happened to those people was anyone's guess, but Owen didn't believe for a second that the cave had anything to do with it, that it needed to be satisfied. That was just superstitious old bull, and he would not be sucked into campfire stories and old wives' tales. He'd been to the cave, had taken one of the shorter tours and seen a bunch of others start. The park rangers kept very good track of who went in and came out… or not. And if there was a "not," you bet your backside they sent people in after them right away.

But no one had been sent in after his cousins. Sheriff Thompson might have told him differently but Owen wasn't sure he could believe him.

Fine, he thought. Sheriff Thompson could suck it. Owen would go into the cave himself. Maybe he hadn't been in it a bunch of times and maybe he wasn't an expert, but he was at least prepared for what he was getting into.

If no one else would look for the girls, he'd do it himself.

FIFTEEN

This time when Sam and Dean pulled up in front of Cinnamon's house her car was in the driveway. It took a couple of rings on the doorbell for her to answer. When she opened the door, there were shadows under her eyes, like bruises, as though she hadn't slept well. She stood aside and motioned them inside. Behind her the cats ran down the hall and disappeared into the house. "Come on in."

"You doing okay?" It was the first thing Sam asked her. He couldn't help himself.

"I'm all right," she answered. "I had some strange dreams, is all." She eyed the brothers. "I'm pretty sure they had something to do with you two, although I can't quite figure them out."

"See anything interesting?" Dean asked.

"Maybe. Can I get you boys something to drink? Have you had breakfast?"

"Yes and yes," Dean answered. "Do you have anything besides coffee?"

"Lemonade or tea." She moved aside and motioned for them

to go into the sitting room. "The lemonade's homemade."

They nodded and sat down, waiting for her to return. In a couple of minutes she came back holding two tall glasses. "It's already sweetened," she said as she put them carefully on coasters, then settled herself in the rocking chair. "I assume you have something to show me?"

Sam nodded and reached into his jacket pocket. He pulled out the pink skull keychain and let it dangle in front of her. "I picked this up in the evidence room. It wasn't easy. Sheriff Thompson is watching over that stuff like it's King Tut's treasure. There's a big pile of things in a back corner, down in a locked part of the basement of the sheriff's building. I yanked this off a backpack that was with a whole bunch of others. No tags, ID, nothing. Thompson claims none of the stuff is traceable to anyone."

"He's lying," Cinnamon said. Her voice was brittle. "It's usually traceable to someone."

"Wait," Sam said, "did you say always? Are you telling us that…?"

"Yes," Cinnamon answered. "I could trace the object to someone who's disappeared."

For a moment neither of the brothers could speak. "Wow," Dean finally said.

Cinnamon clasped her hands, her fingers working against each other. "At this point it wouldn't help. They're… gone."

Sam leaned forward. "What do you mean by gone? Dead?"

Cinnamon's gaze focused on something far away. "I'm not sure," she admitted. "I wouldn't be able to say unless I touched something of theirs. But… yeah. I'm pretty sure they're all dead. Call it intuition."

Sam offered her the keychain again, leaning forward so she could reach it. "Then here," he said. "Take this. Tell us what you see."

The woman reached for it then hesitated, her fingers wavering in the air as if she was about to touch something that would give her an electrical shock. After a few seconds, she set her jaw and wrapped her hand around the little pink skull.

For an instant, a fragment in time, Sam thought he was seeing through the psychic's eyes. Then he let go of the keychain and Cinnamon pulled it away. She cupped her other hand around it, then pressed her hands against her chest and closed her eyes. From anyone else it might have looked theatrical, but not her. Cinnamon's expression melted into pain, her eyes squeezing shut so tightly that the veins stood out in her temples. "Oh," she said with a small moan.

"What do you see?" Dean demanded.

"It's… hard to describe," she said softly. "It's so dark, and chilly. Everything is damp."

"Do you see who the keychain belongs to?" asked Sam.

"Oh, no." Cinnamon's voice was faint. "It's—oh my God. No!" Her voice ended in a scream. She twisted in her chair, then jerked backward as if she were trying to get out of something's reach. She screamed again and began to flail at nothing they could see. Her cries had escalated into agony by the time Sam lurched from his chair and pried the keychain out of her closed fist.

"Cinnamon, come back!" he yelled. He let the keychain fall to the carpet then grabbed her by the shoulders. "Come back," he repeated. "Now!" He gave her a small shake, then another one. Her eyelids flew open, although for a long, frightening moment, it didn't seem like she knew where she was.

"What?" she whispered. "Oh..." She gazed at them and before either could ask, she said simply, "Lots of blood. And so much pain."

Sam looked dismayed. "Could you tell who?"

The psychic nodded and pointed to the keychain on the floor. "That belongs to a woman named Rose Foster. She's from Chicago, and she ran away when she was a teenager and got into drugs, was drifting toward this town because it was winter up north."

"When was this?" Dean asked.

"A year ago, give or take," Cinnamon answered. "She was thirty-one, addicted to drugs. She paid for them by sleeping with truckers."

Dean frowned. "I don't remember seeing her name in any of the missing persons records we went through."

Cinnamon shook her head. "She left home sixteen years ago. Her parents thought of her as nothing more than a problem. They were glad she was gone and never reported her missing."

"That sucks," Dean said.

"So what happened to her?" Sam looked at Cinnamon expectantly.

"I don't know the details," Cinnamon told him. "It's like I said—lots of pain and terror. Then just... darkness." She looked again at the keychain. "I just know this was hers, not something that belonged to one of the girls you're looking for."

Sam sat back, the muscles in his jaw tight. "Then we have to go back," he said flatly. "We have to get back into the evidence room and try again."

Dean looked anything but thrilled. "Well, Thompson did say come back anytime."

Sam glanced at him. "Somehow I don't think he really meant that."

Sixteen

They stuck around Cinnamon's house for another twenty minutes, just to make sure the woman was all right. Whatever she'd seen when she'd touched that skull keychain had taken something out of her. A little chunk of energy, brain cells, hell—in their line of work, she could've literally lost a few years off her life. Even so, it didn't take long for her to recover and she was out on the porch lifting a hand in farewell as they pulled away.

Sam and Dean headed right to the sheriff's office, but they should've known better. When they got there and went up to the door, it was locked and the office was dark. A well-used sign was taped inside the glass.

Sorry, We Are Closed.

For Emergencies Dial 911.

"Now what?" Dean asked.

Sam pushed on the door but, of course, it didn't open. "Can't say I ever saw the police shut down for the weekend."

"I guess that's life in Brownsdale," Dean said. "What do

you think? Time to go caving?"

Sam checked his watch. "Maybe," he answered. "Let's head back to the motel and get everything together, double check the supplies and the gear. Then we'll see how much time we have. The last thing I want to do is get stuck in the cave after nightfall."

"What's the difference? It's gonna be dark in the cave whether it's day or night outside."

"True," Sam agreed. "But we're not even sure where the Crystal Cave entrance is and this park is immense. Let's start by scoping out the maps. We'll look it up, plan it out, then drive the route. That way when we're ready to tackle the cave itself, we won't waste a bunch of time driving around and trying to find an entrance nobody around here wants us to know about."

The countryside that had seemed so lush and beautiful when Sam and Dean had first driven into town a few days ago now looked vaguely menacing. With clouds blocking the sunlight and a hefty breeze pushing through the branches and bushes, the shadows off the roadside looked longer and deeper, darker. The outside temperature had cooled as well. They'd gone back to the motel, changed out of their suits and spent a good hour poring over the maps they'd bought at Go Cave Wild, highlighting the routes with a fluorescent orange marker. When they started getting the caving stuff together, however, they realized it would take at least another hour to get properly geared up; ultimately they'd agreed to find the entrance tonight, then tackle the cave itself early in the morning.

"You know," Sam said now, poking at the map unfolded on his lap, "neither of these entrances are that close to town."

"Yep." Dean watched the road as he navigated the curves. The heavy cloud cover had brought an early dusk, the perfect time for a deer to jump in front of the car. "A hell of a long hike. Maybe they got a ride."

"Maybe." Sam glanced at his brother and for just a moment, Dean looked back. "But who gave it to them?"

They found the main entrance to Mammoth Cave National Park without any trouble, following road signs to glide through the open gate and note the large sign that announced the park closed at six p.m. It was already going on four o'clock. They parked and got out of the car, then followed the main path that led to the cave entrance, scanning the warnings and instructions along the way. After a bit they came to a section where the trail was lined on each side with a chain separating the path from the surrounding brush. About thirty or forty feet ahead they could see the final leg that led to the entrance of the cave. A park ranger stood on either side of the path; one held an iPad-sized computer covered in protective plastic and made a notation every time someone went into the cave. Although there was a steady drizzle and an early, unpleasant dusk had slipped in, judging from the number of cars in the parking lot, there were still a lot of people in the park.

"So they keep tabs on who goes into the cave," Dean commented. "At least late in the day."

Sam studied the two rangers. "Maybe. Or they might be there all the time. The pamphlets say that Mammoth Cave gets more than two million visitors a year. The entrance to the cave is gated off and locked every night."

"You want to go in?"

Sam shrugged. "Not here at the main entrance. There are too many people, plus I think we should do the full drive and try to find the entrance to Crystal Cave first. I have a feeling that's where they'd want to explore. With it being closed off there wouldn't have been anyone around to keep them from going off the main paths. How much more of an adventure would it have been to go in without anyone knowing?"

Dean just looked at his brother. "A deadly one."

"True, but what kid thinks about the future in situations like that, right? The mind doesn't focus past the fun you're planning to have."

"I'm thinking they found anything but fun."

Dusk was bleeding into night around them and the heavy woods on either side of the road were little beyond smears of blackness when Sam and Dean finally saw a sign that pronounced CRYSTAL CAVE AHEAD. But the sign was old and dilapidated and they almost missed it in the headlights. When Dean slowed the car, the brothers could barely read the painted wood board that was so worn by the weather that long strips were peeling off both sides and dangling in the wind.

Dean arched an eyebrow. "This looks promising."

Slowing the car to a crawl, a few minutes later they saw

another sign. It was much like the first, except this one had a red banner plastered diagonally across it that read CLOSED.

"Exactly the sort of thing that teenagers love," Sam said. "An off-limits adventure."

"We've got about a mile to go," Dean said. "Then turn to the right."

It didn't take long to find it. They spotted the rusted gate despite the weeds and heavy kudzu. A thick chain had been tightly wrapped around the two sections and secured with a hefty padlock. Even if they'd been able to get the gate open, the driveway beyond was choked with brush and boulders that were too big for the Impala to drive over, so Dean rolled slowly past and pulled off the side of the road.

"Let's go check it out," he said. "Not go inside, just see if we can find the entrance. Reconnaissance."

Sam nodded and reached for the passenger door handle, getting the door open just enough to make the door light come on. But before Dean could swing open the driver's side, someone stepped in front of it. The door thudded against the person's body and Dean found himself peering up and through the two-inch gap between the top of the window and the car's roof.

"Y'all going somewhere?" came Sheriff Thompson's voice from outside the car. He stepped forward with enough power to force the door closed again, then stood there, staring at Dean through the glass. His lean face, all shadows and angles, was barely visible in the glow from the interior light.

Dean's face darkened and he rolled down the window; his other hand folded around the leather cover on the steering wheel, tightening until his knuckles turned white. "Is there a problem, Sheriff?"

"Don't tell me you two were thinking of going in there?" Thompson inclined his head toward the gated-off path to Crystal Cave, his eyes picking up a fleeting sparkle as he moved.

Sam leaned forward but Dean spoke first. "We were just going to check out the entrance, make sure it's boarded up the way it's supposed to be."

"Oh, it is," Sheriff Thompson assured him. "Nice and tight."

"We'd like to see for ourselves."

"Afraid I can't let you do that." Thompson's voice was absurdly jolly, as if he were enjoying himself immensely. "For your own safety, of course."

Dean ground his teeth and his hand went to the door handle, but Sam elbowed him. "Sorry, Sheriff, isn't this the best time to look around?"

"Well, there's no good time at all to be poking around Crystal Cave," the sheriff told them. "It's closed, has been for years. This part here has passages that are unstable and dangerous, come down on a person's head in a heartbeat. That's why it's closed. The entrance is secured and no one's allowed in." He gave them a severe look. "No one and no exceptions."

"But we're investigating the disappearance of the Dietz girls," Dean began. "We—"

"I know that," Thompson interrupted. "You told me all that before and I heard you. I'm not a stupid man, but I'm beginning to question the ability of y'all to understand things."

Heat flooded Dean's face. "Now wait just a minute—"

"No, you wait." Thompson held up one finger, like he was talking to a couple of disobedient kids, while his other hand dropped to the weapon on his hip and unsnapped the strap securing it in the holster. "I'm well aware that you claim you're from the FBI—and although I haven't had the chance yet, you can bet your asses I'm going to verify that—but I will not put up with you digging around in parts of the cave that aren't safe, taking up what little resources I have left when I have to send a search party after you. I won't hesitate to put you both in a cell and call your supervisor up in D.C. or wherever the hell your home office is. I'd sure rather do that than have to report both of you missing." He bent so he could stare at both Dean and Sam. "Or worse, dead in the cave. Am I clear?"

Dean's teeth were clenched so hard the muscles in his jaw were visibly twitching. "As mud," he ground out. "But I still think—"

Sam leaned over and cut his brother's words short. "Sheriff Thompson, I assure you we're just trying to help. We just want to find the girls."

The sheriff looked at them a moment more, and for a second the hard line of his jaw seemed to relax. "If you really are set on going in there, come by the station and we'll give you a map. Only a fool would go in there without one, especially if you decide to do it on your own."

"Sure," Sam said from the passenger seat. "We'll do that."

The lawman gave a curt nod. "Y'all have a good evening. I'll follow you back to town to make sure you stay safe. This road can be treacherous."

* * *

"I don't believe it. The son of a bitch threatened us," Dean said in amazement. "He threatened us."

"Are you talking about saying he'd call our supervisor, or that we might disappear?" Sam asked. His voice was mild but there was a steely tone of control to it, like he was barely holding his temper. "Or that he looked like he was going to pull his gun on us?"

Dean glanced at the rearview mirror, his face twisted in a scowl. "All of the above."

Behind the Impala, the headlights of the sheriff's car were unwavering, always keeping a distance of about ten feet behind the Impala's bumper. Not only was he a tailgater, but Thompson was keeping his brights on, probably just to annoy the hell out of Dean. It was working.

Sam turned on the seat and squinted at the back window. His face was lit like it was daylight. He touched his hand to his forehead in a mock salute, but the back window was speckled with raindrops so the lawman behind them probably didn't see it. He turned and faced the front again. "Nothing we can do about it. A shoot-out with the local sheriff is not at all a good idea. An even worse one would be him finding out we're not FBI at all. No telling what he might do then."

"I don't get it," Dean said. "The local law usually works with us. What is it about Brownsdale that makes the people so different?"

Sam was silent for a long time, then he finally answered, "The cave."

SEVENTEEN

Owen had never been in a cave by himself and, in fact, had only taken that one short park tour, the one he'd told the FBI agents about. He'd watched some movies, the standard horror flicks that made the rounds, but the ones that had interested him more were factual, like National Geographic specials. Those were fascinating, as were all the books he'd gone through since he'd moved to Brownsdale. He'd learned so much, and the potential for more knowledge just kept increasing exponentially.

Not that it was doing him a lot of good right now.

Nevertheless, Owen kept going, fueled by hope and desperation—a little of the first and a lot of the last. He'd finally got it out of the sheriff that someone had seen the girls in this area and had reported that Marley and Fallon had climbed over the gate and headed down the path. He should have probably called those FBI agents but the sheriff had said he'd talk to them and Owen's panic had become so overwhelming with this new information he'd had to do something immediately. The desperation had been growing since that first day, when he realized that they weren't in the house. If worry had a physical form, it would be like the Blob, that gelatinous mass that had grown so out of control in the old Steve McQueen movie.

How long had he been in here? Hours, probably, but he resisted the urge to stop and click the backlight on his watch. It would be disheartening to do that and find it had really been only forty-five minutes. Could that happen? He didn't know for sure but he thought so. There was no real sense of time down here, just the need to go forward. He was not claustrophobic, but he could, at least in these surroundings, understand why some people felt that way. A lot of folks would think of it in terms of the weight of the Earth pressing down on them, smothering them with mass and the simple truth of their own insignificance. He didn't. As a child, Owen had often blocked any and all sources of outside light in his room and cocooned himself in his sheets, letting the feeling overtake him that he was floating, just him, in a shell of protection swinging through the never-ending, star-studded ribbon of eternity.

Eventually he made it to the chamber indicated on the map he'd been given. It was beautiful, but Owen didn't have time to be impressed by Mother Earth right now. He pulled out the map to double check it and saw that everything matched and the only way to continue was the nearly hidden tunnel on the far left. All the others were marked as collapsed and impassable. If the girls had been in this cave, that was the only way they could have kept going.

Switching off his flashlight to save batteries, Owen took a quick drink of water, then knelt at the opening. His headlamp picked out the way ahead, small, uneven, and studded with rocks. Yep, just like a cave tunnel. No way was this walkable—he could start it on all fours, but only for a few feet. Then he'd have to make like a worm and crawl.

Okay, then. Owen knelt and pushed himself inside.

Moving at a pace likely much slower than a professional caver's—he was a bookworm, after all, and exercised only when some online article made him feel guilty—Owen felt it when the tunnel started to decline. There wasn't anything to see beyond the light cast by his headlamp, but he slowed even more. The reward for his caution was not tumbling over the edge when the tunnel he was in abruptly ended.

Owen pulled out the higher-powered flashlight and aimed the beam below. He could see the ground but it was difficult to estimate the distance. Definitely too far to jump; someone experienced might be able to climb down, but that someone wasn't him. Just in case, he had brought a decent length of nylon rope and a couple of Camalots, spring-loaded devices that could be slipped into cracks and used to securely hold ropes in place. After a careful inspection of the rocks surrounding where the tunnel ended, he found a fissure that was perfect to set a cam in. He threaded the rope through and secured it, then pulled it back up and put fist-sized knots every couple of feet; even if he managed to rappel down, something he'd never in his life tried, he wasn't foolish enough to think he would be able to pull himself back up without hand and footholds. There was the girls to think about, too; if—when—he found them, they would likely be dehydrated and weak. The rope would guarantee he could get back up quickly and go for help.

Taking a deep breath, Owen let himself slide over the edge, keeping his feet together until they hit the first knot. When he had a good hold on the rope, he let his feet go, feeling for the next one, back and forth, hands first, then feet, until his boots landed on solid ground. When he looked up and his headlamp followed the rope and picked out the tunnel entrance overhead, he guessed he'd come down about fifteen feet. No broken bones, not even a scrape—not bad for an exercise-challenged nerd.

When he checked his surroundings, Owen discovered he was in a chamber that wasn't very big, not at all like the many magnificent rooms of Mammoth Cave, or even the chamber he'd been in before this last tunnel. Wherever the ceiling was, it was out of range of both his headlamp and the flashlight, but he could easily see all the walls around him. For a disappointing moment he was afraid the map had been wrong, meaning his search had come to a premature end and he would have to turn back, then he spotted a small hole where part of the wall and ground came together. When he inspected it closer, he exhaled in relief. Right where it was supposed to be. So far he hadn't even needed the paint—in all instances, he'd gone the only available route and not had to make any directional choices. That meant there was only one way out.

Before going inside, Owen stood and let his flashlight play over the walls again, then paused when the light ran across the rope he'd left hanging. How, he wondered, had the girls gotten down here? He'd been told that the other tunnels in the preceding chamber were all collapsed and this was the only one that was passable, and he'd taken all that as word. For the first time, though, he was starting to have doubts. Maybe he should go back and check those out, just to be sure. On the other hand, if he did and found they went nowhere, how much time would he have wasted?

For a few moments Owen was stuck with indecision. Thirteen-year-olds, he reasoned, were strong and loose-limbed. Even himself, as much as he was not in particularly good shape now, had been like an oversized Gumby doll back then, all flexibility and rubber bones. How many times had he done headers and crashed into stuff while skateboarding, with or without protective gear, and come out of it with nothing more serious than a few bruises? Marley and Fallon had probably climbed down; as stupid as it seemed to Owen, to the girls it had likely been just one more exciting part of their huge adventure in Crystal Cave.

Yeah, one for the memory album all right.

He sighed and crawled into the opening.

Eons later the tunnel began to widen. Checking around himself, it wasn't long before Owen was able to rise to his hands and knees, finally getting his belly and thighs off the damp, biting rocks. A short while later, he was able to stand and stretch his stiff, cramping muscles. He got out his flashlight and clicked it on, adding its stronger glow to the light from his headlamp.

He was in another chamber. This one was enormous and beautiful, full of colors that sparkled when his flashlight beam played over them; reds and yellows, layered and splashed into the gray tones of huge boulders and pillars. More beauty that Owen barely registered; instead, he wandered among the stacked rock formations and boulders that were bigger than he was, looking for anything that might indicate his cousins had been here before him. There was a sort of natural staircase to one side and he climbed halfway up, then turned back. So far he'd found nothing, no sign that a human being had ever been so far into this cavern, and his disappointment was so profound that he lost the strength in his legs and fell to his knees. He'd been so absolutely sure he would find them and be able to get them back to their parents. To think that belief had been useless made him almost unable to breathe. He—

Somewhere above him, something moved.

Owen jerked back to his feet and swung his flashlight wildly around, then forced himself to stop. Calm down, he told himself. This deep into the cave, it's probably just a bat. He listened carefully as he let his flashlight beam roam the rocks, but there was nothing beyond the constant sounds of dripping water all around him.

What if it was one of the girls? What if they were hurt, or had succumbed to hypothermia, had run out of food? The notion was too close to the unthinkable—that they might be dead—and it pushed him over the edge to full panic.

"Marley!" he shouted as loudly as he could. He hauled as much of the cold, damp air into his lungs as he could, then bellowed again. "Fallon!"

His voice had been so loud and out of place in the quiet of the cave that it made his ears ring, but he didn't care. He kept yelling their names, over and over, running a few feet up the stone rocks, then trying again. He filled the chamber with so much noise that the sound waves bounced against the rocks and seemed to multiply, completely covering the other, more furtive noises around him, until it was way too late to run.

Then Owen's screams became completely different.

Eighteen

Michael Thompson followed the car with the two FBI agents in it. He'd driven this road a thousand times or more in his career—several times today, as a matter of fact—and the silver sedan rode the dark curves of rain-slicked Route 70 with ease.

At first his mind was blank. No thoughts, just the view through the windshield and the steady thwap thwap of the windshield wipers. It was like a calming mantra, that sound, easing out how pissed off he was that those two agents were poking around the old Crystal Cave entrance, not to mention his outrage that they were in Brownsdale in the first place.

Thompson kept on their bumper intentionally, and also kept his high beams on. It wasn't so much petty—all right, maybe a little—as it was him trying to teach them a lesson; he could be as much a pain in the ass to them as they were to him. Or were they used to resistance from the locals when they were investigating a case? He didn't think so. It was likely no one ever questioned them, much less did a background check to make sure they were legit. The one with the short hair always had this barely concealed look of outrage on his face when Thompson made them hit the brakes. Deputy Sloane had told him about the reaction he'd gotten when the two had shown up and tried to get into the evidence room. Talk about a sense of entitlement. Those big city cops probably always acted that way, Thompson thought, like the small towns that made up the backbone of America owed them something. Good luck with that attitude.

He saw movement in the car ahead of him on the passenger side but there was too much rain to know exactly what they were doing. Probably holding up a hand to shield their eyes from the too bright lights hitting the rearview and side mirrors, or maybe they were flipping him off. Thompson didn't care. Let them be uncomfortable. He'd been that way ever since he'd spotted the two men leaving the library.

Owen Meyer.

The thought of the librarian made Thompson wince. This is what happens, he thought, when outsiders come in. Scratch that—not just moved to town, but thought they were part of the town. The people who made up Brownsdale came from families that had been in Edwardson County and the surrounding area for hundreds of years, back to when this area had first been settled. That included his family, the Thompsons. Anyone could read the proof in the church cemeteries all over town, headstones that dated back to the seventeen hundreds, a damned long time before the county or the town was established, or before the surrounding farmland got divided up by the government as a means of political power and taxation.

Thompson followed the agents' car around another dark curve, his driving on autopilot while his brain worked over the problem of Owen and his cousins. It had been clear the boy wasn't going to shut up about it, and Thompson didn't expect him to—no one would if people they loved had gone missing. Plus, the worse was yet to come—he'd been notified this morning that the parents of those girls had been told about the situation and would be in Brownsdale as soon as they could. They hadn't made it in today, but he'd put his next paycheck on them arriving first thing tomorrow morning. There were going to be a whole lot of questions to answer and he'd better have his story down ramrod straight. One slip-up and everything could fall apart. Everything.

More curves, more blackness, the sound of the car's tires swishing through the water on the road's surface. He tried to think through every question he could imagine he'd be asked.

Thompson could think of a million they would ask, starting with when they were last seen, then going over what the girls had been wearing, to what time they'd been reported missing. But the big one, the mother of all mothers...

What are you doing to find my daughters?

What, indeed?

He had his answers all planned out, and in support was his yellow legal pad with page after page of scrawled notes, the log of his phone call times to his deputies, even a spreadsheet on his computer. The supposed search parties, who was involved, the times, what they had done—all of it in excruciating detail. He only had to make sure that the parents—what were their names? Ray and Lena Dietz, that was it. He just had to make sure they never spoke to any of his deputies but Ken Sloane. While he had no doubt the others would back him up if he instructed them to, Thompson felt they were too nervous, too scared; someone would slip up and there it would all go: hundreds of years of keeping Brownsdale safe, the last few of which had been despite that fool Beau Pyle's effort. Thompson could swear every time Pyle tried to do something, or to fix something, he just screwed it up worse.

For God's sake, the man was old, too old for this kind of responsibility. The problem was he had no one to pass it on to, no sons or even a nephew somewhere. God's punishment, that's what that was, retribution for him doing Miss Ellison so dirty all those years ago. In any case, that's when the Thompson family was supposed to step in, and if Beau had bothered to check the founder's documents in the vault at City Hall, he would know that. Or maybe he did, but he'd just set blinders on himself in that regard a long time ago. He and Beau had never gotten along, way back to the time when Thompson had first joined the sheriff's department. Beau Pyle thought Thompson was cold and heartless, maybe even vicious. But that wasn't true, not at all. Thompson was a Brownsdale son all the way, and he was loyal to this town no matter what. Didn't matter, though. Pyle would never willingly pass his responsibilities to the Thompson family, and let's face it: there was no one else with the balls enough to take this on.

So Thompson had moved in on his own, stepping in to make sure the cave was kept satisfied and under control. Not talking with Beau, or even telling him what he was going to do. Take the reins and ride.

Thompson sighed, his gaze never leaving the back of the Impala in front of him. If it hadn't been for its taillights, the car would have been invisible. Beau Pyle, the FBI, the parents of the Dietz twins coming tomorrow—he couldn't blame any of it on anyone but himself. But damn it all, he'd never seen them before.

How was he supposed to have known those girls were Owen's relatives?

NINETEEN

Cinnamon Ellison puttered happily around the kitchen in her little house on B Street. Her charming house looked small on the outside, but the room was bright and spacious, decorated in white and cheerful yellow. True to her country roots, Cinnamon liked to cook. She was good at it, too, although she kept that fact to herself. She knew how the people in town talked about her, calling her that crazy spinster, that old lady who thinks she's psychic. Except, of course, after events like that leaky oxygen tank at the nursing home, and half a dozen more. She hadn't bothered telling the Winchester brothers about all of them. She still couldn't quite believe how they explained the monster hunter label that kept floating around in her brain, but she had figured out their real names.

Back in the day, Cinnamon Ellison had been just a normal young lady, like her sister Brenda, who was ten years younger. The fifties and sixties had been a great time to grow up in a small town like Brownsdale. Their parents, along with the churches and the other people in town, had worked hard to keep it that way: small, friendly to townsfolk, blatantly unwelcoming to people who tried to be more than tourists— outsiders. Like anything, the plan worked on some teenagers, like Cinnamon; on others, like Brenda, not so much. Television invaded everything, and while Cinnamon was finding out she had... abilities, Brenda was growing up a little wild and too fast, discovering pot—back then there were a couple of good old boys who were growing a patch of it about a mile off Route 183—and finding that she liked it; discovering Beau Pyle and finding that she liked him even more.

The only problem was that Beau Pyle was Cinnamon's boyfriend.

Confused and terrified by the visions and intuitive jumps starting to blossom in her head, Cinnamon tried to stand up to her younger sister. But Brenda, dark-haired and exotic-looking, passionate to her core, had only laughed at her and said, "If he's meant for you, he'll stay with you." Brenda wanted to experience anything and everything, with no limits on her self-declared freedom. She'd inherited their mother's green eyes, where Cinnamon, despite her spicy name, was pale and blue-eyed, like their grandmother. Brenda danced like a graceful gypsy to the rock and roll blaring from the car radios, while Cinnamon wouldn't have been caught dead on a dance floor.

In short, Beau Pyle dropped Cinnamon like a hot rock. Like Cinnamon, he was ten years older, and he and sixteen-year-old Brenda drove off one Saturday night and got married in Bowling Green. Cinnamon's mother wailed long and loud when she got the call from Brenda—who honestly thought she'd get congratulations—while Cinnamon stayed in her room for a week and wept quietly into her pillow. She fought the bitterness that wanted to insinuate itself in her heart for years, especially when Beau and Brenda moved back to Brownsdale two years later, and if nothing else her growing psychic abilities were at least an ongoing distraction.

Nothing, however, would ever compensate for the self-consciousness she'd felt, the heart-stabbing embarrassment of knowing that every time she heard someone whisper behind her back, they were saying, "That's the Ellison girl. Her younger sister ran off with her boyfriend."

She should've moved away, she would have moved away, but Brownsdale was all she'd ever known. She loved the town, the surrounding Mammoth Cave National Park, the soul-deep call of nature and history in it. And if the people in town didn't exactly support her, their basic presence comforted her. The Ellison family dated back to the eighteen hundreds, not quite as far as Beau's, but enough. Sadly, she'd never married, never had any children; neither had Brenda, who'd left Beau ten years into the marriage and moved to Louisville with a car salesman. She and Cinnamon exchanged Christmas cards every year, but despite trying, Brenda reported that she'd never gotten pregnant.

The Ellison line would end with them.

And Beau... ah, Beau. Some, it seemed, were doomed to spend a lifetime regretting hasty decisions. He had, on more than one occasion—okay, dozens—told Cinnamon he had made an enormous mistake in choosing Brenda over her. He'd sworn he would never date another woman, and incredibly, he'd meant it. He loved her, he said, and if she'd just give him a chance, he'd prove it.

My sister's leftovers.

That was the phrase her pride had blazed into her mind decades ago, when Beau had first come back, and that was also what she'd told those Winchester boys. It was the reason, even though, yes, she did still love Beau Pyle, had always loved him, she could never take him back.

She wished she could be like Brenda, not caring what people thought as long as she was happy inside. Brenda was what she was, but Cinnamon could never be that. Extroverts like Brenda flitted through life on the wings of attention, thrived on it; but people like Cinnamon, introverts, preferred not to be in the spotlight because they were happier that way. What Brenda had done by not just stealing but marrying her older sister's boyfriend had been the equivalent of putting a permanent spotlight over Cinnamon's head. She was forever embarrassed in her own skin, forever the sly focus of attention wherever she went in town. She could never be happy being herself, because that person was gone. Now, and forever, Cinnamon was what Brenda had made her. Her true self was gone, and the wanton disregard that Brenda had shown about this still to this day infuriated Cinnamon. Just infuriated her.

Cinnamon blinked and rubbed a hand across her forehead. She had worked herself into quite a state, hadn't she? Her temples were throbbing with a stress headache, something that only happened when she really got ticked off about something... and yeah, that was usually Beau Pyle.

"Stop it," she told herself aloud, using her sternest teacher voice. Before her retirement two years ago, Cinnamon had taught middle-school English. The people in Brownsdale might look at her a little sideways, but they seemed to trust her not to talk crazy to their kids. She took a deep breath to ground herself. "Move forward, not backward." That was a favorite quote from a book she'd read. Just another way of saying there was no sense dwelling on the past, but less clichéd.

The pounding in her head lessened as she inhaled and exhaled, concentrated on calming herself. This was her home, her life. The one she had made for herself despite the past, the one she had furnished with the things inherited from her parents as well as the things she loved the most. The kitchen was the heart of it, filled with light as the west-facing windows, framed by homey white and yellow checked curtains, let in the last, bright rays of the setting sun. It was time to make dinner, something tasty but not too unhealthy, something a lot better than what you could get at any of the restaurants in town.

Shrimp, Cinnamon decided. Something fancy. She pulled a half-pound of frozen shrimp from the freezer and dumped it into a colander, then ran cold water over the pile to thaw it. Then she carried another colander out to the backyard, where she took her time in her small garden, harvesting several cups of golden grape tomatoes along with a generous handful of pineapple sage. Back inside, she got the rest of the ingredients from the refrigerator, chose a box of pasta from the pantry, and put a pot of salted water on the stove to boil.

While the water was heating up, she got out a big cutting

board and set it on the table. Pulling everything together, she sat down to start chopping. First, she would—

Blackness.

Where was she? She couldn't see anything, even her own hand in front of her face. It was there, yes—her fingers, prodding at her own face, her nose, her chin. Was she dead? Unconscious? No, that couldn't be, or she wouldn't... what? Know who she was, herself?

Cinnamon stretched out her arms cautiously, first in front, then to the sides... nothing. Vertigo hit her, hard, and she let herself sink, but carefully, to her knees. What if she bent and felt nothing, just kept on going down, forever? Floating or something, in some kind of eternal limbo?

But no—there was ground beneath her, grainy and full of tiny stones, larger rocks. She was chilly, too, the cold air surrounding her raising gooseflesh along her arms and chest. At least the ground comforted her, held at bay, for now, the idea that she was dropping into hell or something equivalent.

Cinnamon tilted her head to one side, listening. But there was no sound except her own steady breathing. She didn't feel panicked or frightened, just curious, so after a few moments she went to all fours and carefully started crawling, using her hands to make sure there was solid ground in front of her before each forward movement.

The tunnel, if that's what she was in, seemed to go on forever. She kept at it, not knowing what other option she had beyond giving up, but gradually she slowed before coming to a complete stop.

"This is ridiculous," she said out loud... or at least she

thought she did. She heard the words in her mind but they seemed to have no substance, again as if she were sitting on a pedestal in some great, black void. She was just to the point of deciding it was a dream when voices, young but not childish, slid through the darkness and into her hearing. Whispers and giggles—she was hearing a couple of girls, somewhere in the darkness ahead.

Girls?

Suddenly Cinnamon was scrambling forward as fast as she could. Pain scissored through her knees and the palms of her hands as she clawed at the ground, not nearly as cautiously as she had before.

"Hello?" she cried. "Please stop! Where are you?"

But the unseen girls only laughed and talked, their words happy but too far away to be intelligible. Cinnamon had no doubt it was the Dietz twins—who else would it be?—and she crawled faster, ignoring the sharp rocks stabbing into the thin skin covering her kneecaps, the painful gashes opening in her palms.

"Hello?" she screamed again, and then the ground dropped away.

Cinnamon flailed at the nothing around her, then tumbled, bouncing off invisible walls but feeling no pain with each impact. The stinging in her knees and palms was also gone, just vanished along with the surface upon which she had been crawling. She knew she was turning because she could feel the dizziness build up in her head, like she was blindfolded and on one of those balance-defying carnival rides that had always made her want to vomit afterward.

Lights, then, blinking here and there in the void around her, winking in and out like faint stars above the blowing branches of a tree as her turning came to a stop. For about ten seconds—or was it a year?—all she wanted to do was float, drift weightlessly and peacefully through nothingness. Was she dead? Was this what heaven or hell or the nothing in between was like? She felt no pain, no tears, no fear. All was good and she could have felt like this forever…

Except then she started to spin all over again.

Around and around, harder and harder, until she wanted to die, to pass out, do anything to make it stop. With it came the sensation of falling, of plummeting to something unknown so far below her that she had no concept of it.

Abruptly the make-believe stars above her winked out and the blackness began to lighten, fraction by fraction, bleeding at the edges into something that resembled the shadows cast by dancing firelight. She hit the ground—if it was, indeed, the ground—with a lung-crushing thud. Her eyes had been scrunched shut but now they flew open. At first she was so shocked by the impact that she couldn't breathe, was certain that every bone in her body had been broken. But still, there was no pain.

Now she could feel the ground beneath her, that same surface of grit and tiny pebbles. She pulled herself into a sitting position and peered around. There was a fire down here, in this cavern or whatever it was she had fallen into, over by the far wall. Around it, appearing as nothing more than silhouettes between her and the fire, were shapes. Short, thick, some hunched over, and they looked nothing like human beings. Whatever these things were, they didn't know she was here. She hadn't made any noise, or at least not enough to be heard above the noises they were making on their own. What were those terrible sounds? Grunting, cracking... chewing. She had to get out of here. Get away from those creatures, those beasts, before they saw her. But how? She didn't even know where she was.

She had to be in the cave somewhere—it was the only explanation. She inched her way backward, feeling with her hands, nearly holding her breath. Then her hand landed on a rock that was larger than the rest, smoother. No, it felt oddly shaped, long. She glanced instinctively behind her and in the barely there light cast by a fire that was a good thirty feet away she realized her fingers had come down on some kind of animal bone.

No, not animal at all. A human bone. And there were more of them scattered next to it, a lot more, across the floor around her and piled against the walls, too. So many. And despite herself, despite all her efforts to remain undetected, she gave a small surprised scream. Unlike before, when she couldn't find a voice for her words, this one came out shockingly loud.

It was enough. Her head snapped back toward the figures at the fire and she realized they had turned toward her and frozen in place.

Then they started moving in her direction.

The fear that swept over her was, in a word, paralyzing. She toppled backward, unable to move, to breathe, to run. She could only lie there helplessly while things unknown, black cutouts against the fire, moved silently forward until they stood over her.

Cinnamon Ellison came back to herself with a shriek. She was in her kitchen, sitting in the same chair that she had been in when she had... what? Blacked out? She was still holding the knife she'd been about to use on the vegetables, and now she dropped it on the tabletop. Her fingers were chilly and stiff, like they'd been holding it for hours. When she ran a hand across her forehead she found it sheeted with cold perspiration. Her heart was racing and she pulled in air, trying to compose herself. The kitchen smelled of hot metal and when she turned her face toward the stove, she realized that the water she had put on for the pasta had completely boiled away.

She stood to go to the stove and stumbled as her knees almost gave out. When she looked at the wall clock she realized she must have been out of it for hours. She didn't recall what time it had been when she started cooking but the water in the pot was gone and the leeks on the cutting board were dry around the edges.

It didn't matter anyway. She had lost her appetite.

Cinnamon shut off the burner and left the pot to cool, then put away the ingredients for her supper, figuring she could make the meal the next evening. Then she did something she hardly ever did: poured herself a generous glass of port from the bottle she kept in the sideboard for the extremely rare occasion when she had company. She took the glass and sat in the rocker in the front room. After a few moments she got up and moved to the wingback chair because the rocker reminded her too much of that same swinging sensation she'd had in her vision. She would have liked to go outside, but the mosquitoes would make her miserable. It was a comfort when the cats came out and curled around her ankles, soothing her with their presence.

Stuck inside the house, she stared into space and tried to understand the things she'd seen in her head, and why they'd appeared to begin with. That wasn't too hard to guess—it was because of the girls, of course. In her vision she'd assumed it was their voices she'd heard somewhere up ahead, although she'd never actually set eyes on either one. What she had seen was indescribable, the stuff of nightmares and hellish children's fairytales. But did it really have anything to do with the disappearance of the Dietz twins?

God help them, she had to believe it did.

TWENTY

"I am not going back to that restaurant," Sam said stubbornly. "I want something light for breakfast this morning. In fact, I just want coffee."

"Man cannot live on coffee alone," retorted Dean. "At least have doughnuts." He was dressed in his customary T-shirt with a blue and white button-down shirt over it. He looked raring to go as he yanked on a brown jacket that was comfortably worn at the edges.

"A muffin, and that's it."

Dean looked at him. "Aren't you ready?"

"Do I look like it?" Sam pushed his hair, still damp from the shower, out of his eyes and yanked on a pair of jeans. "Who the hell gave you a double shot of adrenaline this morning?"

Dean stuffed his hands in his jacket pockets. "What's the matter? Didn't you sleep okay?"

Sam's expression was incredulous. "Me, sleep? All that crap that you eat—do you have any idea what kind of bodily noises you make at night?"

Dean grinned. "The body does what it does to digest, brother. Blame it on the awesome food in this town. Maybe you ought to eat more like I do. I feel great." He bounced on his toes impatiently.

Sam yanked on a brown and white checked shirt. The skin under his eyes was puffy. "Not in this lifetime… or any other. I like my arteries clear."

"Yeah? Look who's sleeping and feeling fantastic—" He jerked his thumb at himself. "—and who feels like a piece of flattened road kill."

Sam's mouth fell open. "What?"

Dean shrugged. "That's what you look like."

"Nothing like a little brotherly love," Sam grumbled.

"I calls it as I sees it."

"Does the word filter mean anything?" Sam tugged on his shoes, then stood.

Dean grinned again and pulled open the motel door with a flourish. "Only when it applies to cars."

Monday-morning Brownsdale was quite a bit more awake than on weekend mornings. The buildings along Main Street were old with tall, thin windows on the upper floors that meant the rooms inside were probably tiny and had twelve-foot ceilings. All the diagonal parking slots in front of the shops were full, even at this mildly early hour. A few cars cruised along the street, presumably hunting for the next free spot. Dean pointed at an old-fashioned movie theater as they rolled past it. The movie advertised on the marquee was *The Cave*. "You gotta be kidding me," Dean said. "That was a great flick—scary as hell—but it's at least ten years old."

"It's a theme, I guess." Sam eyed the theater as they rolled past. It had a red and white striped awning below the marquee, which stuck out from the front of the building. Together the two structures sheltered the sidewalk so people would be protected from rain. "Maybe playing to the tourists."

Dean scanned the sidewalk but there were only a few pedestrians; everyone seemed to be inside somewhere. "What about the people who live here?"

Sam shrugged. "They probably go down to Bowling Green, which is an enormous city compared to this place. It has malls and movie theaters."

"Brownsdale does have a good restaurant."

"And we're not going there," Sam said. "Just head toward the sheriff's office. We'll stop somewhere and pick up coffee and doughnuts."

"Powdered sugar."

"Whatever." Sam kept his gaze focused on the scene outside the window. The tiny downtown area was already gone, traversed in literally sixty seconds; now businesses were spaced apart, interspersed with small houses. A small blue house had a Marathon gas station on one side and a lot with an ancient barn that was slowly collapsing on the other.

They rolled on without speaking, and it wasn't long until Dean spotted a minimart. "There," he said. "Powdered doughnuts, here we come."

"I'll wait here."

"Coffee?"

"And a muffin. Something healthy."

Sam frowned as he watched his brother head into the store, but the sour look on his face didn't hold. Dean was a good guy, and he was the best big brother he could be, given their circumstances. Was there darkness inside him? Sure, but Sam knew there was darkness inside himself, too. Hell, there was darkness inside everyone; some people were just better at controlling it. So far on this trip, neither of them had mentioned the Mark of Cain, the source of the First Blade's power. If Dean wasn't going to bring it up, then neither was Sam. Cain had transferred the Mark to Dean and neither brother had figured out how to get rid of it, so talking didn't do any good anyway. It was like emptying a revolver into a ghost—you made a lot of noise but in the end, the ghost was still a ghost and the only thing you'd managed to do was waste your bullets.

Sam waited, tapping his fingers on his knee. He could see Dean through the window, but he didn't seem to be doing anything. He had one, no, two small boxes of doughnuts in one arm, with some kind of oversized, plastic-wrapped lump balanced on top of it. In his other hand was one of those cardboard carriers for multiple cups of coffee, but instead of going to the register, he looked like he was staring at... what? A rack of fishing magazines?

Sam saw his brother glance to his left, over by the checkout counter. There was a young girl there, leaning forward and talking to the cashier, punctuating her conversation with little flutters of her left hand. After a moment, Dean moved to the register and Sam saw him flash the girls his biggest and best smile.

Uh oh, Sam thought.

"Good morning, ladies," Dean said. Instead of smiling back at him, they just stared. What happened to southern hospitality and friendliness and all that happy sappy? Maybe he had something in his teeth—no, he'd brushed thoroughly and hadn't eaten anything after that. He tried again. "Looks like it's going to be a nice day."

The girls, both in their late teens, glanced at each other then looked back at him. "Sure," the one behind the counter finally said. Then she added, "Good morning to you, too," as though she finally remembered he was a customer and she was supposed to not ignore him. She had streaked blonde hair that looked like it could use a touch-up, and there was no name tag on her red shirt—too bad. Using a person's name always made them feel more obligated to talk to you. She glanced at the stuff in his arms. "Will that be it?"

Dean let the two packages of powdered doughnuts and the lemon-berry muffin—the healthiest thing he could find for Sam—tumble to the counter, then set the coffee holder next to them. "Yeah." He kept his smile going and glanced at the other teenager, a girl whose brown hair was edged in a luminescent blue that matched her eyeliner. "Did I hear you saying someone else disappeared?"

Blue-haired girl frowned and backed up a couple of steps. "You're not from around here," she announced, as though there was an audience. Before Dean could respond, she hurried to the door and pushed it open, tossing a quick, "I'll see you later, Margie," over her shoulder.

When Dean looked back, Margie—he assumed that was her name—had narrowed her eyes and was watching Dean like she thought he might suddenly start turning cartwheels in the middle of the nearest aisle. Dean blinked and tried to look innocent. "Did I say something wrong?"

"Never seen you in here before," presumably-Margie said. She pulled the first box of doughnuts closer and scanned it. "You're passing through."

It was a statement, not a question. In the space of five seconds, Dean felt like he'd been accused of something unknown, tried, and found guilty. Still, he looked at her steadily. "Does it matter? I was just commenting on something I overheard you two talking about."

"I guess that's town business," Margie said as she scanned the other box. She put the muffin over the scanner next and in his peripheral vision, Dean was certain he saw her fingers contract on the plastic, then she punched in the charge for the two coffees. "That'll be twelve dollars and fifty-three cents." She intentionally looked away as she brought up a plastic bag and put the stuff inside.

Dean pulled out his wallet and his FBI badge at the same time. "I'll ask again: did I hear you say that someone else has disappeared?"

Margie stopped and stared at the ID badge for a moment, then pushed the bag toward him. Her face remained expressionless. "That's a question you need to be taking to the sheriff's office, mister. My dad works there, Deputy Sloane. You can talk to him."

Brick wall, Dean thought. Now I know where she gets her

sparkling personality. He put away his badge, then paid for his items. When he picked up the bag and coffee holder and turned to leave, he smiled at her again. "You have a nice day, Margie." He wasn't surprised when she didn't answer back.

"What were you doing in there?" Sam asked as Dean slipped behind the wheel and handed him the bag and coffee.

"Scoping out the local gossip," Dean said. "Which unfortunately came to a standstill when I, a lowly out-of-towner, had the nerve to try and join the conversation."

"Yeah?"

"The cashier and that other girl were talking about somebody disappearing in town."

"The twins."

"Nope." Dean started the car and backed out of the spot. "They distinctly said somebody else."

Sam frowned. "That's not good."

"Definitely breaks the pattern," Dean said. He pulled smoothly onto the road. "Let's head to the sheriff's office and see if we can get him to let us back into that evidence locker, get that over with. That's where Margie told me to go, anyway." At Sam's questioning look, Dean added, "The cashier. Turns out her father is Deputy Sloane."

"Okay." Sam dug into the bag and looked inside. "What the hell is this?"

"A lemon-berry muffin," Dean answered. "It was the best looking out of what they had."

"It's smashed."

"I knew she didn't like me."

* * *

Sam was picking at the too-sweet muffin when Dean drove past the library. He glanced at the building then sat up straight. "Whoa—slow down."

Dean automatically applied the brakes. "What's up?"

Sam twisted around and stared out the back window. "Turn around and go back. Something's not right."

Dean didn't argue, just swung the car in a wide U-turn at the next intersection. "Where am I going?"

"The library," Sam answered. He pointed. "Look, there's some kind of sign on the door. Pull into the parking lot."

Sam swung open the door before Dean brought the car to a complete halt, then hurried over to the entrance. A piece of notebook paper had been taped to the outside of the glass. The printed font was the same as the one on the sheriff's department sign, but that was probably just coincidence.

Closed until 2:00 P.M.

Please come back.

He stared at it for a few moments, frowning, then made his way back to the Impala. When he relayed what it said to Dean, his brother just shrugged.

"It's no big deal. Didn't Owen say his aunt and uncle would be in town by today? He's probably with them. In fact, I wouldn't be surprised if we got to meet the family at the sheriff's department."

But when Dean pulled into what had become their customary spot across from the sheriff's office, the only cars in the private lot next to the building were two of the official silver sedans. There was another car a few slots down from them, but it was a silver Ford Escort with a rental

THE USUAL SACRIFICES   155

agency sticker on the back window.

"What does Owen drive?" Dean asked.

Sam shook his head. "Honestly, I have no idea. Never asked him, never saw it. I assume he was parked around back the day we visited the library."

Dean's face darkened but he said nothing as he and his brother got out and walked across the street. The lights were on inside and in the gloom cast by a sky filled with heavy gray clouds, the place almost looked welcoming. That notion went out the window when they opened the door and stepped inside. No one was at the front desk but they could hear muffled but clearly raised voices through the wall. It sounded like several male voices and one female, two clearly angry and one in a lower tone that was unmistakably placating.

Sam and Dean waited, not sitting down. After about five minutes, the interior door opened and Deputy Sloane strode out, then jerked when he saw them.

"What do you two want?" he asked, not even trying to be cordial. "We're kind of busy right now."

"I can hear that," Sam said. "I'm afraid we need access to the evidence room again."

Sloane gave an exaggerated sigh. "Can't you come back? We—"

"No," interrupted Sam. "It's FBI business and it can't wait."

The deputy wiped the back of his hand across his forehead, as if whatever was going on beyond the back wall had made him nervous enough to sweat. "Have a seat. Sheriff Thompson is the only one who can take you, and he's occupied right now. I'll let him know you're here and he'll be out here as soon as he's done." He shot them a resentful look. "He might be a while."

"We'll wait," Dean said. He made no move toward the chair.

"I figured you would." Sloane dropped into the chair behind the desk and began typing something into the computer, steadfastly ignoring the brothers.

Sam sat down and folded his arms, watching his brother watch the deputy. Dean's gaze was fixed on the lawman like a predator's, a cheetah tracking the movements of a baby eland on a breezy African plain. He was kind of enjoying the way Sloane started fidgeting under Dean's non-wavering regard, and had to stop himself from grinning outright when the deputy finally sighed.

"Look," Sloane finally said. "Give me a break and sit down, would you? I swear the sheriff will be with you as soon as he can."

"You said you'd let him know we're here," Dean said in a brisk voice. "You didn't."

"Right." Sloane pushed himself out of the chair. "Be right back." He pulled out a key and went through the door. A moment later the volume of the voices coming through the wall lowered. It was only a few seconds before Sloane came back. "The sheriff said to give him five minutes."

Dean nodded, then went over and sat, slouching in the chair. Sloane had lucked out; between the computer monitor and a stack of upright notebooks and folders on the desk, the older Winchester brother's view was cut off. Sam, though, could still see the deputy, who glanced at him every now and then.

True to his word, at the five-minute mark the door opened

and Sheriff Thompson motioned them to come through. They followed him down the hallway. This time one of the doors on the left was open; as they passed, the brothers caught a glimpse of the room, inside which was a small oval conference room table. Two people were seated on one side of it, a man and a woman. The woman was holding her face in her hands and her shoulders were shaking as the man rubbed her back.

"Mr. and Mrs. Dietz?" asked Sam quietly.

"Yes." The sheriff didn't elaborate, just led them through the same door at the far end and down the stairs to the basement. "I don't know what y'all are looking for, but I can't spend a lot of time down here with you. I'm sure you get that." The man motioned to the upper floor with his head. "Edwardson County policy says I personally have to supervise all outside people, whether they're official personnel or not, while in this locker. So I'm asking you, nicely, to get your business here over with as quickly as possible."

"Of course," Sam said. He motioned to the caged area. "We're going to need to look in there too this time."

With a frown Thompson unlocked the steel door. "I don't have time for you boys to keep coming back here on fishing trips. If you're looking for something specific—"

"We're all on the same side, Sheriff," Sam said levelly. The other man didn't reply, just took a stance inside the door while they moved down the aisle of the sectioned-off area. With Dean at his heels, Sam headed straight to where all the miscellaneous backpacks and odd items were heaped. This time he didn't bother pretending about shoelaces or anything else, just squatted and began to poke through the things at eye level.

After a few minutes the sheriff shifted. "Well?" he asked, impatience clear in his voice. "The Dietz couple is waiting for me upstairs and I already told you, we didn't find anything that belonged to those girls. I don't have any idea why you even want to look at this old stuff anyway."

Sam opened his mouth to reply, then his gaze returned to an old green backpack that looked like it had at least fifty patches haphazardly sewn on it, some barely holding on by a few worn stitches. "We're almost ready," he said blandly.

That had to be it, Sam reasoned. He would have remembered the dull army green decorated with patches that ranged from aliens flashing peace signs above the words Far Out to unicorns and bright, crazily stitched slices of fruit. But... was that dirt on the edge of one corner? Blood? Or both?

Sam looked back at Thompson. "We'd like to take a few things with us," he began. "We—"

"That's out of the question," the sheriff interrupted. His normally cool gaze went frigid. "Right now, anyway. That involves a crap ton of paperwork that I just don't have the time to do right now. In case you forgot, this department is neck deep in the search for two missing girls, and their parents are upstairs." The lean man put his hands on his hips. "Now, if you care to come back, say on Friday, I'm sure I'll be able to tackle it then."

Dean's eyebrows shot up. "You're saying you're confident you'll find those girls by Friday? What makes you say that?"

"I never said that at all." It was clear Thompson was getting frustrated. "Don't go putting words in my mouth." He stepped to the side, a clear indication he was ready for them to precede him out of the enclosure. "What I'm saying is that by Friday we ought to be in a better position to deal with things that aren't critical. Like y'all wanting to look at things found on the side of the road and whatnot."

If Dean's eyebrows could have gone higher, they would have. "I'm real sorry that you don't consider the FBI's part in the investigation of those girls disappearing critical."

Sheriff Thompson blinked, then recovered. His expression had gone harder than it normally was. "There you go again." His words sounded like they were coming through gritted teeth. "Putting words in my mouth. I really hate that." He inhaled, a visible effort to keep calm. "Of course your participation is important. But this stuff here—" he gestured toward the pile of unlabeled items—"is just detritus, things left behind. They're nothing but a big waste of time."

They had thought about it before, but now Sam couldn't help voicing the question. "If I remember correctly, these things are… disposed of after six months."

"That's right." Thompson's eyes were steely.

"So if someone were to find a body out there in the park that was, I don't know, a couple of years old, no one would ever know if it was connected to anything that you might actually have had in this building?"

Sam had known it would be a mistake, and the change in the sheriff's demeanor was instantaneous. "I don't like what you're insinuating, Agent." His emphasis on the last word was outright biting. "As I've said, I have things to attend to, and while you may believe digging around a heap of lost and found articles is significant, my emphasis right now is on dealing with parents who are on the verge of hysteria." With his right arm, Sheriff Thompson pushed open the door, hard enough to make it clang against the enclosure itself. "It's time for you two to be on your way."

Dean looked at his brother, but he knew it was useless. Short of bodily tackling the man, they were out of here. And they probably wouldn't be allowed to come back.

Sam stood and made a show of brushing dirt from his hands. "Right," he said. "We totally get it."

He and Dean moved out in front of the sheriff, who had the door locked and the key pocketed in seemingly record time. "I believe you know the way." When they ascended the stairs, the older man snapped off the lights behind them, then shadowed their steps down the hallway. The Dietz couple was still in the conference room. The man had his arm around his wife's shoulder and was talking softly to her. When the brothers would have stopped at the doorway, the sheriff was suddenly there, a human shield keeping them from the twins' parents.

"No," he said acidly.

"You're impeding a federal investigation," Dean shot back.

"Maybe so, but in my opinion all you're going to do is confuse the issue and make the situation worse for these good people. If you don't like it, have your supervisor call the county attorney. I answer to him."

There wasn't much either of them could say to that so they kept walking past the sheriff, whose back was as stiff as a column of concrete. The lawman followed them out, and when they were in the front office he yanked the door closed behind them with a final-sounding bang. Deputy Sloane barely glanced at them, but Dean could've sworn there was a hint of nasty laughter in his eyes. He said nothing as they stepped outside and the door closed behind them.

"That was useless," Dean said as he pulled the car keys from his pocket.

"I wouldn't say that," Sam responded. Dean shot him a questioning glance, but Sam just kept walking toward the Impala, his gaze straight ahead. Finally, when they'd both climbed into the car and shut the doors, Sam looked at his brother and grinned. He held up his hand and Dean saw a patch, rumpled from where it had been wadded into Sam's pocket, dangling from his first two fingers. It was a small but goofy thing showing a girl's hand with sharp pink fingernails, two roses on each side, and the slogan Don't Gimme a Cause to Use My Claws across the bottom in purple script. The overall shape was a heart and it had frayed threads across the upper right side. "I pulled this off one of the backpacks," Sam told him. "Either it wasn't there yesterday or I missed it when I zeroed in on that keychain."

"It's not the most well-lit place in the world." Dean studied the patch but didn't touch it. "Or maybe our favorite sheriff didn't expect us to come back," he suggested.

"Bull's eye." Sam carefully placed the patch on the seat between them. "I thought I saw dirt, maybe even blood, on the bottom of the backpack."

"Not good," Dean said as he started the car.

"No," Sam agreed. "Not at all."

"You think we can figure out a way to talk to the parents?"

Sam turned his head and stared out the window, his gaze going back to the window of the sheriff's office. "If we can figure out where they're staying."

"Must be local. Owen's house?"

Sam nodded, then shook his head. "Exactly."

Instead of starting the engine, Dean's fingers tapped absently on the steering wheel. "Why wasn't Owen in that conference room with the sheriff and Mr. and Mrs. Dietz?"

Sam looked at him in surprise, then scowled. "That's a damned good question."

Dean's face was carefully expressionless. "So if Owen isn't in there, and he isn't at work, then where the hell is he?"

"Home? He gave us his address, I think I saved it." Sam poked at his phone for a bit, then said, "Got it. I'll plug it into the GPS and… there we go."

Dean backed out of the parking space and headed toward Owen's place, following the directions Sam supplied. Fifteen minutes later they pulled into the driveway of a single-story house with white siding and a low-maintenance metal roof. The small covered porch was clutter free; the yard was the same, green and neatly mowed, the edges soggy with water from the recent rain. The carport was empty.

"Looks like we're out of luck," Dean said.

Sam pushed open his door. "I'm going to take a look around."

"Okay." Dean put the Impala in park and cut the engine, then got out and followed him.

Sam and Dean walked through the carport and around the back of the house, stepping lightly across a muddy part where the carport ended and a raised back porch started. Like the front, the back porch was empty—no lawn chairs or plants, not even a portable grill even though there was a large concrete patio.

"I guess he doesn't spend much time out here," Dean said. He stepped off the porch and pushed at a weed trying to grow in one of the cracks on the disused patio.

"Definitely a nerd." Sam gazed at the backyard, but like the front, there wasn't much to see. Just flat green lawn, no fence, a couple of trees, and a pile of tidily collected tree branches. He tried the back door, and when the door pushed open, he wasn't really surprised. Brownsdale had less than a thousand people in it and Owen lived on the outer edge of town; the door to this house probably hadn't been locked since it was built.

He was on the edge of the kitchen when he stepped inside. "Hello?" he called. "Anyone home?" He knew there wasn't, but hey, when you're going into someone's house without an invitation, you have to maintain courtesy. "Hey, Owen, it's..." Sam had to pause for a moment to remember. "Brian and Roger, from the FBI."

No answer.

Dean glanced around the yard, checking to see if the neighbors on either side were around; he didn't see anyone and the houses were pretty far away to begin with, so he slipped in behind his brother and pushed the door closed behind him.

They were in a good-sized room with a white tin ceiling and a tiled floor, pretty fancy stuff and unusual for a home built after the nineteen-fifties. On their left was the kitchen:

standard layout but very clean; Owen was clearly as neat and well organized in his home as he was in his office at the library. A dish towel was folded tidily over the edge of the double sink. There was a small kitchen table with three chairs under the window, but the only things on it were salt and pepper shakers. When Dean looked closer, the pepper shaker was only half filled but he saw a sprinkling of white around the full salt shaker, as if it had tipped over. To the right was apparently a dining room, but there was nothing in it except a stationary exercise bike facing the window; earphones hung over the handlebars but they weren't plugged into anything. The bike was fitted with a book holder and Dean thought that probably got more use than the music on Owen's phone or an MP3 player. Sam walked over to look at the piece of equipment and changed his mind; the seat and handlebars were covered in enough dust to make him think Owen hadn't used it in at least a month.

"Looks like working out isn't high on Owen's to-do list," Dean said from behind him. He walked over to the doorway and scanned the living room, which had the same tin ceiling but nicely polished wood floors. The front door had an oval inset of cut glass. There was an overstuffed couch and matching chair with the coffee table in front of them positioned in the center of a colorful braided rug; one wall was lined with shelves stuffed with books. A small flat-screen television on a stand was against the smallest wall, but it clearly wasn't the central focus. "Nice place."

Sam nodded. Then, just because he felt he should, called out again. "Hello? Owen?"

Still no answer. They moved down the hallway to the left, finding two small rooms. One was clearly Owen's office, neat and organized like everything else in his life; the other was the room the librarian had made up for his two cousins. It was cute but not overly girly, with matching curtains and bed covers. There was enough clutter to tell that Marley and Fallon Dietz had been staying here—a few books open, some small stuffed animals tossed in the corner, clothes piled in a basket between one bed and the wall. A lot of pillows and, of course, more books and interesting knickknacks placed on shelves built into the walls. In the center of those was a cloth-covered table that apparently served as a desk. The cover on one of the beds was the tiniest bit rumpled on one corner, as though someone had lain on it after it had been made but not quite straightened it out.

Sam stepped inside the room, then went over to the shelves and scanned the books. His gaze stopped on a big coffee table book about Mammoth Cave, then on another one two shelves down. There were half a dozen tomes about the cave, which wasn't surprising since it was the main attraction around here. The books were all still shelved but that didn't mean anything as the twins might have looked at them then put them away.

After a few moments, Sam and Dean backed out of the girls' room and went back the way they'd come, going down to a large bedroom at the opposite end of the house, obviously the master. The room was well-lit by a triple window on the front of the structure and the platform bed inside was neatly made with a masculine black comforter. A dresser, a chest of drawers, more bookshelves. Dean checked out the top of the dresser and saw a few things anyone would expect in a guy's bedroom—a bottle of inexpensive cologne, a sports watch with a rubber wristband, a small men's valet. While Sam looked in the closet, Dean flipped the valet open and found the standard stuff: another watch, a couple pairs of cufflinks, nail clippers, a wood-grain pocketknife, some change. Nothing in the room seemed out of the ordinary until Dean looked down.

"Wonder what shoes he changed into," he said, using one foot to prod at a pair of athletic shoes that looked like they'd been kicked off.

Sam had left the closet and wandered to the other side of the bed. "Look here." He pointed to a pile of clothes on the floor. "That doesn't seem like Owen," he said.

"Maybe he was in a hurry."

"To do what? I'm guessing that Ford we saw across from the sheriff's office was his aunt and uncle's rental car, so he didn't pick them up from the airport. They would've called him as soon as they got the news back in Arizona, so he had plenty of time to get ready for their arrival."

Dean frowned. "You think he ran?"

Sam shook his head and led the way back to the kitchen so they could go out the way they'd come in. "No. If he was going to do that, he'd have taken off the day they disappeared. Instead he reported them missing. And I don't believe for a moment he did anything to them."

"Then what?"

They walked back to the car and Sam met Dean's gaze over the roof. "I think he went into the cave to try and find them."

TWENTY-ONE

Sam and Dean decided to run by Cinnamon's house before going to the cave, to see if she'd be willing to take a look at the patch that Sam had filched from the evidence locker. By the time they got there, the rain had changed from a nebulous drizzle to a full-on downpour and the temperature had dropped by a startling fifteen degrees. The sky looked like a dirty comforter ripped apart by a rabid animal, filled with globs of shadowy gray; they couldn't see lightning but thunder swelled at irregular intervals, a celestial banging that was hard to ignore. The early afternoon storm made it seem like dusk, but the windows in the psychic's house were lit, the glow fragmenting across the Impala's rain-splattered windshield.

Dean pulled up as close as he could, but Cinnamon's car was in the driveway; they would still have a good twenty-some feet dash to the front porch.

Dean squinted through the windshield. The rain was so

heavy they couldn't see the porch clearly. "It won't be the first time we've gotten wet."

Sam pulled in a breath, getting ready. "And it won't be the last."

He reached for the door handle but a sudden rapping on Dean's window made them both jump. When Dean's face whipped toward the glass he saw the water-diluted figure of someone outside under the shelter of an oversized black umbrella.

The person knocked on the window again. "Come on!" They could barely hear Cinnamon's voice above the hammering of rain on the Impala's roof. "I'm getting soaked out here!"

Dean opened the door and Cinnamon reached past him and tossed a second umbrella at Sam. Dean clambered out and crab-walked with her to the porch; normally he wouldn't have cared about a little rain, but this was more in the mode of God turning on the faucet to wash Noah's ark out to sea. Sam was right behind them, almost slipping on the wet concrete of the porch.

"Close the umbrellas and leave them on the porch," the older woman yelled. Thunder almost drowned out her next words. "And for crying out loud, don't forget to wipe your feet."

Sam and Dean followed her instructions, then stood inside the door after she pushed it closed behind them. There was an oak coat rack next to the door and Cinnamon pulled a towel off one of the brass hooks and handed it to Dean. "You'll have to share," she said as she slipped off her shoes and pushed her feet into a pair of slippers at the base of the rack. "Haven't seen a storm this bad in quite a while. It's like a bad omen."

Dean gave the sleeves of his jacket a cursory wipe, then tossed the towel at his brother, who did the same. When Cinnamon headed toward the kitchen, Dean stuck the towel on an empty hook and he and Sam followed her. "Bad omen for what?" Sam asked.

She shrugged and pulled a metal teapot off the stove, filling it with water from the tap. "Nothing, I guess. Or maybe just for the poor folks who've gone missing." She set the teapot on the stove and twisted the knob underneath it, holding it there until the burner finally lit. "I mean, how could you find anything in this deluge, right?" She turned to look at them. "Would you sit down, please? I can't stand people who hover. They make me anxious."

The brothers glanced at each other but didn't argue, each sinking onto one of the wooden kitchen chairs. She fiddled around her kitchen, getting out mugs and setting one in front of each of them without bothering to ask if they wanted anything. While the water was heating she pulled a little basket from one of the cabinets and put it on the table in front of them. Inside was a selection of tea bags, and a few seconds later she added a plate with a pile of cookies on it.

"Homemade," she said. "Oatmeal raisin."

Dean grinned and went for the plate. By the time the teakettle started to whistle, he'd already happily ingested two and was working on a third.

Cinnamon plucked the kettle off the burner and came over to the table. "Pick a tea," she commanded. "No is not an acceptable choice. It's a miserable day outside and hot tea will warm your bones."

There wasn't anything to be gained by arguing, so each of the brothers picked out a packet of plain tea, opened it, and draped it over the edge of their mug so Cinnamon could pour the boiling water. When she'd finished, she put the kettle on a cold burner on the stove and returned to the table, settling onto a chair across from them and dunking her tea bag up and down. Finally, she said, "I assume you boys came by because you have something to show me."

They looked at each other, then Sam cleared his throat and pulled the patch out of his pocket. "Yeah," he said. "This." He slid it toward her on the tabletop, but she made no move to touch it.

She narrowed her eyes. "What makes you think this belonged to the right person?" For a brief moment, Cinnamon's eyes squeezed shut, as if she'd felt a sudden pain. "Not that there's a wrong person," she added. "What I meant was—"

"We understand," Sam said. "Everyone is important."

She nodded. Her expression was grim as she stared at the slowly browning liquid in her cup.

"This has to be hard for you," Dean said after a moment. "Seeing inside another person's head, sometimes at the worst time of their life…" His voice trailed off.

Cinnamon inhaled. "It is that," she agreed. "People think it would be great to read minds, to know what someone else is thinking, but they forget that you'd get the bad with the good. And I'm not talking about the juicy stuff either, all the naughty middle-of-the-night crap. Most of the time that's the easy part—I just ignore it, push it away; unless, of course, it folds in with more evil stuff. The hard part is the darkness in every soul. The guilt, the anger, the envy. Knowing that, feeling it, is debilitating. It takes something vital out of you. And that doesn't even touch on the... end."

Sam studied the psychic. "Death? Do you see beyond it?"

"God, I hope not," she said flatly. "Because all I've ever gotten a glimpse of is bad."

Sam's gaze met Dean's. His brother looked like he wanted to say something but Sam's warning look shut him down; instead, he stuffed the rest of the third cookie into his mouth.

Cinnamon sighed and it made the brothers realize just how tired she must be of it all, although the definition of that was still in question. How many years had she been questioning the disappearances in this town, or at least wondering if she should, or even could do something to put a stop to them? On the other hand, maybe all she felt was helpless, possessed of a skill that no one in the so-called real world even believed in. No matter what she'd done in the past to help, neither of them could picture Sheriff Thompson welcoming her offer of assistance; he would've laughed, then told her to get lost and stop meddling in the affairs of the sheriff's office. That would have been the nice part. After that he would have told her, no doubt in his most courteous voice, to stop impeding their investigations.

Cinnamon pressed her lips together, a movement that made her look more tired than ever. She was dressed in polka dots again, this time in jeans topped by a blouse with a bright green background for the dots. That same purple and white-dotted scarf was wrapped around her neck and the combination of purple and green wasn't a good one; it made the pale skin on her face look sallow and thin to the point of translucence. The delicate veins along her jaw crept upward, faint bruised-looking lines of red, green, and purple.

"Let's just relax for a few moments," Sam said. He swept the patch off the table and tucked it back into his pocket. "Enjoy the tea and the cookies." He plucked one from the plate and took a bite. "These are seriously delicious," he told her. He glanced at Dean. "Just ask him. He's the connoisseur of baked goods." In response, Dean snagged his fourth one and toasted her with it.

"Thanks. I made them this morning. Something to keep me occupied while I waited for you two to get here." Cinnamon chose a cookie and took a small bite. She smiled faintly and some of the tension seemed to go out of her. "They are good, aren't they? My mother's recipe."

They sat in companionable silence for a while, drinking the tea and working on the plate of cookies. Dean could have easily polished off the entire pile—would have, in fact—had Sam not kicked his ankle under the table when he reached for one of only two that remained. Instead Dean pulled his hand back and wiped his fingers on his jeans.

Cinnamon eyed him. "Would you like a napkin?"

He grinned at her and shook his head. "No, thanks."

"You have crumbs around your mouth."

Dean automatically wiped the back of his hand across his mouth. "Not anymore."

"Don't mind him," Sam said. "He was raised by wolves."

Cinnamon chuckled as she stood and gathered the mugs. As she touched Sam's, her finger brushed across the edge and she blinked. For just a second her hand shook.

"You all right?" Sam asked.

The older woman pulled herself up and carried the mugs to the sink. "I'm fine, Sam," she said. "Thanks for asking."

Sam sat up on his chair and twisted to look at her. Cinnamon stood at the sink, carefully rinsing the mugs after setting the used tea bags aside. "Cinnamon…"

Without turning to look at him or Dean, she raised a hand. "Don't bother," she said. "I just figured out who you really are. You told me you were monster hunters and I believed you, but the rest of it just fell into place." She turned her head and her eyes met Dean's. "Sam and Dean Winchester. Brothers. Monster hunters—famous ones, at that. That's pretty amazing."

Sam pushed his hair out of his eyes. "Not as amazing as what you can do," he pointed out. "We have to mostly figure it out on our own. You can… what? Just touch someone? Or something that belonged to them? And then you know everything."

"Oh, not even close," she responded. She gave a raspy laugh. "Yeah, I'll get the name, generally be able to figure out who they were—or in your case, are. Maybe some history." She shook her head. "If I was on a television show, it'd be called Psychic Lite. Except that I always manage to get the details about the bad parts, the horrible things that happen to people." She plucked a dish towel from the counter and dried her hands. "Why can't I get good memories? You know, like when a woman gets married, or a man holds his newborn son?"

"That sucks," Dean said.

Sam said nothing. He couldn't help wondering if she

wanted to see memories like those because they would bring balance to the horrific things she usually saw, or because she'd never experience them herself. Either way, he felt bad for her.

"All right," Cinnamon finally said. She gestured at them to follow her and the brothers rose. "Let's go and get this over with."

They followed her to the front room, where they all sat in the same spots they had before; it was getting to be a pattern. "Let's have it," she said resignedly.

Sam pulled the patch from his pocket again, unfolding it and offering it to the psychic. He stretched it out so she could see how it was worn along the edges but still bright, still full of the kind of attitude so common among today's kids.

"Well," Cinnamon said. "That's quite unusual. Where did it come from?"

"A backpack in the evidence locker," Sam told her. "We were there this morning."

"Yeah," Dean put in. "And Sheriff Thompson was as congenial as he always is."

"No doubt." She considered the patch but made no move to take it out of Sam's grip. "Then I guess you heard the news?"

The brothers looked at each other. "No," Sam said. "There's nothing—"

"Wait," Dean interrupted. "We stopped at the minimart this morning and I heard a couple of girls talking about someone else going missing. I asked but they wouldn't talk about it, even when I told them I was FBI." Dean's mouth went down at one corner. "The cashier's name was Margie. She said her dad was Deputy Sloane and I could go ask him."

Cinnamon nodded. "That girl's just as friendly as her father."

"Yeah, I noticed that. I knew there was no way he'd say anything to us if we asked," Dean leaned forward and clasped his hands between his knees. "So who disappeared?"

Cinnamon eyed them, then took a deep breath before she answered. "Owen Meyer."

Dean jerked at the same time Sam sat up in shock. "What? When?"

"No one really knows, except he didn't show up for work this morning. An administrative assistant at City Hall was calling around this morning to see if someone was willing to go sit in the library until this afternoon. There's a junior librarian but she's part time while she's working on her degree; she's in class this morning up in Bowling Green."

"That explains the sign on the library door," Sam said.

Dean's forehead furrowed. "It also explains why he wasn't at the sheriff's office with his aunt and uncle, remember?"

"Yeah."

"I had a vision last night," Cinnamon said. Her voice was so soft her words could barely be heard. "I don't know for certain, but it might have been about Owen."

Sam and Dean studied her for a few seconds, then Sam said, "Let me guess. It wasn't good."

She shook her head. "No."

Dean glanced at his brother. "Is he..."

"I can't say," Cinnamon answered. "It was from someone else's perspective." She swallowed. "It didn't end well."

Sam winced. "Can you tell us what you remember?"

The white-haired woman rubbed her fingers hard across her forehead, as though she was trying to massage away a headache. "Everything was black, but I knew I had to be in the cave. I was crawling around, couldn't see anything, but then I heard laughing. You know, like kids do, and I called out but no one answered. Then I fell." Her hands started shaking and she clasped her fingers together to stop them. "No sense going into the real horrible details, but it ended with me being surrounded by bones—human ones— and these..." Her voice faltered.

"Yes?" Sam prompted. He knew it was a hard thing for her to recount but they needed to know.

She took a deep breath. "Animals, or creatures, or... something. I don't know exactly. I only got a glimpse of them at the last second, right before I pulled out of it, but I could tell they'd been... been chewing, they'd been eating—"

"Okay," Dean interrupted. "I think we get the picture."

Sam studied her. "Did you actually see the girls? Or anyone else?"

"No. Just those things."

Sam sat back and let her recover, at the same time thinking about what she had told them. Something inhuman in the cave... demons? Or something more tied to the earth itself, like bat creatures?

Cinnamon made a visible effort to sit up straight on her chair, then cleared her throat. "Did you talk to them? The girls' parents?" Her eyes were bright.

Sam shook his head. "No way. Thompson wouldn't let us near them."

"But Owen wasn't there."

"Nope," Dean answered.

"He must be devastated right now," Cinnamon said. "He adored those girls."

Sam's fingers were absently working at the patch, smoothing out the wrinkles. "You sound like you know Owen pretty well."

Cinnamon sat back. "Well enough, I suppose. I like to read but I'm one of those old-fashioned people who check out books from the library rather than buy them, and I don't own an e-reader. Maybe it's a budget thing, or maybe it goes back to my childhood. Back then libraries were great places where you went to do your homework, learn about countries you'd probably never get to go to." She reached up and tapped the side of her head. "Use your imagination. Owen was trying to bring all that back. Even though Brownsdale is small, he had ideas for so many programs—things he said would get the kids interested in reading again, teach them that the world out there wasn't something unattainable." She was silent for a moment. "I guess now all that'll go in the trash. Not much outreach in this county, I'm ashamed to say."

Sam looked at her steadily. "You keep saying was, like you've already decided Owen is never coming back."

"Or that he's dead," Dean added.

Cinnamon let her head drop forward, then rubbed hard at her face, as though she was trying to wipe away some emotion too personal to share with them. "It's not my decision," she said quietly. "Whatever's happened is already done. Nothing we do can change that."

"And what happened is…?" Sam let the question go unfinished.

"I don't know." Cinnamon sounded defeated. "I guess I

could find out, but I'm not sure I want to. These things...
they have a way of ending badly in Brownsdale. Very badly."
She paused. "At least if I mind my own business, make sure
to stay away from anything that might have belonged to him
or whatever, then I can tell myself that he just... left. Maybe
went to Bowling Green, or Louisville. That he decided this
rotten little town wasn't where someone like him, someone
with heart, wanted to spend his life."

"Like everyone else in town." Sam looked at her and she
flinched.

Dean leaned back on his chair. When his brother didn't add
anything more, he asked, "And what happens when you do?"

The psychic looked confused. "Do what?"

The older Winchester brother looked at her intently.
"Touch something of his. He was the librarian. Are you never
going there again?"

"Well, I—"

"How strong is your power, anyway?" Sam suddenly asked.

"I don't have any powers," she protested. "That's ridiculous."

He waved away her words. "Power, skill, whatever.
Semantics don't matter here. We gave you a keychain and you
were able to tell us who the woman who owned it was and
that she died a year ago." Sam's gaze was hard, unrelenting.
"What happens if you go to the grocery store and the last
person who used the cart was Owen Meyer? What then?"

Cinnamon shook her head, a sharp jerk left and right. "It
doesn't work like that," she said. "Whatever I touch has to
have belonged to the person who owned it exclusively. I don't
just walk around having visions all the time!" Her voice was

climbing. "It doesn't work like that," she repeated.

"Okay, just hold on, Sam," Dean said. His voice had a placating tone to it and he rose and stepped toward her chair. "Let's not get her all flipped out."

"Don't touch me!"

"Whoa," Dean said, and back-stepped. "My bad."

"Look, I'm sorry," Sam said. He grabbed Dean's wrist and tugged on him until his brother sat down again.

Cinnamon covered her face with her hands. "Never mind," she said in a muffled voice. "Just give me the damned patch and be done with it." When she pulled her hands away, her eyes and nose were red as she struggled not to cry. "It's not going to be good, but I guess I can't say no, can I?"

The brothers looked at each other, then Dean focused again on her. "We can't force you to do anything."

"But I'll have to live with myself if I don't," she said. "You might not believe me, but a lot of the time that's not an easy thing to do." The older woman inhaled deeply, then let out her air in a slow, controlled breath. "I'm ready," she said simply, and held out her hand.

Sam frowned and looked down at the patch in his hands, then back at her. "Are you sure?"

Cinnamon gestured at him impatiently. "Come on already."

Almost reluctantly, Sam stretched out his hand and let her take the patch. For a moment, nothing happened. It was almost as though she had managed to erect some kind of metal force field, a barrier to keep herself safe from the memories infused into the brightly colored threads.

Then her face crumpled.

She began to shake, hard, making the rocker she was sitting in visibly vibrate. Her fingers spasmed and she clutched the patch, smashing it into a wad in her palms. With no warning, her head snapped backward and her eyes rolled up until all the brothers could see were the whites floating against the pale skin of her face. Her skin, her hair, her eyes—they were all white, making her look like a tortured ghost.

Reflex made Dean lean forward and reach for her, but Sam stopped him. "Bad idea, dude. You might stop what she's seeing… or get pulled into it."

Dean sat back down, but he still looked ready to leap forward. "This doesn't look good."

"Just hold on, give it a minute."

Cinnamon's mouth was closed, her lips pressed together so tightly that they were as pale as her skin. It was like this time she was fighting not to scream, was somehow determined to stay in whatever crazy and horrific scenario was playing out in her head. Then she began to pant, harder and harder, and sweat broke out on her forehead; another few seconds and her feet drummed against the wood floor as though she were running for her life. Her hands, one still clutching the patch, gripped the arms of the rocking chair. Her feet pounded in front of her, faster and faster, until they were just a blur, and her breathing took on a ragged, gasping note.

Dean couldn't stand it any longer. "Cinnamon," he said, and grabbed her by one wrist before Sam could intervene. "Cinnamon, wake up!"

Her eyes flew open, then shifted to focus on him. Then she did the last thing he expected: she bared her teeth and lunged at him, shooting forward and ramming him in the shoulder hard enough to make him stagger backward, pinwheeling his arms to maintain his balance. "Hey!" he yelled. He tried to grab her again, but he was off balance; he tilted and started to go down. Cinnamon lurched past him, headed for the front door, while Dean ended up on his backside on the floor next to the chair he'd been sitting on a moment before.

Cinnamon clawed at the front door, but before she could yank it open Sam was behind her; he wrapped his arms around her waist and lifted her off the floor, then spun and headed back to the sitting room, trying to get her to the middle of the floor where she wouldn't break anything. She flailed like some kind of gigantic spider, arms and legs going in every direction. And when Sam thought it couldn't get any worse, she started shrieking.

The sound was loud enough to make Dean wince, but Sam didn't dare let her go. She started punching backwards, trying to hit his head over her shoulder. She wasn't missing, either.

"Get that damned patch out of her hand!" he yelled at Dean.

Dean scrambled forward, but the psychic was giving it everything she had, hitting and clawing, kicking out with both feet, and all the while making a hideous screeching noise that sounded like nothing human. Dean caught a double groove across his cheek as he tried to duck her blows but finally managed to grab her hand. She was holding the patch in a death grip and no matter how hard he tried, he wasn't going to get it free unless he broke her fingers. "I can't get it free!" he hollered in frustration. He looked toward Sam just as Cinnamon's head shot forward and her forehead slammed into his chin.

Dean reeled backward and for the second time ended up on his ass on the floor, this time in the middle of the doorway to the sitting room. The walls revolved around his head and for a crazy moment his brain told him he was on a Tilt-A-Whirl, then his hands slapped against the floor and he shook his head. His chin ached massively.

"Hey, you okay?"

Dean rubbed his jaw and looked up. Sam was standing there with his arms still holding Cinnamon firmly around the waist. This time, though, his arms were relaxed and the small woman's feet were draped loosely over Sam's shoes. Her head was slumped forward and her arms dangled at her sides; head-butting Dean's chin had knocked her out cold.

"Ow," Dean muttered. "Did you hit me?" He pushed himself to his feet.

Sam snorted. "You wish. Just so you don't have to admit she glass-jawed you." He inclined his head toward the rocking chair. "Come on, help me get her back in there before she comes to."

Dean grabbed Cinnamon's ankles and they carried her over to the rocker and set her into it as gently as they could. Dean looked at the unconscious woman warily. "Think we should tie her up?"

This time Sam actually laughed. "Oh, this is one for the record books. A hundred and seventy-five pound expert hunter gets cold-cocked by a ninety-five pound woman."

Dean glowered at him, then realized the side of his face was stinging like he'd been sandpapered. When he touched his cheek, his fingers came away bloody.

"Damn," Sam said. "She really did get you good."

Cinnamon's voice cut Dean off before he could answer. "Couple of nasty scratches," she said calmly. "There's hydrogen peroxide below the sink in the bathroom down the hall. You'll want to clean those out real well. You look like you're getting a bruise on your chin, too."

Dean instinctively jerked at the sound of her voice, then realized Cinnamon was sitting motionless on the rocker, looking up at them both. "Welcome back," Dean said. "You really had us going."

The woman looked down at her hands and frowned, stretching her fingers. When they followed her gaze, they realized the patch had fallen free when she'd been knocked out; it lay in a creased clump on the front hallway floor. Sam started to go get it, but the psychic's voice stopped him. "No, throw it out. I never want to touch that thing again."

Sam glanced at her, then scooped it up. "Okay."

She adjusted herself on the chair and gave a little groan. "I feel like I've gone three rounds with Muhammad Ali."

Dean gave her an irritated look. "You're not the only one."

For a moment, she actually grinned. "Sorry about that."

"Can I get you something?" Dean asked. "Water?"

She shook her head. "Skip it. How about I just tell you what I saw, then you two be on your way. I'm sure you're both great guys, but I really can't say it's been fun."

Dean nodded, resisting the urge to agree. His jaw hurt enough that he didn't want to talk.

For a second she stared at her fingers. "I've got blood

underneath my nails," she said faintly. She raised her eyes to Dean's. "I'm so sorry."

He shrugged. "I'll survive."

Cinnamon curled the fingers of both hands into fists, then took a deep breath. "Okay, I'll tell you what happened to the girls, at least the best I can, but you're not going to like it."

"I figured as much," Sam said. "Are they dead?"

The psychic nodded, her eyes haunted. She tried to speak, then had to take another deep breath. "It was horrible," she finally managed. "Bloody and horrible."

Dean scowled. "How?"

Cinnamon bit her lip. "That's just it, I don't know exactly. I saw… shapes, forms in the darkness. Smoke from what looked like small fires, maybe from camping."

"Inside the cave?" Sam asked.

She nodded. "Yes… at least I think so. I didn't see any trees. Then again, it was so dark." She closed her eyes momentarily. "But yes, inside the cave. It had to be." Her eyes opened again. "I remember the walls, cold stone, the feel of moisture against my palms." Her fists unfolded and the thumbs of each hand rubbed against her palms, as if she were reliving the sensation. "So cold. So frightening."

"Go on," Dean encouraged.

The woman licked her dry lips. "I—I mean they—were running from something. They couldn't see what it was, but they heard… sounds. Terrifying sounds."

"And you heard these, too?" Sam asked. "In your mind?"

She nodded. "You have to understand," she glanced at Dean, her voice almost pleading, "I didn't just hear them. I was there, with them, in the cave. So scared I almost couldn't breathe." She blinked rapidly, as though she was trying to clear her vision. "The patch was Fallon's," she said. "She got it at this crazy little resale shop in Nashville the last time her family visited there. Three years ago, I think. It's hard to pinpoint."

"And Marley?" Dean prompted.

"She was there, too. The both of them. Running as fast as they could, trying to get away from... something." Cinnamon frowned, her eyes taking on that same faraway look they'd seen the first time they'd showed up at her house. Her gaze cleared. "I—they—never got a good look at what grabbed them from behind."

"Crap," Sam murmured, not because the girls hadn't seen their attackers but because he knew what was coming.

"They were..." She swallowed hard, and for a moment she looked like she might throw up. She took another deep inhalation as she forced her voice to stay level. "They were hauled backward in the dark by things... big, strong things. There were so many of them that they got turned around, slamming into each other because it was so dark you almost couldn't see anything. They were pulling on the girls from every direction like they were the object of some kind of vicious tug of war. In the end, they were literally ripped apart. It was like I was the one screaming, along with my sister—Marley. I felt the pain Fallon was in, all of it, until everything went black." She was silent for a few moments. "I think I went a little crazy because of it. I didn't mean to hurt you. I didn't even know I was doing it."

"It's all right," Dean said, and he meant it. "I know what

it's like to get… taken over by things you can't control."

"I hope you don't end up with scars."

Dean shrugged. "Won't be the first time." He was silent for a moment. "You're sure the girls are dead?"

Cinnamon nodded and drew her hand across her forehead, letting her fingers linger as if she had a sudden headache. "As sure as I am about anything I see that I can't actually prove. Which is a lot, when you think about it."

"Cinnamon," Sam said, moving forward until he was sitting on the edge of his chair. "Can you tell where in the cave they were?"

"No," she answered. "I don't know the cave at all. But…" She turned her head and her gaze stopped on something across the room. She stood, still unsteady, and made her way to the side table where the snow globe rested on its brass base. When she reached toward it, Sam couldn't help tensing. But Cinnamon picked up something smaller that was behind it and held it up for Sam and Dean to see. It was another sphere, this one made of solid crystal rather than glass; its smooth surface was not quite translucent, shot through with veins of milky white. It was small enough for Cinnamon to curl her fingers halfway around it when it rested on her palm. "Yes," she breathed.

"What?" Sam prompted.

Cinnamon went back to the rocking chair and sat, looking down at the stone in her hands. "My mother gave this to me when I was ten years old," she told them. "I was just starting to… see things, and she told me it came from Crystal Onyx Cave, what they now just call Crystal Cave." She turned the orb over on her palm, fingers running over the cool stone.

'I guess you'd call this a crystal ball, although I never used it in the traditional sense. Occasionally, though, I'd play with it and get flashes of… I don't know. Intuition, I guess, extra insight that almost never made any sense." She looked up and met Sam's gaze. "Once in a while, though, it would be like the final piece falling into a puzzle. Like now."

He looked steadily back at her. "And?"

"They were in the part of the cave system that this came from," she said. "Crystal Cave—the one that's been closed off."

"We were already guessing that," Dean said. "But how did they get there? That's a hell of a long way from town. How did they even know where it was?"

Cinnamon frowned and closed her eyes, trying to pull in the memories from before the girls' lives had ended in terror and tragedy. "I… can't tell," she finally said. "The brain puts memories in a sort of filing system ranked by importance. A momentous event can just sort of flash out the things that preceded it, or came after it."

"And momentous can mean good or bad," Sam said.

"Yes."

"Can you get anything at all from that thing that you didn't pick up from the patch?" Dean asked.

Cinnamon closed her eyes. She sat there for several minutes, with her only movement being her fingertips playing over the surface of the crystal ball. The brothers stayed quiet, letting her concentrate; Dean was just thankful she wasn't having the same reaction to the sphere that she'd had to that damned patch.

She'd been quiet for so long that her voice, although it was faint, startled them when she finally spoke. "Someone drove them there. Someone they trusted."

Both the brothers frowned. "Owen?" Sam asked.

Cinnamon shook her head. "No, someone else."

"That's weird," Dean said. "Who else did they know i town? I thought they'd only been here a couple of days."

"I don't know." Cinnamon's forehead was creased as sh visibly struggled to remember. "All I can see is that the didn't think twice about accepting a ride. I can't even see if i was male or female, just that they were dropped off right a the entrance, the one that's supposed to be boarded up." Sh opened her eyes. "I'm sorry. What happened after they got ir the cave blots out everything else, just wipes it all out."

"Can you at least tell how long they were in the cave befor they ran into whatever those things were?"

She shook her head again. "No, although I think it was while. I remember they were happy. They were talking, like girls do. They were exploring and having a good time." The psychic looked up at the ceiling, as though she was trying to see inside her own brain. "I think they might have crawled somewhere in the cave, through a small tunnel or something."

The brothers looked at each other. "Maybe that explains it," Sam said. "Whatever's inside that cave is too big to get out."

"But what about all the other people who have disappeared?" Dean asked. "Plenty of adults who were a lot bigger than a couple of thirteen-year-old girls."

"True." Sam looked frustrated.

"It's a cave," Cinnamon reminded them. "There are probably dozens of ways in and out, maybe hundreds, known and unknown."

"Also true," Sam said.

Cinnamon stood and returned the crystal orb to its place on the side table, then gazed at them. "I know what you're going to do," she said. "And it's not a good idea. In fact, it's an awful idea and it'll only get you killed."

Sam met her eyes and didn't look away. "So you've seen our futures?"

The psychic shook her head. "No, and I don't want to. I don't have to. I appreciate your determination, but if you two go into that cave, you're going to end up like all the others."

"Are you sure?" Dean's voice had that stubborn tone to it, the one where he wasn't going to change his mind.

"No, I'm not. And I'm not going to touch either of you to find out. I've been through enough." She made her way slowly back to the rocking chair, using one of its arms to steady herself as she sat. "I'm not a young woman anymore, and I don't think I have the stamina, the strength, to continue digging into other people's minds. It's too taxing, too painful." She'd started rocking but now she stopped and stared at them. "Look, if I thought getting down on my knees and begging you would change your minds, I'd do it. Please don't go into Crystal Cave. It won't do any good. It won't stop the disappearances, and you'll just end up being two more people added to the list."

Sam shook his head. "I'm sorry, Cinnamon. We can't let this go. Whatever's in that cave has to be stopped. It's—"

"Bad," she finished for him. "I know that. But I don't know that you can put an end to it."

"We have to," Sam said.

At the same time, Dean said, "Oh, we will."

Sam looked at his brother, then back at Cinnamon. "Wh
he said."

There was no doubt at all in his voice.

TWENTY-TWO

Cinnamon Ellison watched from her front room window as the Winchester brothers backed out of her driveway. The rain was still heavy but both had refused her offers to walk them to the car with an umbrella, or to borrow the umbrella and return it later. If braving the conditions of the Mammoth Cave system wasn't fazing them, she imagined a little rain didn't even register. All that water made their black Impala—she remembered the make and model from back in her younger days—gleam like some kind of sleek, furtive military vehicle, something built long and stealthy to deal with things like the monsters the Winchesters supposedly faced all the time. If only that were true, she thought. If only those two young men could somehow drive that car into the heart of the mountain itself and use it to conquer the darkness that festered and grew at its center.

She gave herself a mental shake and turned away from the window. It felt chilly in the house, or perhaps that was just her own body's reaction to the psychic trauma she'd inflicted upon it. Stopping in the hallway, Cinnamon turned the thermostat up a couple of degrees to chase away the dampness the morning's storm had brought. Funny how it could be hot and humid outside, but the old houses, ones like hers, always seemed to cool when it rained. Maybe that coldness was a byproduct of certain parts of humanity, a notation in the physical world of how some human beings lacked empathy.

She knew other psychics—in this day of the Internet, how could she not?—but few seemed to truly understand how enormously strenuous having these abilities could be. That, of course, made her doubt the veracity of most of the online "friends" she had made on Facebook. Almost all of them had come via word of mouth, rumors about her or referrals from someone who knew about something she'd done. She saw a lot of advertising and self-aggrandizement in the About sections of those pages, from claims that people could be reconnected with lost loved ones, accurate tarot card readings, to predictions of the future. All, in her opinion, questionable just by the fact they had been posted to begin with. She made no such statements, said nothing about her abilities or, and this was rarely asked about, her limitations. Her profile simply noted she was retired and that was that. She didn't have the Facebook account to advertise or make money from her talents—she'd never, ever, taken a dime in relation to that. She just had it because it softened each day's long hours into something bearable and lessened her loneliness. In fact, she hardly ever posted, just read about the things that happened in other people's lives, listened to their complaints—which most of the time were about the silliest, most trivial things imaginable—looked at the pictures of their husbands, wives, kids and pets, and contemplated how they could not realize their own stupid luck in having such full lives.

The sound of the furnace kicking on in the too-silent house startled her and Cinnamon gave herself a mental slap for being morose and self-pitying; neither would do any good. If she wanted to feel better then she had to do something about the situation that was weighing her down, to at least try and change an outcome she was all too sure was going to come true.

With the air in the house warming up and the cats following her, she went into the bedroom and changed her clothes, picking out clean jeans and a heavier tunic sweater that was red and came down to mid-thigh. She pulled on boots that would keep her feet dry, then retied her purple dotted scarf around her neck. So what if it didn't match—it was her favorite and it kept her neck warm. That done, she went into the bathroom and rinsed the dried sweat off her face. Patting her skin dry, she inspected her image in the mirror. Not a bad face for a woman her age, she surmised. High, lined forehead, lots of wrinkles and crow's feet around her eyes, smile lines on either side of her full mouth. A face with character, hair that had started to go white in her early fifties and had been complete by fifty-five. Her eyes, however, blue and sharp and bright, had not seen enough of the good things in the world. Those had seen only Brownsdale, and while there were certainly a lot of decent enough people living in the town, the sins of those who were bad far outweighed the good.

God, even though she loved Brownsdale, how she wished

she had gotten out of here. Not just decades ago, but a full half-century in the past. Back at the height of her shame—where would she have gone, who would she have become had she simply gotten on a bus and gone east, or west, or anywhere?

A foolish question, Cinnamon thought as she stared at her reflection, because it could never be answered. The past was as set in stone as an ancient marble statue. The stone might crumble, but it could never change what it had been.

But the future…

Cinnamon combed her hair and pulled it behind her head in a small, loose knot, just to keep it out of her face. She put a touch of gloss over her lips and called it good, then retrieved her purse and keys. Her umbrella wasn't great shelter but it got her to the Prius and inside and kept her from getting soaked. The inside of the car was steamy and hot so she started the engine and let the defogger blast the windshield with cold air until it cleared.

There was only one person who knew the cave well enough to make a difference, maybe, in what fate had in store for those Winchester boys.

It was the last thing she wanted to do, but Cinnamon set her jaw, put the car in drive, and headed into the rain.

The drive to Go Cave Wild was as uneventful as driving to the grocery store or going to get gasoline; if Cinnamon expected something wild and grand to happen on the way, a bolt of lightning splitting the roadway in front of her, or a werewolf leaping out of the woods and landing on her windshield—something the Winchester brothers would have her believe was not impossible—she was disappointed. There was rain, a lot of it, and nothing else but some distant thunder. The nonstop rain had driven a lot of the townsfolk inside and what few shoppers were on the main thoroughfare scuttled along like they were in fear of doing a Wicked Witch of the West meltdown. Most of the stores were open except for a few businesses that used Monday and Tuesday as a faux weekend to make up for working on Saturday and Sunday.

Beau's shop was maybe ten stores down from the old cinema. At one time there had been a black and white striped awning in front of it but Beau had taken it down about ten years ago, saying it made everything so dark that people passing on the sidewalk didn't pay any attention to the store. At the same time he'd redone the old interior, driving away the dimness inside and out with extra lights and lots of neon. She still remembered his words: "Just because I sell spelunking supplies doesn't mean the place has to look like the inside of a cave." Even now, with the pouring rain between her car and the storefront, Go Cave Wild was the brightest and most welcoming on the street.

Cinnamon had found a spot four slots down from the store. Resigned to getting soaked even with her umbrella, she tugged her scarf tighter around her neck then opened the driver's door just enough to shove the umbrella outside and open it. The rain hammered down on the plastic, surprisingly loud and ferocious, but she wriggled out the smallest space she could, pushed the door shut and scurried down the sidewalk.

Before she could reach for the handle, the door opened.

Beau stood there with his arm outstretched, holding it in place while she ducked inside, almost like he'd known she was coming to see him. Which, of course, was impossible.

Of course.

"Here," he said. "Let me take that for you."

Cinnamon gave him the umbrella and watched as he opened the door again and gave it a brisk shake. That done, he pulled it back inside and leaned it against the wall to the right of the entry. In only a few seconds, a puddle formed at the tip but he paid no attention.

"Come on," he said congenially. "It's warmer in the back, away from the door."

She followed him without saying anything, noting the way he was still strong and straight-backed. Exercise, she thought. She knew he hiked almost every Tuesday and Wednesday, the days when the shop's business was slowest and he had a young man, a hiker himself, who worked the counter. She didn't know if that meant he was in the cave every week— he seemed a little too tanned for that—but he still had the reputation of being the go-to person if you wanted something a lot more interesting than one of the regular park tours.

Here and there throughout the shop were chairs, almost like one of those bookstore-coffee shop combinations in the bigger cities. He led her to a spot by a bookshelf filled with hiking and cave texts, where two worn but comfortable-looking plaid armchairs were arranged around a battered circular table. "Please," he said. "Sit. I have a pot of coffee, just made fresh."

"No, thanks," Cinnamon said as she let herself sink onto one of the chairs. Although she mostly drank tea, she did like the occasional cup of coffee; right now, however, her nerves were already tight enough to make her skin tingle and her fingers tremble. She kept them shoved in her pockets to make sure he didn't see how nervous she was. This morning's mental excursion had done a fine job of setting her on edge and, like always, just being around Beau Pyle put a swarm of half-agonizing, half-pleasurable butterflies in her stomach. When he looked at her questioningly, she managed, "I already feel waterlogged."

Beau glanced back toward the counter. "Do you mind if I...?"

"Of course not." She watched as he went and poured coffee for himself, then carried his Mammoth Cave National Park mug back and sat in the other chair.

They stared at each other for a long moment and Cinnamon realized she couldn't remember the last time they had met like this, face to face and without other people around. Sure, there were town functions now and then where they ended up in the same room, but they always avoided each other. She knew he was in church every Sunday, knew precisely where he sat; she also knew that he did so to make sure she had the chance to get out of there without having to talk to him.

"This is a surprise," Beau finally said. "Never expected to see you come in the shop."

She didn't answer because she couldn't; she kept searching for the right words to say what she needed him to know but she couldn't find them. It was crazy enough that she was here, that they were across from each other—she'd sworn so many years ago she would never speak to him again—but it really frosted her that he still had the same effect on her, after all these years and after having run off with her younger sister.

"Yes," she finally said. Her tone was curt but it was the best she could manage.

He looked at her expectantly, adding, "There must be something you want, Cinnamon. You wouldn't be here otherwise."

Damn him for being so reasonable, so calm and clear-headed. She could barely organize her thoughts. Inside her pockets, she let her stiff fingers relax, then purposely dug the nails into the tops of her thighs through the fabric. The pain wasn't terrible, but it was enough to give her something on which to focus.

"I have a problem," she said. "There's something I'd like your help with."

His look of disbelief was almost as comical as it was genuine. "Me?"

"You sent two men to my house," she continued. "You told them I was psychic."

He nodded. "Yes. They were from the FBI."

Cinnamon shook her head. "No, they weren't."

His expression melted into outrage. "But they showed me identification." Then the color drained from his face. "Did they hurt you? I never meant to—"

She held up a hand to stop him. "I'm fine. And even though they aren't really FBI agents, they're..." She tilted her head, trying to find the correct word. "Good guys," she finished. "Their names are Sam and Dean Winchester." She met his gaze. "But here's the thing," she told him. "They're looking for those girls. And they're going into Crystal Cave to try to find them."

Beau nodded. "Right. They wanted gear, so I laid it all out for them, made sure they had the right stuff, a couple of good maps. I offered to guide them but they didn't bite."

"They're going to die in that cave, Beau. Just like the girls."

He stared at her in shock. "Oh my God, Cinnamon. What are you saying? You know what happened to them?"

Cinnamon let her gaze drop to her lap. She'd put her hand back inside her pocket, and now she could see her fingers moving under the fabric of her sweater, nails again pressing into her own legs. "Yes. I saw it."

He looked confused. "You saw—"

"In my head," she said impatiently. "Come on, Beau. Get with the program. I told them you didn't really believe I was psychic, but that's a lie, isn't it? You do believe. You always have."

Beau's mouth opened and hung there for a second, then closed with an almost audible snap. "Yes." There was a long, uncomfortable silence between them, then Beau said, "You knew I was going to leave with Brenda, didn't you?"

"Yes."

He let out a breath, loud, frustrated. "Then for God's sake, why didn't you stop us?"

Cinnamon shrugged. It was a careless gesture but the emotions she felt were anything but. "I couldn't have done anything. You'd made up your mind."

That last sentence hung in the air, heavy and insinuating. Cinnamon herself wasn't sure exactly what it meant: that he'd made up his mind to go—he had—or he'd made up his mind he wanted Brenda rather than her—he also had.

"I'm sorry," Beau said. His voice was hoarse and he sounded like he was putting everything he had into not crying. "I've told you before. I screwed up, Cinnamon. I made the worst mistake of my life."

"Yes," she said quietly. "You did." She looked to the left, back toward the front of the store, then inhaled. "But that was a long time ago. Right now, you need to help those two young men."

He nodded. He leaned toward her on his chair and his voice was steady again, even though he had folded his fingers together so firmly that the knuckles were white, the tips red. "All right, what do you want me to do?" Then his well-worn face tightened. "Wait—you said you know what happened to those two girls?"

"Yes. Like I told you, they're..." She started to tell him, then found she couldn't just blurt out the words. They were simply so terrible that they stuck in her throat and hung there. She'd once had some kind of allergic reaction in a restaurant and found herself, for a long forty seconds, unable to swallow the food in her mouth or breathe, no matter how much she tried. Trying to speak now was like that. She tried again, forcing it out. "They're d-dead. Something in the cave..." She couldn't say, just couldn't. "Took them," she finally blurted out. Her forehead was sheathed in perspiration again and panic rose in her chest, a perfect and completely intense fear that she was going to relive the girls' last moments. Now, and perhaps every time she thought of them.

Dear God.

Blackness started to creep in at the edge of her vision and she sucked in air, then Beau's voice yanked her back to the present. If they hadn't had such a monumental thing between them, she would have hugged him. "Took," he repeated. "By that, you mean what? That they got lost?"

Cinnamon shook her head, inhaling raggedly. "No." Her voice had dropped to a whisper but she didn't have the strength to make it louder. "Worse than that, Beau. Much worse."

He scowled and looked down at his hands, but didn't say anything. "Oh," was all that came out after a few moments.

She stared at him, but he didn't lift his head. "Have you been anywhere else this morning? Out for breakfast?"

"No," he answered. "Why?"

"The way I understand it, the whole town's talking about it," Cinnamon began.

"Aren't they always?" he grumbled.

She might have smiled if what she was about to tell him wasn't so awful. "It's Owen," she said. "He's gone, too."

Beau's head snapped up. "What?"

"He didn't go to work and didn't call anyone to let them know he wasn't coming in. His aunt and uncle flew in this morning and were at the sheriff's office, but he wasn't there with them."

"Where do you think he is?"

Cinnamon lifted her chin. "In the cave, Beau. He went in at the old Crystal Cave entrance to try and find the girls."

Beau swore under his breath. "What the hell's the matter with people? You can't just go off half-cocked like that. The cave's too big, too unforgiving. It's a four-hundred-mile underground trail with no landscape markers."

"Which is exactly why I'm here." Cinnamon's voice was urgent. "Those girls went into the cave and now they're dead. Owen's gone after them—I'm sure of it—and if you don't stop them, those two men are also going in there. Beau, this has got to stop."

He blinked at her. "What are you talking about?"

She flicked her hand at him impatiently. "Oh, knock it off. You know damned well what I'm talking about. The town, the cave, whatever the hell you want to call it. It feeds on people somehow, sucks them in and never lets them go. It's been that way for I don't know how long, but now it's out of hand. It's bad enough—terrible, in fact—that it takes people who've had the rotten luck to pick this place to pass through, but these are children, Beau. Children who are related to people who live here. And other folks, those young men, who just want to help."

Beau stood and rubbed his lower back. His coffee sat, cold and untouched, on the table between them. "If those guys aren't FBI, then who are they?"

Cinnamon opened her mouth to answer, then hesitated. Yes, Beau believed that she was psychic, that she somehow knew things that other people didn't. But how far did that go, really? Would it stretch enough to accommodate the types of creatures Sam and Dean Winchester claimed to fight? Or would her long-ago boyfriend and lover think she'd finally fallen off her proverbial rocker? "They're from a… different agency," she finally offered. "I gave them my word I wouldn't say." A lie, yes, but if any statement could be considered a white lie, this one could. After all, Sam and Dean were the good guys.

Weren't they?

Yes, she firmly believed that. While being good or evil wasn't a rigid choice—there were too many levels in between—her gift always seemed to have her back in knowing the kind of person she was dealing with. "Look," she said now, "are you going to help or not, Beau? Tell me now, because if you aren't, I need to go to the park rangers and ask them."

"You'll get nowhere," Beau said flatly. "I don't know how, but Sheriff Thompson's got all those people following his orders. Why do you think there was never any call for volunteers to join a search party?" When she just stared at him, he answered his own question. "Because there never was a search party. And anything otherwise he's told anyone, including Owen and their parents, is a bald-faced lie."

Cinnamon didn't know what to say to that, and it didn't matter anyway. What mattered was right now, what might be happening to Owen even as they spoke, and the two young men who planned to go into that cave of death.

She pushed to her feet and picked up her purse, then looked into his eyes, something she hadn't done for more years than she could track. "What should I do now, Beau?"

He inhaled. "Go home." Although she felt like she should have known it was coming, Cinnamon was still surprised when he reached out and took both her hands in his. "Where you'll be safe."

"Safe?"

Beau's eyes took on a faraway look, one that she knew she

had experienced many times herself. "I need to know that you aren't going to do anything crazy, like go to the cave yourself."

"Of course not. I haven't been in it since I was in my forties."

"Promise me."

She frowned. "I promise, Beau."

"Not even in the park."

"Okay. I'll just head home." She was silent for a moment, still aware of her cool hands held in his larger, warmer ones. "You'll call me?" she finally asked. "When you find those young men?"

He held her gaze. "Will I?"

"What?"

"Find them, Cinnamon. Will I find them?"

She squeezed her eyes shut for a second, then opened them. "I can't tell," she said. "There are so many variables in what you're going to do that there's nothing for me to see. It'd be like trying to tell you which way the branches of a tree are going to grow."

"Impossible," he said in a low voice.

She nodded. "Beau, be careful. The cave—it's dangerous."

He moved toward the front door, gently pulling her with him. "I know. Anyone who understands nature will tell you that a cave is a living thing, and this one has always been one of the more hungry ones." They stopped and looked out the window, where the rain was still pounding down, then he bent and retrieved her umbrella. "You still need this."

"Thank you."

Beau pulled the door open for her. "Home," he reminded

her. "You promised. I'll call you after everything's done."

Cinnamon turned to step outside, then stopped and looked back at him. On impulse she reached up and touched one of his cheeks with her fingertips, the way she had way back when they'd been going together. She didn't miss that her fingers were thinner and her skin fragile and veined; under the tips, the surface of Beau's lean face was lightly grizzled but surprisingly soft.

Fifty years, she thought. Fifty years wasted.

He caught her hand in his, then brought it to his lips and brushed a kiss across her knuckles before releasing her. "Don't worry," he said. "I'll take care of this."

Cinnamon inhaled, then faced the rain and opened her umbrella. "Don't make me wait too long for your call," she said without looking at him. "I did that once, and I don't want to do it again."

TWENTY-THREE

After Cinnamon left the shop, Beau flipped the toggle switch on the neon sign in the front window, ducking his head back outside to make sure the blinking red Open was replaced by the standard blue Closed. The sign was over twenty years old and the switch was tricky sometimes; at his age if it said Open and no one could get in, they were likely to think he'd had a heart attack and call 911. It would sure tick him off to come back to work this afternoon and find the front door busted in. And he damned sure planned on being back, because for the first time in… well, it felt like forever, he had something to live for.

He had everything he needed at home, so he locked up the shop then made his way around the back of the building, where his old Land Rover was parked. In terms of today's vehicles, it wasn't that old—fifteen years—but he had used it hard in that decade, going up back trails and unmarked, unpaved roads. He'd kept it reasonably clean and saved the front leather seats by encasing them in full seat covers; he'd also lightened the wear on the carpet by putting in heavy rubber mats. His preference for the outdoors still took its toll, though—the paint was nicked in a thousand places from rocks and scratches from bushes. The bumpers were dented from God knew what, and even the interior, try as he had to keep it looking new, had ended up with scratches and scrapes in various black plastic areas. His favorite parts of the Land Rover were still the leather-covered steering wheel, parking brake handle, and gear shift. There was just something about the feel of leather that made you confident you could proceed with strength. Crazy, perhaps, but there it was. Hanging from the rearview mirror in a small net sling was the baseball from his last day as pitcher on the Edwardson County high-school team. It was a great many decades previous, but damn, he'd had a terrific arm.

Beau was home in fifteen minutes, hopping from one big paving stone to another between his car and his house, trying not to track mud in from the rainstorm. Being an old bachelor might mean you didn't have to worry about things like keeping the house as clean as you should otherwise, but it also meant that the only person wiping mud off the floor was him.

This place wasn't big but it was his. He'd bought it from an auction house back in 1996, and its unhappy first owners had retaliated against the bank's foreclosure by completely trashing the inside. Outside it was a nice-looking little house with a purple metal roof and matching shutters, doors and windows trimmed in white, and siding that was a lavender color. But inside had been a nasty surprise, indeed. The rooms had been filled with garbage and filth, doors ripped from cabinets in both the bathroom and kitchen, junk piled into the sinks and the bathtub. Buying the house at auction had meant Beau couldn't see the inside beforehand. Beyond the obvious expenses of painting, putting in new cabinets, replacing the missing appliances, and swapping out the stained linoleum and carpet for new stuff—all remodeling he probably would have done anyway—cleaning up his place had cost Beau only energy and elbow grease. At the end of the project, he'd had a nice little home, clean and just the right size for him; he'd kept the original color so that his neighbors, whom he assumed already talked about him with the rest of the town, would have new gossip fodder, wondering why on earth a man would live in a purple house.

Beau pulled the door shut against the relentless rain and shrugged off his jacket, draping it over a wall hook next to the door before pulling off his boots. He left those on the mat and padded across the living-room floor; outside came a crack of thunder that was strong enough to make the floor vibrate. As he did every time he stepped through the kitchen doorway, even after all these years, he got a flash memory of how the room had been the first time he'd seen it. Seeing that image in his mind—the trash-littered floor and countertops, the cabinet doors hanging askew and moldy dishes in the double sink—made him appreciate the transformation.

Now it was a welcoming room with refinished cabinets that were well taken care of and walls painted white. It had a white linoleum floor that was clean and the counters were uncluttered, with only a few necessary items kept out. The appliances were a little dated and the counter was Formica, but they served him just fine—he didn't have any use for fancy granite and a high-end stove and refrigerator. Most of his cooking was done in the microwave, so that and the coffee pot were the two most important things. Every now and then he got to feeling lonely and felt the house balloon around him, like the emptiness was expanding; when that happened he pulled his notebook of old recipes out of the cabinet over the fridge and did a little baking. His mother's recipe for sweet Amish cornbread was a good one, or his grandmother's chocolate pie.

Today he went to the farthest wall cabinet and opened it, studying the contents before carefully choosing a number of high-energy snack packages and some jerky. He set those aside and pulled out some of the other supplies he might need, including spare batteries and a small first aid kit. Finally he added a couple of folded thirty-nine gallon plastic bags, the heavy kind used for yard waste.

That done, Beau headed to the bedroom, trying to ignore the aching in his lower back, hips and knees, all courtesy of the chilly rain that had been falling for the last twenty-four or so hours. The dampness was already making him feel his age; God only knew how he'd feel a couple of hours from now, when the cave's constant fifty-four degree temperature had time to work its way past his clothes. He made a side trip to the bathroom and swallowed a couple of buffered aspirin, then decided to include the small bottle in his supplies.

He'd done this same selection of cave exploration clothes and supplies a hundred times or more, but he was smart enough to know this time was different. This wasn't a fun excursion to check out an unexplored side channel that the park had blocked off to the general public. Yeah, he'd probably be going down just such a tunnel, but he was planning on going a lot farther and deeper—as deep as was necessary—to stop those two young men and hopefully find Owen Meyer. He might find the girls, but since he trusted Cinnamon implicitly, he didn't really want to… not after hearing what she'd described as their fate.

The gloomy day made his bedroom feel almost like night, so he snapped on both the overhead and bedside lamps. Then he went to the closet and retrieved the gear he was going to need for his upcoming expedition, laying it all out on the bedspread to make sure he didn't forget anything. He started with his helmet and the attached headlamp, one of the oldest pieces of caving gear he owned. He added a sturdy flashlight and old knee and elbow pads from his early caving days, back when the exploring had gone into tougher parts of the cavern. That stuff went on one side; on the other he placed his clothes: polypro long underwear, heavy flannel shirt and pants, coveralls, a pair of thick socks and heavy gloves. His caving boots were in the front closet.

Before he changed his clothes, Beau knelt and dragged his equipment box from under the bed. He frowned at the fine layer of dust on the brown-painted top. He liked to go twice a week but these days he was finding it more and more difficult on his body.

Beau inhaled deeply, then unsnapped the latches and lifted the lid. Looking at the contents was like looking at the inside of an old, familiar drawer. Everything was there and in fine shape, and he began to pull out the last things he would need to complete his preparations: his compass, folding multi-tool, survival hiking knife, a small roll of duct tape, a hand-line and carabiner, a small but super-absorbent towel, a couple of small candles and waterproof matches just in case, a pack of flashlight-activated glow-in-the-dark chalk, a full pack of hand warmers, half a pack of twelve-hour light sticks. He didn't know how long he would be in the cave, but chaos theory always seemed to apply—if something could go wrong, it would, and he had no intention of finding himself inside that cave system with no light source. Most folks would go in with about sixteen ounces of water; he knew better, and would grab his two one-liter Platypus bottles off the hallway closet shelf on his way out. Completing the gear was the old nylon pack everything would go in. It was worn and stained, and he considered it lucky enough that he wouldn't go into the cave system without it.

That done, Beau closed the box and shoved it back under the bed, then gathered everything together from the kitchen and the bedroom and stowed it in the pack. He went to the bathroom and stripped off his clothes, avoiding his image in the mirror. He didn't need to see himself to be reminded that no matter what he told himself or how he insisted he felt, he was old. His "lucky" seventy-seventh was coming up in another two weeks.

Back in the bedroom, Beau pulled on the clothes he'd set out, then tugged on the overalls and zipped them up. Like the pack, they were well-used, dotted with stains that washing couldn't get out. Like scars, they showed his experience.

Already sweating, he swept up the rest of his supplies and did a quick double-check of the bedroom and kitchen to make sure he hadn't forgotten anything. With everything ready, he shoved his feet into his caving boots and laced them up. Then he stood and took a deep breath, mentally going over his gear list a final time and steadfastly ignoring the voice of doubt that wanted to creep in, the one that was whispering about his age and his strength—or lack of it—and how he was being an egotistical old fool to think he could go into the cave and save anyone.

With a final glance back at his comfortable living room, Beau Pyle grabbed his small load of gear and the two water bottles off the closet shelf. Then he shoved the other stuff on the shelf aside so he could reach an object he'd traded a high-end caving helmet for about ten years ago. He took it down and examined it carefully, hoping he could find a way to pack it so that he wouldn't end up killing himself. Everything in hand, he locked up the house and headed to his Land Rover.

He might be a fool, but he was going into that cave a well-armed one.

TWENTY-FOUR

"What do you think?" Sam asked. "Do I look like Floyd Collins?" He was standing across from Dean in the hotel room, geared up for their coming excursion into Crystal Cave. Since he had no desire to get stuck in some frigid tunnel made of rock, Sam had followed the cave store owner's directions to the letter. He had on the heaviest pair of jeans from his suitcase, a green and white plaid flannel shirt over a warm T-shirt, and wool socks. The jacket he'd chosen was a brown nylon thing that was a little thin, but it ought to keep him decently warm and if he had to squeeze through any kind of narrow space, at least it wouldn't add any inches to his girth. Now he grinned at Dean from under his brand-new white caver's helmet.

"Who's Floyd Collins?" Dean asked absently. He didn't even look up from where he was fiddling with the zipper on his waist pack, which was—big surprise—bulging with various packages of junk food snacks.

Sam made an impatient noise. "Really? Only the guy who

first owned the land that Crystal Cave is on. I read about him in the tourist pamphlet. He was exploring a new way in and got stuck in there, died before the rescuers could get him out."

Dean finally looked up at him. "Stuck. In the same cave we're going into."

Sam had no choice but to nod.

"And you want to look like this Collins guy why?"

"Well, I…" Sam's voice trailed off. "No reason."

"Right." Dean looked down and finally managed to force the corner of a candy bar into the pack so he could tug the zipper past it. "You got all your stuff?"

Sam looked around. "Yeah."

"Then it's on to the cave." Dean swept his car keys off the dresser and headed toward the door.

Sam followed. "Let's go by the sheriff's office first," he said.

Dean turned to look at him in amazement, stopping just under the edge of the roof. "Why? Because they've been so cooperative?"

"I want to see if he really does have maps that show Crystal Cave," Sam said. "If he does, I want copies."

Dean shot him an I-think-you're-crazy look, then dashed for the car. Sam waited until his brother was inside and had unlocked the passenger door before making his own run for it.

When he was settled inside with the door closed, Dean said, "I thought we had what we needed from the caving shop."

"Maybe," Sam said. Just a couple of seconds outside and their hair as well as the shoulders of both their jackets were soaked. "But I still want to check. And if the sheriff does have maps, I want to see if they show where the search parties—if they really did exist—went."

"I'm beginning to feel like I live at this place," Dean muttered as he pulled into their parking spot.

"I'm sure they'll do everything to make you comfortable," Sam said as he studied the building across the street. Through the gray sheets of water, he could see there were lights on in it. A good sign.

"Funny."

"The sheriff sounded pretty fond of you last night," Sam shot back. Before Dean could retort, he had opened the door and made a run for it through the downpour.

"Smartass," Dean said anyway, then dashed after him.

Sam was waiting for him under the covered entrance. "Why is it you never park on this side of the building?" he demanded. He gestured past where a wheelchair ramp angled down, then turned into a parking area. "It's a lot closer, you know?"

Dean shook his head. "No guaranteed way out."

"You just pull around—"

"Nope. Based on our friendly relationship with the law around here, I want to know I can always get the car out without having another vehicle block me in. I especially don't want to get pinned in behind a building that doesn't have a clear line of sight to the street. Which would be this one."

No argument there—Dean would always be extra careful when it came to Baby—so Sam just nodded and pulled open the door. Dean trailed after him, then they both stopped when Deputy Sloane looked up from where he was flipping through something in a file cabinet. He didn't bother with niceties. "What can I do for you, Agents?"

"We spoke with the sheriff last night," Dean said. "He told us to come by and pick up maps of Crystal Cave."

Deputy Sloane's gaze was emotionless, but at the same time mocking. "Right. Sheriff Thompson mentioned he *talked* to y'all." He put just enough emphasis on the word *talked* to let them know he was aware it hadn't been a friendly conversation. "You'll have to wait while I find them. I wasn't going to bother unless I was sure you wanted them."

"We do," Dean said. He kept his tone even but his half-lidded gaze made his dislike of the deputy clear.

Sloane ignored Dean's look. "Have a seat," he instructed. "I'll be back in a few minutes."

"Thank you," Sam said politely, while Dean fought the urge to tell the man to take his time; mouthing off would make it far too likely Deputy Sloane would leave them sitting there for as long as possible. It was a given that the reception area was monitored on security screens in the back, and as long as no one else came in, Sloane could leave them out there as long as he pleased.

Neither brother said anything for a while, then Sam sat forward on his chair. "Only one sheriff's vehicle in the parking area," he said.

"That you can see."

"True," Sam agreed. "But let's assume I'm right and Sheriff Thompson isn't here. Besides," he inclined his head at the door behind the desk, "Deputy Dog there is acting like he's not."

"Okay," Dean said. "What's your point?"

"I'm wondering if he's out escorting Mr. and Mrs. Dietz," Sam said thoughtfully. "Or if he's actively looking for Owen and his cousins."

Dean snorted. "More likely he's kicking up his feet at home, watching reruns of cop shows."

Sam squinted at him. "Seriously? You really think he's the type?"

"No clue." Dean shrugged. "I just like making fun of him."

Sam rubbed at his temples. "If you could leave the twelve-year-old you behind for a minute and go back to adulthood to help me out, that would be awesome."

"But the younger me is so much more fun."

"But the older you is just a little smarter," Sam shot back. "So back to what I was saying."

"Is Thompson out looking for the girls?"

"Or Owen?"

"Right." Dean's gaze wandered over the framed certificates on the walls, but without much interest. "Personally, I don't think he gives a damn about any of these missing people," he finally said. "As for the girls' parents, he probably just wants to do whatever he can to get them out of his hair."

Sam nodded thoughtfully. "Right. Owen aside—not that he doesn't matter—if it were your kids, would you take no for an answer?"

Dean looked at him steadily. "No. Not now, not ever."

"Right. Neither would I. So where are they?"

"Where are who?" Deputy Sloane's voice cut in before Dean could answer. Neither of them had heard the door unlock and he was standing in the open doorway. His face was expressionless but his eyes were hard and suspicious. In one hand was a stack of folded maps that looked like they'd seen better days. "If you fellows have a question, all you have to do is ask."

The Winchester brothers stood at the same time. "Lena and Ray Dietz," Sam said. Thanks to being startled, his voice had a sharper edge than he intended. "We were wondering if Sheriff Thompson was with them. We need to talk to them."

Dean glanced at him in surprise, then recovered quickly. "Yeah," he said. "Since the FBI has its own investigation going on this case, we have to interview the girls' parents."

Deputy Sloane pulled the door shut behind him, then locked it and stuck the key back in his pocket. "The sheriff is attending to other matters right now," he said. "That the Dietz girls are missing is unfortunate—"

"Unfortunate?" Dean echoed in amazement.

"—but it's not the only case the department has. Edwardson County is a large jurisdiction and there are a significant number of illegal activities occurring simultaneously at any given time. The sheriff's department serves over three hundred square miles and twelve thousand people, so while you two have seen only this little office and a few personnel, there's a lot happening behind the scenes." Sloane's cheeks had flushed, but the brothers couldn't tell if it was anger or enthusiasm. To them, he sounded like he was reciting a memorized speech. "There's a lot going on here and only ten people to handle it all."

"I understand that," Sam said calmly. "It's just that we were thinking that three people missing from your town might be given priority over other things."

"Of course it's given priority," Sloane snapped. "The sheriff's out investigating right now. And for your information, he does not believe that Owen Meyer is missing, a word y'all really like to throw around."

"If he's not missing," Dean asked pointedly, "then where is he?"

"Mr. Meyer is an adult," the deputy said in a voice that sounded like it was coming through gritted teeth, "and no one is holding him in this town. I will say, however, that he is a person of high interest in our investigation of the disappearance of his cousins."

"Owen is a suspect?" Dean said in disbelief. "You've got to be kidding."

Sloane glared at Dean. "This is not a laughing matter, Agent."

"I didn't say it was," Dean snapped back. "But it's ridiculous to think he had anything to do with it. He wasn't even there when they disappeared."

"And you know that for a fact," Sloane said flatly. "Then I assume you were there with him in the morning before he went to work, or perhaps you were guests in his house the day before."

Dean's eyes narrowed. "What the hell are you talking about?"

"The fact that he was the last person to see them alive." The deputy's face was so rigid it looked like it was sculpted out of stone. "As far as we can determine, they were last seen in town the same evening they arrived, which was Tuesday evening. That's almost a week ago."

"Tuesday evening?" Sam echoed.

"Yes." Sloane dropped the papers in his hand on the desktop and folded his arms. The stance somehow made him look defensive and intimidating at the same time. "Several people at the Cee Bee grocery store saw them when Owen brought them with him to do some shopping. After that... nothing."

Sam rose to his feet but tried to look non-threatening. "And you don't suppose they could have just stayed home those first few evenings, playing video games, watching movies, doing whatever you do to entertain a couple of kids."

"I don't suppose anything," Deputy Sloane said icily. "I don't get paid to do that. The Edwardson County Sheriff's Department works on evidence, like any law enforcement agency. And so far, all the evidence points to Owen Meyer."

Dean's face darkened and he opened his mouth to argue, but Sam's smooth words came out first. "Well, in the meantime, we'd appreciate those maps." When Dean jerked his head toward his brother, Sam elbowed him sharply, catching Dean hard enough in the side of his biceps to make him grunt.

"That's good," Sloane said. He jabbed a thick finger at the papers on the desk. "I don't have all day to spend arguing with you about this."

"Of course you don't," Dean put in, getting himself another elbow jab.

Sam stepped in front of Dean, effectively putting himself between his brother and the deputy. "So what have we got?"

Sloane shot Dean a final contemptuous look, then turned his attention to the maps. "Okay, I found four, in varying degrees of age. The most current is about fifteen years old.

There are two that are older by a couple of years, and the oldest one dates back to sometime in the sixties, when the park bought the cave and closed it." The maps weren't that large and Sloane unfolded them and spread them all on the desk, the edges overlapping each other. "There's an older one in the back but it's useless."

"Why?" Sam asked.

"All it shows is where Floyd Collins got himself stuck and died, in the shaft they dug trying to reach him."

"He died there?" Dean's eyes widened.

"I told you that this morning," Sam said impatiently.

"Is he still in there?"

"No," Sloane said. "He—"

"I'll tell him about that later," Sam interrupted. "Right now let's concentrate on the maps."

"Good idea," Sloane said. He shot Dean an irritated look. "They might save your asses from getting lost."

Dean's mouth tightened but he didn't say anything, just looked back down at the creased documents.

"Right here," the deputy said, pointing, "is the entrance off Route 70. The sheriff told me you were there before, so you shouldn't have any problem finding it." He glanced up at them, but his face was unreadable. "This map is the newest one, and it picks up right at the entrance, which is about a hundred yards or so beyond the gate."

"How about a key to the padlock on that gate?" Dean asked. "I hate parking my car on the side of the road."

Sloane shook his head. "No can do. The place has been closed so long the sheriff doesn't have a clue where it is. In fact, I don't think we ever had it to begin with. You'll have to climb over."

Dean didn't believe that for a second, but short of calling Sloane a liar—and the sheriff by proxy—there wasn't anything he could do. "All right," he said. He tried to keep his voice amenable.

The big deputy tapped on the paper again. "This here is the main passageway. You follow it in and it opens into a bigger chamber."

"How far in?" Sam asked.

"No idea. As far as I know, none of these maps are to scale."

"So it could be twenty feet or two hundred feet."

Sloane shrugged. "Like I said, no idea. All I can tell you is what Sheriff Thompson told me to pass along. I've never been inside, never been interested enough in the caves to go." He gave them a sideways look. "I can't even figure out why the sheriff wants to let you down there, but that's his pay grade, not mine." When neither brother responded, he continued. "Like I was saying, you get to this bigger chamber. From there you got a choice of a bunch of side tunnels." He squinted down at the document. "It shows four of them. The sheriff himself made notations about each one. According to him, these two on the right are collapsed—you can see where he X-ed out the entrances—so there's no sense in even trying to go there. The other two are open and go on to other chambers and intersecting tunnels. The map shows some of where they lead, but the mapping has never been finished. With it closed to the public for so long, there's never been a need." He shook his head. "I think the two of you are insane for going in there without a guide," he said bluntly. "Sheriff Thompson already ran search parties all through the main Mammoth Cave entrance, which is well-manned all the time, mind you, and searched this one, too. You aren't going to find anything but a hard way to go, and if you're lucky, your own damned way back."

"We'll take our chances," Sam said and reached for the maps.

The deputy gave them to him, then put his hands on his hips. He'd obviously perfected a compassionless cop stare, and he leveled it at them now. "I'm obligated to tell you that Crystal Cave is owned by Mammoth Cave National Park and the sheriff's department is in no way condoning your exploration, nor is it giving you permission. If the park rangers happen to catch you on the property, they might be surprised and won't be very friendly about it."

Dean raised an eyebrow. "Maybe you could call them in advance."

The deputy lifted his chin. "Absolutely. The guy who supervises this area doesn't spend a lot of time in the office, but I'll be sure to leave him a message if he's not available."

Before Dean could start yet another argument with Deputy Sloane, Sam said, "We'll get these back to you as quickly as possible."

"Don't bother," Sloane said. "They're copies. Even the old one—we have at least ten more copies of it. That Floyd Collins fellow dying in there was a big sensation back then, and it started all over again when he was dug up and put on display in a glass-topped coffin."

Dean gaped at him, thinking suddenly of revenants and how they tended to hang around where they'd died, getting angrier all the time. This Collins guy would sure have a lot to be pissed off about. That would explain a lot, maybe even solve the whole case. If Collins's ghost was still in there—

"Don't worry about it," Sam said, and pulled on Dean's arm hard enough to make his brother do a little two-step to keep his balance. "I told you, I'll fill you in on the whole Collins thing later." He looked back at Sloane, who was folding up the maps to give to him. "One last thing, Deputy," he said as he took the documents.

The lawman looked up. "What's that?"

"The Dietzes," Sam said. "We need to speak with them."

"Don't see what point there is in that," Sloane responded. "Just brings it all back and causes them a lot of pain. My opinion—"

"Is really going to annoy my supervisor at Quantico. I don't think you want to do that. This is a federal investigation, Deputy." When Sloane still didn't say anything, Sam pulled out his identification wallet. "I tell you what," he said, "I'll give you his number and we'll wait while you call him and explain precisely why the Edwardson County Sheriff's Department won't connect us with the parents of the two missing girls." He pulled a thin stack of business cards out of the wallet and began flipping through them.

Sloane stared at Sam for a moment, then held up his hand. "Never mind, that's not my place. They're staying up at the Tranquility Bed and Breakfast right off Route 70. It's even on your way to Crystal Cave. The place is private and quiet, and the woman who runs it is taking real good care of them, not even charging for the room." He gave them another flat, blank stare. "That's the kind of people we got in this town, you know."

Sam tucked the ID wallet back into his jacket, then gave the other man a curt nod as they turned to go. "We'll be sure to put in a good word for you."

Dean pushed through the door first, and only Sam heard his brother as he ground out the words, "In hell."

TWENTY-FIVE

Like everything in Brownsdale, the Tranquility Bed and Breakfast didn't take long to find, especially now that the rain had finally dwindled away. It was a white two-story about a quarter-mile off Route 70; the house stood atop a small hill with its side facing the road. The driveway was long and curved, and when Dean drove up it, they saw that the front was a wraparound covered porch from which guests could have a great view of the lush surrounding countryside. An American flag swayed on a pole to the right of the stairs leading to the porch. A double garage with its doors closed was across the driveway, which widened considerably in front of the house. They'd seen only one car, the same silver Ford rental that had been at the sheriff's office, in the paved parking spaces about thirty feet back off the drive. Instead of parking down there, Dean pulled the Impala in front of the garage, blocking both doors.

Almost as soon as they got out, a woman hurried onto

the porch from inside the house, a dish towel in her hand. "Excuse me," she called. "I'm sorry but you can't park there." She motioned back toward the road. "You'll need to move your car down into the parking area."

"We'll just be a few minutes," Dean said. She came down a few steps and looked like she wanted to protest, but Dean gave her his mildest smile, then pulled out his FBI identification. "Sorry to bother you, but we're looking for Lena and Ray Dietz." He whisked his ID back into his pocket.

"Oh, dear." The woman was average height but carrying about twenty extra pounds, with blonde hair that was cut in a short and curly style, now gone frizzy at the edges from the humidity. Her eyes were gray in a pretty, oval-shaped face that would probably be exceptional when she smiled; she was not smiling right now. In fact, she looked like she was about to burst into tears. "Did you find their children?"

"No, ma'am," Sam said quickly. He'd pulled out his ID at the same time Dean had, but she hadn't even glanced at it. "We'd just like to talk to them. Are they available?"

She nodded and tried unsuccessfully to give them a smile. Her fingers were working furiously at the red and white towel in her hands, twisting and untwisting it. "This way, please." She turned and pulled open the front screen door, motioning at them to follow. "I'm Christa Kretschmer. My husband and I own Tranquility."

"Nice," was all Dean could think of to say. Maybe she hadn't realized how it sounded—or maybe she did—but owning tranquility sure sounded like an enormous accomplishment. Sam glanced at him like he was a lost cause and shook his head. "What?"

"What my partner means is it's a beautiful place," Sam said. "How are the Dietzes doing?"

"Not that well," Christa confided. "We have four kids, two still in school, and I can't begin to imagine what they're going through."

She led them through the main sitting room, which wasn't that large but was furnished with highly polished antiques. To their left was a tall fireplace surrounded by a wood mantel, in front of which was a luxurious leather couch and an easy chair with a matching foot stool. To the right was the formal dining room and an antique table around which were six chairs; against the back wall were a matching china cabinet and buffet, both huge and expensive-looking. They went straight across to another door, through a bright, busy-looking kitchen, and stopped in front of another door; through the door's upper window, they could see an enclosed back porch.

"They've been out here all morning," Christa told them in a hushed voice before she put her hand on the doorknob. "I've offered several times to bring them tea or coffee, but they just keep saying no." She almost looked hurt. "The weather's been just terrible—I'm so afraid they'll catch a chill." When Sam nodded sympathetically, she let out a loud sigh, then pulled open the door. "Mr. and Mrs. Dietz?" Christa said in a timid voice. "These gentlemen are from the FBI. They're here to speak with you."

Lena Dietz was a middle-aged woman with brown chin-length hair that was probably impeccably styled in any other situation. Right now it looked straight and lifeless and she had pulled most of it back with a fabric headband; a few strands of bangs hung over her forehead, accentuating rather than hiding the long creases of worry across her skin. Her eyes, brown like her hair, were swollen from crying, her nose red. When Christa's words sank in, one hand, clenched around a crumpled tissue, went to her throat and her body pressed back against the uncomfortable-looking wrought-iron chair she was sitting on.

Ray Dietz stood so abruptly that his chair almost toppled behind him. He ignored it, his terrified blue eyes focused on their faces. He had the body of someone who likes the outdoors, tall and lean but hard; his hair was thinning and the parts of his scalp that showed through were slightly sunburned from their Arizona trip. "Did you find them?" he rasped. "Did you find our girls? Are they alive?"

Sam stepped forward. "No, sir, I'm afraid they haven't been located." He wanted to add the word yet, but given what he knew about the girls' fate he couldn't bring himself to do it. "I'm Agent May and this is Agent Taylor. We'd like to talk with you about the girls, if that's all right."

Sam offered his hand and Ray Dietz looked at it as if he didn't understand what was going on, then visibly tried to pull himself together. He shook Sam's hand. "Of course."

"I'll get you men a couple of chairs," Christa said. Sam glanced at her and nodded; for a moment he'd forgotten she was still there. She walked briskly to the other end of the porch and immediately came back with two folding chairs.

Sam set them up, then glanced at her. When she stayed in place, he said easily, "If you'll excuse us, Ms. Kretschmer?"

"Oh!" she said and blinked rapidly. "I'm so sorry. Of course." She was back through the door so fast it was still on its opening apex when she went through it.

The brothers pulled the chairs a bit closer to the table that sat between the couple. Before either could say anything, Lena Dietz spoke. "The sheriff told us yesterday that they were still searching for Marley and Fallon." Her voice was a monotone, no inflection at all. She sounded hollow, like a computer-generated speaker on a telephone. Her head swiveled as she looked from her husband to them, then back again. "Do you think that's true?"

Dean frowned. "Why would you ask that, ma'am?"

"Because I don't think he is!" Finally, some feeling, but it wasn't the good kind. Her voice had gone up in volume and the last word bordered on a scream, her body rising from the chair in an eerie sort of coordinated movement.

Ray Dietz was up and around the table with the swiftness of an athlete, a person whose reflexes were heightened by something demanding, like racquetball. "Shhh," he murmured into her hair. "Just sit down, Lena. It won't do any good to lose control. Let's just talk it out." He was bent at the waist and holding her, rocking ever so slightly. "Shhh."

His wife sobbed into his shoulder for a few seconds, then wriggled her hand between her chest and his so she could swipe hard at her nose with the nearly obliterated tissue. "I'm okay. I swear." He let her go reluctantly, eyeing her, then his shoulders relaxed and he went back to his chair.

Christa's voice broke the small, uncomfortable silence. "Here you go, Mrs. Dietz." She stepped up from behind

Dean, holding a tray. From it she picked up a small box of tissues and set it on the table, then added four glasses and a pitcher of ice water. "Just in case."

She nodded at the brothers and went back into the house, and Dean's gaze followed her to make sure the door closed behind her. It did, then he realized there were windows on either side of it, both raised about two inches to let fresh air into the kitchen. She was probably listening to every word they said, but that couldn't be helped.

Dean leaned forward. "Mrs. Dietz, what you said about Sheriff Thompson not looking for your daughters, why would you say that?"

"Because he thinks our nephew abducted them," Ray Dietz said before his wife could answer. The man's back was straight and stiff, his chin high. "He's so focused on that idea that even though he claims he's searching, I don't believe he's putting resources into anything. He's utterly convinced about Owen."

"I see," Dean said. "And do you know why he wants to go that route?"

"Because it's easy," Lena exploded. She balled one fist and slammed the side of it against the tempered glass tabletop, making her husband jump. "Because he just wants this whole ugly thing to be over, and that's the fastest, most convenient way to get it done!"

"And what about Owen?" Sam asked. "Where—"

"Oh, and isn't it so convenient that he's gone," Lena said. Her tone was a mix of bitterness and sarcasm. "For the sheriff, I mean."

Sam sent a sideways glance at his brother. "Do you have any idea where he is?"

"No," Ray answered. He didn't look away, just met Sam's gaze with no hesitation. "Just that he wouldn't." At Sam's questioning look, Ray continued. "He wouldn't leave. He wouldn't do anything to the girls."

"And the girls themselves?" Dean asked. "Would they…" He left the question unfinished.

"No," Lena said. Her voice was the firmest it had sounded since they'd arrived and she waved a dismissive hand in the air. "I know all about how people can't tell, parents don't see the signs, yadda yadda yadda." Her gaze was fierce. "I'm not an expert on other parents, but I am a damned good mother myself. I pay attention, damn it. My mother was an intel specialist in the Army, and she knew how to read people. She taught me a few things, and I know my girls. They're happy. They don't do drugs, and they're not depressed or angry."

Dean nodded. "No secrets." He made it a statement rather than a question.

"None that would make a difference," the woman insisted. "All kids have secrets, but Marley and Fallon are both open about their lives. I've taught them they can ask questions about anything and get honest, non-judgmental answers." She gripped the edge of the table and Dean saw Ray's hand reach out to steady it, just in case. "That sheriff—" Lena almost spit the word out—"is not looking for my daughters. Oh, he has all his notes and his files and his answers at the ready, but it's all bull. I'm sure to everyone else he seems sincere, but to me his body language might as well be a confessional video." She inhaled sharply. "And that deputy of his is no better. He's just covering up for his boss."

The Winchester brothers sat and thought about this for a few minutes. "Tell me about Owen," Sam said finally. "We met him at the library on Saturday and he helped us do some research—"

"Research?" Ray asked.

Sam nodded. "About the town and its surroundings, the cave area." It wasn't a lie and it left a lot out, but he hoped he was good enough to fool Lena Dietz, although he doubted it when he saw her eyes narrow almost imperceptibly. "He was pretty broken up about the girls."

"I would expect so," Ray said. "He doesn't have any brothers and sisters and he's doted on them ever since they were born. Everyone in the family was upset when he moved here to take the library job. We all hoped it was just temporary, that once he had it on his resume for a few years he could move back to Dallas and find a good position."

Dean frowned. "Dallas?"

"I know what you're going to say," Lena said. "And it's true he hated big cities—the noise, the pollution, the crowds. He'd always found it overwhelming, maybe because he was an only child and his parents—my sister and her husband—were quiet, bookish people. But he also missed his family, even if it is small, and that was the thing Ray and I hoped would eventually bring him back."

"Since you brought it up," Sam put in, "where are Owen's parents?"

Lena blinked, then exchanged a look with her husband. When she didn't immediately answer, Ray spoke for her. "I'm sorry, I assumed you knew. Owen's mother is brain-dead, the result of a car accident a couple of months before he graduated college. His father spends almost all of his time at the nursing facility with her." At the brothers' surprised expressions, he added, "It was one of the reasons Owen was so insistent about relocating. He came home after commencement and got a job right off, but his girlfriend had gone off to take a job... somewhere, I don't remember. Owen was just rattling around in the family home, mostly by himself. His father told Owen that he should get away from all the sadness, make a new start somewhere else. He came across the job opening here and applied for it on a whim. He was surprised when he was offered the position, but his dad insisted that he go."

"And the rest is history," Sam murmured.

"It was all good until this," Lena said. Her voice had changed; now it sounded brittle, the words breaking off at the edges. "When we found out, at the end of the rafting trip, and we called him... God." She stared down at her hands. "It was so awful. We were mad with fear and grief. The things I said—"

"Were completely understandable," Ray cut in. "We were both hard on him."

"But—"

"I'm sure Owen understood," Sam said gently.

"Too much," Lena said. When her husband looked confused, she added, "He's out trying to find them. I'm absolutely sure of it."

The brothers looked at each other, then back at the Dietzes. "That's what we think," Dean said.

Ray fixed his gaze on Dean. "So what are you going to do about it?"

TWENTY-SIX

"Well?"

Settled on the passenger side of the Impala, Sam looked at his watch. "I think it's past time we head to that cave," he said. He glanced back at the front of the big bed and breakfast and saw Lena and Ray Dietz standing next to the innkeeper. The three were watching them intently. Sam wondered what they would talk about once they were gone, or if Christa Kretschmer would run to a telephone and report the conversation on which she'd eavesdropped—Sam had glimpsed her several times, hanging just beyond the window frame in her kitchen—straight to Sheriff Thompson. Somehow he didn't think so; she might be a bit of a busybody, but she'd seemed genuinely concerned about the Dietzes and the fate of the couple's children.

Dean glanced at the sky. The rain had stopped but it was still overcast. Unless it cleared, and he didn't think there was much chance of that, dusk would come early. "I thought you said we shouldn't be in there at night."

Sam shrugged. "And like you said, inside the cave it doesn't matter. Although Cinnamon said the girls are beyond helping, I'm still holding out a chance for Owen. Plus this time we have Sheriff Thompson's blessing to poke around Crystal Cave."

"If that's what you call a blessing," Dean said wryly. "Don't forget Deputy Do-Wrong's warning about it being park property."

"I'm shaking in my boots."

"Floyd Collins," Dean said suddenly. The Impala was parked about a quarter-mile back on Route 70, pulled as far off the road as he could manage. He and Sam had hiked the remaining distance and were now standing in front of the chained gate that, according to Sheriff Thompson and the maps, would ultimately lead them to the entrance to Crystal Cave. They were fully geared up, packs around their waists, helmets in hand.

"What about him?" Sam asked.

"You said you were going to tell me his story."

"Right," Sam said. He assessed the gate in front of him for a second, then clambered over it and stood, waiting for Dean to follow. When his brother did so, they headed down the path together, helmets swinging as they walked. It was wide at first, as though it had once been a driveway, but it twisted around and began to narrow as the trees and bushes on either side encroached on it.

"About how he died in here."

Sam grinned. "Well, not actually here here. Floyd Collins owned the property Crystal Cave is on back in the early nineteen hundreds, give or take. But the cave was too far away from everything else and didn't get a lot of visitors. Think of it in terms of transportation in the first quarter of the twentieth century—cars, sure, but they probably weren't comfortable and the roads, especially country ones around here, were crude and dusty, hard to travel." He looked over to see if Dean was still paying attention. He was.

"What did you mean when you said he died in Crystal Cave but he didn't die here? That doesn't make any sense."

"Collins was looking for a new entrance to his cave, one that would be closer to where folks could easily get to it."

"So I-65 wasn't built yet," Dean said.

"Oh, no," Sam told him. "The only way to get to Crystal Cave was via Route 255, then finish the trip down a dirt road."

"What about Route 70?"

"Didn't exist back then either," Sam said. "Anyway, Collins found a cave entrance, barely more than a big hole in the ground. He went inside to explore it, but after a couple of hours working himself through a tunnel, he realized he was running out of light. So he turned around and started back out, but he got stuck. Bad luck follows bad—"

"Ain't that the truth," Dean mumbled.

"—and he knocked over his lamp and ended up in total darkness. In trying to get free, he kicked a rock loose from the ceiling and it fell on his leg. It didn't weigh much, but the way it landed, it pinned him tight. He was facing toward the exit with his legs behind him, and he couldn't reach back and get at it. Nothing he did could get it loose."

"Crap," Dean said.

Sam nodded. "He was only a hundred and fifty feet from the entrance when his buddies found him the next day, but the tunnel he was in was so tight they just couldn't get him out. They crawled in and brought him food and water, light so he wouldn't be in the dark, and kept trying to dig in where they could free him. Meanwhile, the newspapers were all over it, lots of coverage, photographs, what have you. The media started calling the hole where he'd gone in Sand Cave." Sam paused for a moment, partly for effect and partly because it was a story that really did have a sucky ending. "Five days into the rescue, the tunnel they were using collapsed in two places and was deemed unsafe."

Dean winced, thinking about how the guy thought he was going to be saved, then was plunged into absolute darkness all over again. "Oh, man. What did they do then?"

"They dug a shaft downward, trying to get in behind him. But it took too long, almost two weeks. He was dead by the time they got there, and their calculations were off anyway— they came in above him and still couldn't get his leg free. They left his body there and filled in the shaft."

Dean squinted at him. "And this Sand Cave is where?"

Sam trudged along the rocky path, watching where he stepped. "About five miles northwest. I looked it up on the computer."

Dean was silent for a couple of minutes as they walked along, then he lifted his head. "Wait a minute. Deputy what's-his-name said something about a glass-topped coffin. How can that be if they left his body in that tunnel?"

Sam grinned in spite of himself. "Good catch. A couple of months later Collins's brother and some friends went back and dug a different shaft into the mountain, managed to get down and recover Floyd's remains. They buried him on the family farm and figured that was the end of it."

Dean looked relieved. "So we're not going to run into some hundred-year-old revenant who's all pissed off because his body was left in there."

Sam frowned. "That's something we probably ought to consider."

"Where's this glass coffin thingy come into play?" Dean asked.

"A couple of years later the family sold the farm. The new owner, apparently being a stand-up and sympathetic guy, dug up Floyd Collins and put him on display in Crystal Cave. Fast forward a few years later, someone actually stole the body."

Dean gaped at his brother. "Seriously?"

Sam nodded. "Hey, I think we're almost there."

"Come on! Finish the damned story."

"All right, all right. They got the body back, but not the bad leg, the one that got stuck. That was never recovered. They put what was left of Collins in a casket that was chained closed, then stuck that in a part of the cave that was secluded, along with his tombstone."

"So it's still there?"

"No," Sam said. "About thirty years later Mammoth Cave National Park bought the property and closed the cave. In accordance with the wishes of the Collins family, they had a crew of men dig out the coffin and stone, and they reburied him in a cemetery. I forget the name."

Dean had a sudden image of the ghost of Floyd Collins

lurching through the secret passages of the cave, searching futilely for his missing leg. "And what you said about revenants—"

Sam shrugged and sent his brother a sideways look. "There could be. How many people have died in this place? At least three we know of. With all the disappearances, let's face it— there's probably been a whole lot more. God only knows what we might find."

Dean couldn't think of anything to say in response. They followed the path up a steep incline as it took a short, sharp turn to the right, then curved back on itself—

And there it was, right below them.

The entrance to Crystal Cave.

Sam and Dean stared down at it. The ground sloped sharply, stopping in a hollow that was at most five feet wide at the base. Sharp-edged rocks littered the angled ground to the left until it met a solid rock overhang, while the ground to the right was more like an abrupt cessation of a boulder that jutted overhead. Gray concrete blocks had been used above the entrance and also to make a supporting wall to the left of the door, while the door itself, rusted steel, was hinged into no more than a thick piece of rotting plywood on the left.

Dean took in the setup, then said, "Is it just me or does it look like a big chunk of the frickin' mountain is being held up by a couple dozen construction blocks?"

Sam's lips pressed together as he studied the door and the geology around it. The main rocks to the left and right were immense and solid, stained gold, pink, and green from water run-off, as were the no doubt old concrete structures.

If nothing else, a long iron bar, at least six inches thick, had been used as a header over the door. But like Dean said, it sure didn't seem like much to hold back a mountain. "It is a little unnerving," he finally agreed.

Even so, the brothers worked their way down the slope, leaning back to maintain their balance. The ground at the bottom was soft mud and they could see the reddish line two-thirds of the way up the door, a clear indication that flood waters regularly accumulated down here; a rusty stain spread upward from the fill line, as if the waters hit with enough force to make a splash pattern. The bottom of the door was so badly rusted that it was dark brown, uneven and flaking away in layers, warped outward and still wet from the recent rain.

They stood in front of the door without saying anything for a few moments, then Dean touched Sam's arm. "Notice anything?"

"Yeah," Sam said. "There's no lock."

Not only was the iron door unsecured, there didn't appear to even be a way to keep it closed. It was also ajar, just a couple of inches, but enough to make an ominous black slash around the top and right side. Sam looked carefully at the wet soil in front of the door, but the rainfall had obliterated any footprints or indication that it had been opened recently.

"Not the sort of place I'd expect the public to have free access to," Dean said. "Especially with all the yammering about how unsafe it is and kids disappearing."

Sam nodded, but instead of commenting, he just asked, "You ready?"

Dean's expression said he'd rather do anything else, but he

nodded. "Why not? I'd say you only live once, but we both know that's not necessarily true."

Sam ignored the quip and pulled on his helmet, fastening the chin strap then snapping on the headlamp. That done, he yanked on his gloves and gave the open edge of the door a test pull. When it didn't move, he braced himself the best he could, slid the fingers of both hands over the right edge, and pulled.

The door gave, but grudgingly. Dean moved to Sam's right and got his gloved hands in there, too; together they fought with the door and the mud that had built up along the bottom edge until they had a two-foot gap.

"I'm already sweating," Dean said. He stuck a forefinger under the front edge of the helmet and swiped at his forehead.

"It'll be cooler inside." Sam reached over and knocked on the side of Dean's helmet. "Turn on your headlamp."

Dean did, then gestured at the door. "Age before beauty," he said.

Sam sent him a bemused glance. "You do remember you're the older brother, right?"

"Well, you always act older, so you might as well get the honors."

Sam rolled his eyes. "Come on."

TWENTY-SEVEN

The Winchester brothers had been in caves before—plenty, in fact—but never like this one. Their experiences tended to be more toward monsters' dens, like the Wendigo, or some of Crowley's rooms in Hell, the ones that had yet to be decorated with anything besides bones and other... unidentifiable objects.

Crystal Cave, though...

Wow.

The entry passageway hadn't seemed promising. Sam and Dean had left the door open because it felt stupid to close it behind them and prematurely cut off their only source of natural light. The path they trudged along was nothing but a long tube of darkness—dark floor, dark walls, dark ceiling—broken only by the swinging, puny-looking cones of light cast by the lamps on their helmets. The soil beneath their feet was loose, the walls and ceiling packed but not permanent, not rock. It had seemed to go on forever, but that was probably just a trick of the darkness: ten feet could feel like a hundred, and a hundred… well. Ad infinitum. In the dark and without professional tools, they really had no way of knowing how far they'd traveled at any given moment. Every time one of them said something, it was like the sound waves dissipated instantly, squeezed away to nothing by the sheer mass of the earth around them. After a few minutes, they stopped talking at all, moving along with only their own shuffling footsteps to break a silence that was otherwise absolute.

"I think the tunnel widens up ahead," Sam said suddenly. His voice was so unexpected that it made Dean flinch. He was glad his brother was in front so he didn't see it.

"Maybe it's the… what did Deputy Dawg call it? Cavern?"

"Chamber," Sam corrected. He kept walking, then slowed after about ten steps and tilted his helmet down so he could sweep the area in front of him. "Yeah, I think this is it. I'm pulling out my flashlight."

There was finally space enough so that Dean could move up and stand next to Sam. He heard Sam switch on his flashlight and saw the glow out of the corner of his eye, then brought up his and hit the button. His mouth dropped open.

No wonder cavers called these areas chambers—no other word was… big enough to describe something like this. Even in the limited light put out by their combined helmets and flashlights, in every direction they turned, the scene before them was breathtakingly beautiful.

"Dude," Sam said. "This is pretty incredible."

"Yeah," Dean agreed. "I've never been fond of tight, dark spaces, but going through that tunnel back there to get to this… it was worth it."

Dean tilted his head back so his light would skim across the ceiling. The beam barely made the distance, providing only the faintest of circles. The rock overhead was at least fifty feet away, maybe more—it was impossible to tell with so little illumination. Hanging from the ceiling were stalactites, thousands of them, in every length imaginable. Some were thin, almost like fragile, straight pieces of yarn, while others had melded together to form chunky points that were a yard or more across where they met the rock above but only dropped a couple of feet.

"It looks mostly black and white," Sam said softly. "Some color, but I wonder what it would look like if we had decent light."

"Right?" Dean pointed his light up to the left, where the rock formations fell in folds like sheets that should be arranged around some immense, god-sized statue. When he and his brother surveyed the chamber floor in front of them, they saw stalagmites of every size imaginable, rock fingers reaching from the floor as if they were trying to touch the stone heaven above.

Where the walls of the chamber met the floor was rocky and pitted, but fairly level. Sam began to pick his way along the right side, weaving among the boulders and formations protruding from the floor. Dean followed, thunking his helmet a few times on the angled walls.

"Watch where you're going," Sam said from ahead. "You might knock some sense into yourself. Or crack your helmet."

"Wise guy," Dean said in a low voice, but it was good advice. "Do we know where we're going?"

"There's a flat spot," Sam said. His headlamp picked out a

low, wide stone a few feet away. "Let's take a look at the maps."

They stopped and pulled out the most recent map Deputy Sloane had given them, crouching so they could spread it mostly flat. Sam glanced from it to the chamber several times, trying to get his bearings. "Okay," he said. "It's just like we were told, four tunnels. According to what Thompson wrote," he pointed, then poked his forefinger at corresponding words penciled on the paper, "those two aren't passable." He and Dean looked at depressions in the chamber wall on the right curve of the wall; they could see rubble and large rocks strewn inside both entrances. "But there should be two more tunnels up ahead."

The brothers scanned the chamber, combining their helmet lamps and flashlights to get the best view they could. Now that they had stopped moving, they could hear water dripping in dozens of places around the chamber; their moving beams of light sparkled off drops of water making slow treks down the stalactites to eventually fall to the lump-covered floor. Beyond the stalagmites the floor dipped downward in the roughly oval-shaped chamber; the sloping sides were pocked with shadows cast every time one of their beams cut across a rock formation. There was definitely water down at the bottom, black and forbidding.

"Some kind of underground lake?" Dean asked. He had visions of an ancient sea creature, the North American version of the Loch Ness Monster, a long, slimy neck slowly unfurling from the black water. Or a dinosaur, the offspring of some long-extinct creatures stuck under the earth for millions of years. Blind. Hungry.

"I don't think so," Sam said. "I think it's run-off from the rain the last couple of days."

Dean looked at him in disbelief. "You have absolutely no basis for that."

Sam looked back, one corner of his mouth lifting. "Maybe not, but I bet it sounds a hell of a lot better than whatever you're thinking." He tapped the map to turn Dean's attention away from what could very well be a bottomless lake and back to what they were doing. "They look evenly spaced apart but the scale is screwed up," he said. "Just like we were told. The chamber's big but I think I can almost make out the other side, which means that the first of the remaining two tunnels shouldn't be too far ahead."

"Right." Dean squinted into the darkness, but it didn't help; he still couldn't see a thing past the relatively weak lights of their headlamps and flashlights. "And how are we going to choose which tunnel is the right one?"

"No idea," Sam answered. "Let's get there first, then we'll figure it out." He picked up the map, folded it, and slid it into the back pocket of his jeans. "Let's go."

"I wish that thing showed something useful," Dean said. "Like where each tunnel goes and whether or not we're going to die at the end of one. So, you know, we could avoid exploring that particular passage."

Sam had to laugh, but it sounded strained. "Too bad Cinnamon's crystal ball wouldn't work for anyone but her. We could've brought it with us."

"It would've worked for us," Dean said. "As a weapon."

"Right."

Moving slowly along the wall, this time Dean kept one gloved hand in front of him, skimming along the surface of the rock over his head to catch any protrusions before he could whack his helmet against it. Ahead, Sam was doing the same, plus taking care to shine a light in front of him before he took each step.

Trundling along, thinking about where to put his feet without spraining an ankle or worse, Dean drew up short when Sam suddenly said, "Stop."

"What is it?" Dean tried to peer past Sam but his headlamp kept reflecting off the back of his brother's jacket, washing out everything around it. "You see something?" Dean hated the uncertainty he heard in his own voice but he couldn't help it; the unrelenting dark was like being in a void. It felt as though nothing outside of their circle of light existed.

"This has to be the first of the two passageways," Sam said. His words sounded a little weird, like the sound waves were veering off somewhere instead of bouncing around the chamber.

Dean pointed his flashlight at the ground and carefully moved up next to Sam before bringing it back up. He played the beam along the wall, seeing the blacker, ragged hole his brother was talking about, then more beyond that. One, two—

"There's an extra one," he said. "You can just make it out down there. The entrance is on the other side of where that rock slants out from the wall, very easy to miss. Three in total, not two. Or five if you count the two that are blocked." He glanced at Sam, but Dean could barely see the outline of his brother's face when he frowned. "Unless most of them dead end pretty fast, I don't think we can cover all of them in one trip."

"The map shows where each one goes," Sam said. "But that extra one…" Dean heard him draw in a breath, then after a moment's thought he said, "Let's check them out first. Then we'll decide."

Dean started to step forward but Sam beat him to it, his stride long enough to put him in the lead. "So you're like, what?" Dean asked crankily. "Chief Spelunker? And please don't say Floyd Collins."

Sam chuckled. "I always wanted to be an explorer," he said over his shoulder. He was almost to the first open tunnel.

"Great." Dean moved after him, trying to place his feet where his brother's had been. "Couldn't we have just gone hiking? At least then we wouldn't have the weight of the world on our shoulders."

"Sometimes it feels like that anyway." Sam's footsteps stopped. "Okay, door number one. The question is, what's behind it?"

Dean stopped next to Sam and they shone their lights into it. There was nothing there except for a long, ragged tube into the earth. It might've been made by a giant worm except it had too many jagged edges.

Dean squeezed his eyes shut for a second, then opened them. Great. Now he was thinking about giant worm monsters.

"Okay," Sam said. "Let's check out the next one."

And they did, with the same result: Nothing to see here, folks, please move on.

Finally, they stood on either side of the third tunnel, the one not on the map Sheriff Thompson had set aside for them.

"Do you think he knew about this passageway?" Sam

asked. "He had to know we'd find it if we went into the cave."

Dean shrugged, even though the movement couldn't be seen in the darkness. "I think he knows everything," he said flatly. "Where the girls are, what happened to them."

"And Owen?"

Dean scowled. "Maybe, although Owen trying to find his cousins might not have been on Thompson's flight plan."

Sam shone his flashlight into the tunnel and rotated it, training the light carefully along the ground, sides, and ceiling. Dean added his, and the combination of all four lights, as it had in the previous four passageways, showed nothing but rocks and dirt.

"Well?"

Sam exhaled. "I have no clue," he admitted. "They all look the same. Like they're man-made, or they've at least been worked on so that people could pass through. Maybe they were, to the extent the map shows, and the expeditions were abandoned."

"Maybe it wasn't safe," Dean pointed out. "Two of them have already collapsed, which could mean the ceilings in all of them aren't that stable."

"Right," Sam agreed. "And if you think about it, there's no guarantee this third tunnel is the one left off the sheriff's map. It could've been any one of the others."

Dean didn't know what to say to that. "Let's just go back and look at each one again," he suggested. "Maybe—"

"Wait," Sam said. "What's that?"

Dean turned and his gaze followed where the beam of Sam's flashlight was pointing, where the wall met the ground about fifteen feet beyond the third tunnel. He added his beam and saw immediately what Sam had discovered…

A fourth passageway, barely more than a hole in the ground two feet high. It might have been a yard across but the entrance was shaped like an elongated oval that had been sliced in half lengthways.

Dean moved over to it, squatting next to Sam to shine light into it. At first glance, it didn't seem to be anything but a deep depression that went nowhere; then they saw that it was, indeed, a full passageway, and it turned sharply to the left then angled down. The ground was pitted with rocks, like the others, but they were smaller and pushed to the side, leaving little piles that looked as though someone—or something?—had dug their way into it.

They looked at each other, then back at the very dark hole in front of them. "And then there were four," Dean said.

Sam glanced back into the opening, then dropped to all fours and crawled a couple of feet into it. After a moment, he backed out and held up something for Dean to see.

An earring.

"I've seen this before," Sam said. "One of the twins—I don't know which—was wearing these in the photo on Owen's desk at the library."

Dean glanced at it, then shook his head. "So much for four-leafed clovers bringing luck."

"No kidding." Sam tucked it into the pocket of his jeans. "I think our choice was just made for us."

He didn't want to tell Dean that the tunnel entrance looked a lot like the opening to Sand Cave, where Floyd Collins had died. After all, it was just coincidence.

TWENTY-EIGHT

"I've died and gone back to hell," Dean said to himself. He was low-crawling through the tunnel behind his brother; he felt the press of rocks and pebbles through the fabric of his jacket and jeans. His forearms and the front of his thighs were aching and bruised, and he had to keep himself from grunting with pain every time he dragged himself forward.

"What?" Sam yelled ahead of him. "Did you say something?"

"No," Dean hollered back. "Just remarking on our lovely surroundings. By the way, is this going anywhere?" The chilliness of the cave's temperature had worked its way past his clothing, especially the single layer of denim, now dampened from crawling, around his lower body.

Sam stopped in front of him and Dean almost ran into the bottom of his brother's shoes. "It has to, right?" came Sam's muffled answer. "We saw the earring."

They had put away their flashlights to conserve them, and

now Dean scanned what he could see of the passage they were in. There's wasn't much around them but shades of gray dirt and rock. "Unless it was a plant." He heard Sam mumble a couple of swear words, then his brother started moving forward again. He thought again of Floyd Collins, cold, thirsty, and in blackness somewhere under uncountable tons of earth. At least the channel hadn't narrowed to where they'd come to a standstill, or worse, felt like they were stuck. The instant he thought it, Dean wished he hadn't; the universe had a way of kicking people in the ass when they were stupid enough to count their blessings.

"I see something," Sam called back. "It's pretty wide up ahead. I think—" His voice cut off with a grunt and a spray of dirt as he suddenly disappeared from Dean's sight. Somewhere in the darkness ahead Dean thought he heard his brother cry out.

"Sam!" Dean bellowed, and scrambled forward as fast as the tight space would allow.

"I'm all right!" Sam called. His voice sounded far away. "Don't—"

Too late.

Propelled forward by his legs, Dean's upper body followed a short decline, then surged out of the tunnel and onto… nothing. He felt like he hung in mid-air for a long moment, like one of those crazy talented basketball players taking a shot—Michael Jordan, maybe—then his own weight dragged him over an edge and he fell.

He turned in mid-air, flailed for half a second, then landed butt-first on top of Sam. The air went out of his lungs and from underneath him he heard Sam's second yell of surprise. Momentum yanked his head backward and his helmet slammed against the ground. He saw lights flash—from somewhere he remembered being told that was the brain banging against the inside of the skull—and then he just lay there, stunned and staring upward.

The ground beneath him was lumpy but not particularly hard, then it began to move. Something pushed hard at his shoulder. "I know you're alive," Sam said with a groan, shoving harder. "I can hear you breathing. Get off me."

Dean inhaled, then pushed himself to his bruised elbows. "I'm all right, thanks for asking." He stared upward, straining to see something in the wan light that was still, thankfully, coming from his helmet lamp. "How far did we fall?"

Freed of Dean's weight, Sam sat up. "Far enough so we can't reach the ledge, not so far that anything is broken."

"You hurt?"

"Now that you ask, I felt okay until you landed on me. You really need to stop eating all those cheeseburgers."

In spite of their situation, Dean grinned. "I can't wait to get another one of those Big Cave Country Breakfast Sandwiches."

Sam rolled to one side, turning his face so his helmet lamp swept overhead. "I can't wait to watch you, since it means getting out of here." When he saw there were no overhanging rocks, he got to his feet. Upright, he let out a painful breath. "Yeah, gonna feel this in the morning."

Dean pulled himself up next to his brother and scanned their surroundings. Another chamber, this one taller than it was wide. His headlamp could just pick out the walls around them, all shades of varying gray and black, but when he looked up the beam dwindled away to nothing. At least the floor was flat, no dipping down into some bottomless, wet abyss. If he moved his head really slowly and followed the light from his helmet, he could spot the small, darker circle of the tunnel he and Sam had fallen from. Puddled on the ground beneath it was a tangle of rope, useless to them since they had no way to attach it to anything overhead. "Where the hell are we?"

Sam frowned. "I'll check the map, but I don't have a lot of hope." He pulled the document from his back pocket and unfolded it, then took out his flashlight. The stronger light reflected off the paper and made him squint before he could fully focus on it. "Uh oh."

Dean had been carefully feeling his way along the wall, but he jerked his face back in Sam's direction. "What's wrong?"

Sam crouched and tried to stretch the map out as flat as he could on the ground. "Take a look at this," he said unhappily as Dean came back and crouched next to him. "Man, we should've taken a closer look at this thing back at the sheriff's office."

"Don't tell me," Dean said. "We've had it upside down the whole time?"

"No, but look there. Look really close." Sam brought the beam down to the map, so close it was almost touching.

Dean did, but still couldn't see anything. "What am I supposed to see?"

"Correction tape, that stuff that offices use to cover up mistakes. Here," he pointed. "Here, and here, too. The map has been intentionally changed. The tunnel we're in is this one, which has…" Sam unclipped his helmet and took it off, then held the map up in front of it. The light came through like a weak x-ray and they could just see faint lines and a couple of words under the thin strip of white tape.

Dean peered at it. "What does that say?"

Sam held it closer, then farther, trying to make it out. After a moment, he said, "I'm pretty sure it says drop off. And look here." He lowered the map and showed it to Dean again. "This area has been drawn in, over the tape."

Dean rubbed his chin. "And that's where we are now."

"Yep."

"Great." Dean watched as his brother put his helmet back on. "Game stats: Sheriff Thompson: one. Winchesters: zero."

"I prefer to call that the final score."

Sam and Dean whirled, then craned their necks to see above them. "Who's there?" Dean's loud, deep voice bounced off the rock walls.

Someone laughed softly, then they saw a watery circle of light wink on overhead. Its glow was just enough to illuminate the entry tunnel. Someone was looking down at them but it was impossible to identify the person; all they could see was the silhouette of a helmeted head.

Well, not that impossible.

"Sheriff Thompson," Sam said. He didn't sound surprised. "I assume you've come to rescue us?"

"Never assume, Agent." As the figure moved a little closer to the edge, the man's voice became recognizable. "You know what they say about that."

"Really? You're going to rely on clichés at a time like this?"

Thompson laughed again. "There's nothing more reliable than a good old-fashioned adage. You know, like—"

"Spare us the gloating," Dean cut in.

"Such a sore loser," the sheriff said. They couldn't see his expression but his voice was edged with smugness.

Sam glared up at him. "What are you doing here? You knew we'd end up falling with no way to get out, so why follow us?"

Thompson didn't even hesitate. "To finish you off, of course. After doing a little checking, I've come to the conclusion that you two are not FBI. I don't know what your business is here and I don't care, but I won't have you somehow figuring out a way to get free and showing back up in town, crying about how the sheriff's department gave you a map that made you fall down and go boo boo." There was a pause, then he added, "I have enough trouble trying to figure out how to get rid of the parents of those girls."

Dean's face was hard. "You going to kill them, too?"

Thompson chuckled. "Don't be stupid. They're just an unexpected turn of events, that's all. A problem to be dealt with. Eventually they'll accept their kids got lost in the cave and go away. There's not much they can do about it, is there?"

Sam looked at Dean out of the corner of his eye. "If he starts shooting at us, we're like ducks in a pond," he murmured.

Before Dean could reply, the sheriff's voice boomed out again, followed by the all too familiar sound of a slide being pulled back on a pistol. "I can hear you down there." He actually sounded happy. "Your voices carry. It's like a big old auditorium."

Dean turned his head toward Sam. Before his brother could react, his hand whipped forward and shut off Sam's headlamp. He grabbed for the switch on his own helmet and dived sideways at the same time, hitting the loose-packed ground hard on his left side and feeling the air whoosh out of his lungs just as his light blinked off.

"Nice try," Thompson called out from above.

Without warning the light from the overhead tunnel tripled, temporarily blinding them in the nearly absolute darkness. Dean thought he could actually feel the surface of his eyeballs sizzle. He spun and faced the wall, scuttling along it like a sightless crab; somewhere to his right he could hear Sam doing the same.

There was a shot from above, and the chamber carried the noise and magnified it, making it sound and feel like a small explosion. Dean yelled in surprise, then something whizzed by his head and ricocheted off the rock. Like he'd told Sam, ducks in a pond—a very small pond.

To make sure it didn't get lost in the tunnel—yanked out of his waistband by a jutting rock—Dean had shoved his gun into a side pocket in his jacket. His fingers tore at the fabric as he tried to get to it, but the gloves that had protected his hands were now a hindrance. He scraped the side of his face against the wall, then instinctively ducked as another shot boomed through the chamber. Another set of ricochets followed, and Dean was sure he felt the sting of spraying rocks on the side of his neck. Damn, that was close.

Almost completely opposite him, Sam already had his gun out. He brought it up but Thompson jerked the spotlight in his direction; the sudden light was like the flash of heat in night-vision goggles—intense and painful. He pulled his head down like a frightened turtle, and just in time; Thompson's next shot bounced off the rock next to him, grazing the sleeve of his jacket. Sam leapt into a sort of modified baseball slide, going chin first into the rock-filled dirt but toward the center of the chamber rather than along the wall. He felt the skin along his jaw open in half a dozen places, but at least they were just scratches and he didn't have a bullet wound. Yet.

On the other side of the chamber, Dean raised his weapon and fired at the tunnel opening above, using the light as a guide. He missed the light, but heard Thompson swear as chunks of rock blew out around him. Dean aimed again but made himself pause and count to give Thompson time to crawl back to the opening—one, two, three. Then he squeezed the trigger three more times. Although the light didn't go out, it bounced wildly and flickered and Dean heard Thompson cry out.

With Thompson's light pointing in another direction, Dean could just see Sam, and he sprinted across the chamber to get to him before Thompson got himself back together. He didn't know for sure if one of his bullets had struck the sheriff—and if it had, the upward angle was too sharp for it to have been a good hit—so they needed to do anything they could to get out of this predicament.

Dean caught his brother by one arm. "You all right?" His voice was barely audible.

"Yeah." Sam switched positions, grabbing Dean's jacket and pulling him along the wall. Dean followed his brother's lead, all the while looking up to monitor what was going on with Thompson. When Sam stopped, Dean bumped into him and almost fell. "Watch out," Sam whispered. "Look, it's not very big but there's an opening here. Maybe a way out."

"Like the one we used to get down here? Great." Overhead, the light wavered—Thompson was picking it up, getting ready to aim it back in their direction.

Dean started to bring up his gun again, but Sam pulled on his shoulder. "Forget him for now. We have to get out of here." Before Dean could protest, his brother yanked him to the left and pushed him down, propelling him into a darker spot in a rock wall of shadows. Caught off guard, Dean crawled blindly forward; he reached to turn on his headlamp then reconsidered, not wanting to give away what they were doing.

In the chamber, Sam crouched in front of the newly discovered opening and aimed his gun at the overhead tunnel. He couldn't see Thompson, but he knew they didn't have much time. The sheriff would fire a couple of shots to make them go on the defensive, then find them with the spotlight and aim to kill.

He heard a muffled sound as Dean pushed himself forward and hoped his brother was far enough in that there was room behind him. When Thompson's initial shots came, Sam gritted his teeth and had to will himself not to duck, or even flinch— he needed to keep his aim, the position and the angle, true. It went against every self-preservation instinct he had, especially when the four set-up shots thundered against his eardrums and were followed by the whining zings of the bullets ricocheting around him—it felt like he was putting a target on himself in the middle of a war zone. Still Sam held, unmoving, arms raised and gaze fixed, knowing that once the lawman got the light in place, he would most likely be blinded by it.

The glow overhead went from diffused to bright and vicious in the space of a millisecond, showing everything on the floor of the chamber, including Sam. He didn't blink, he didn't move, he didn't breathe.

Sam's ears were still ringing from the noise of Thompson's shots, so he couldn't count on hearing anything to tip him off to Thompson's position. He certainly couldn't see him; in this blackness, looking at the spotlight was pretty much like staring straight into the sun. All he had to go on was instinct. If it was him, how long would it take to—

Sam fired.

Four shots, no hesitation between squeezes of the trigger. The high-powered lamp shattered and the light went out with a hiss that sounded very much like an electrical short. At the same time, Thompson screamed. Not like his previous yelp of surprise, but a genuine sound of pain.

Sam grinned savagely and spun, dropping to the ground and launching himself into the opening. He moved as fast as he could, scrunching along like a fat mole forcing its way through a tunnel it could barely fit in. There was no light in front of him, but he could hear Dean somewhere ahead.

The noise in front of him stopped. "Sam?"

"I'm here," he said in a stage whisper. "Keep going."

The rustle of clothes against soil resumed. "I can't see a thing. Did you get him?"

Sam pushed on. "Yes, but I don't think I killed him. The angle was too much and I couldn't see."

Dean didn't say anything for a second. When his voice came

again, he sounded surprised. "The tunnel is angling down."

"Okay," Sam said. He was still whispering but growing more confident. "Give it another ten or twenty feet, then I think you can turn your headlamp on."

Dean didn't respond, but after a long pause, Sam saw a glow not too far in front of him. It was just a brightness around the outline of Dean's body as he crawled and it moved crazily, but Sam didn't know the last time he'd felt so grateful to see light.

Forty-some minutes later they were still crawling, and Sam wasn't nearly as pleased. Everything on his body hurt except his hair, and for all he knew, that was next. His brother had to be just as uncomfortable but he wasn't complaining, so Sam wouldn't either... even if he did feel like his spine was full of glass shards and his joints were pieces of cracked ice.

Finally he couldn't take it anymore. "Hold up," he called as he came to a stop. Soreness pulsed through his muscles. "Water break."

Dean's movement halted. "Man, I thought you were going to keep going forever," he yelled back.

"You see anything up ahead?" Sam snapped on his headlamp—there didn't seem to be any sense in using a light just to see the bottom of Dean's shoes, so he'd been saving his battery, just in case.

"Nothing." Dean still wasn't complaining, but Sam thought he could hear a note of discouragement in his brother's voice.

"We have to keep going," Sam said before Dean could add

anything else. "We'll find something."

"Maybe we should turn back."

Sam's jaw tightened. He'd wondered the same thing, but the reality of it was harsh. "First of all, we can't actually turn around. We'd have to somehow push ourselves backwards the entire way." He waited for a moment, but all he heard was a grunt… enough to let him know Dean was as uncomfortable as he was. "Secondly, we don't know if Thompson is coming after us."

"You said you shot him."

"True, but I also said I didn't think it was fatal. My guess? It'll slow him down but that's all. He can't take the chance we find another way to make it out of here and tattle on him. He'll have to finish it, and he'll have to make sure we're dead. If either of us meets him head on in the tunnel everyone will end up dead and our bodies will rot under this mountain."

Dean was quiet for a long time and Sam let him be, let him think things through. "The tunnel started going back up a little while ago," he finally said. "It's not a big incline but if it keeps going, we eventually have to poke out of the ground somewhere, right? Like gophers."

"Right," Sam agreed. Despite himself, the image of their heads suddenly popping out of the ground made him grin. He snapped off his headlamp. "Let's move."

TWENTY-NINE

Michael Thompson slumped against the wall, gasping, in the darkness of the tunnel that the two fake FBI agents had fallen from. He was about three feet back from the first edge, the one that opened to an incline and ended in the second edge, the one they had both stupidly gone over. Like lemmings, one following after the other. As his mom used to ask in response to his childish declaration of "All my friends are doing it!"

If all your friends jumped off a bridge, would you?

Clearly these two hadn't gotten the memo in their "FBI" training courses.

All that was great, but the truth was Thompson wasn't feeling particularly smart at the moment, with a chunk of his left arm gone, his blood running into the dirt, and pain throbbing all the way down to his fingertips. He'd heard them scrabbling around in the dark but the sound had quickly faded; they must have found the opening, the only one besides the one Thompson was sitting in, that led out of the chamber down there.

The USUAL SACRIFICES 265

Good.

He'd tried to take care of them the easy way, the most painless way—for them, anyway—but he was not without a follow-up plan. It was true that he hadn't factored in the furrow high on his upper arm, but he was resourceful and he would deal with it. Losing a little blood was nothing compared to the shambles his life and his town would be in if those two made it out of Crystal Cave.

He forced his breathing to slow, trying to get a handle on the trip-hammering dance his heart was doing in his chest, then snapped on the lamp on his helmet. He'd kept it off— and a wise choice that had been—so as not to make his head a target, but now that the spotlight was gone, it and his flashlight were his only sources of illumination. He needed to see to be able to fix himself up.

There wasn't a lot of room in the tunnel and Thompson could only sit hunched over. He dug the first aid kit out of his pack and opened it. Not much in the way of help since people didn't count on getting shot inside a cave tunnel, but there were a bunch of Band-Aids, antibiotic tubes, and whatnot. When he examined the wound, it wasn't as bad as he'd thought it would be, about two inches long and a half-inch wide. Yeah, it would eventually need stitches but he wasn't going to bleed to death. In fact, he felt a little ashamed at his reaction, how he was dealing—not very well—with the pain. In the movies people always gritted their teeth and kept going. Fun to watch, but this was real life.

After shrugging out of his jacket, he tried to set his jaw against the pain as he pulled on the torn fabric of his shirt to widen the opening so he could get to the wound. He ended up yelling anyway, shocked all over again at how much it hurt. He had clamped his gloved right hand over it from the beginning, and now he was dismayed that it looked like it was starting to bleed again. He found a gauze pad in the kit and ripped it open with his teeth, then pressed it over the wound. Impatient, he dumped the contents of the kit onto his lap and dug through all the pieces. There were alcohol pads—like he was foolish enough to use those—and a thin roll of medical tape, but he thought his arm was probably too wet for it to stick. Then he spotted an elastic wrap with a couple of clips, the perfect thing to hold the gauze in place. He wrapped it nice and tight, trying to ignore the way it throbbed once he was finished. Getting back into his jacket was another exercise in mental fitness, but he kept telling himself that the pain was good. It would help keep him focused.

That done, he inserted a full clip into his pistol, got the first aid kit repacked and stowed, and he was ready to face the next big task: getting down to the chamber floor and following them.

Thompson used his flashlight to make a careful examination of the tunnel exit and finally found a crack he could hammer an anchor into. He'd considered pulling out Owen Meyer's cam and ridiculous, amateur knotted rope—but it was so dark he knew those fake FBI guys would probably miss it. He'd take it down once he'd used it to climb out and they were dead It wasn't a long way down, only about fifteen feet, so he hadn't had to drag along a lot of equipment— just enough to get him down and back up, in case he had to. Good thing he'd thought about it ahead of time. He fastened his rope into a double length and dropped it over the side, then fought to get into his climbing harness. Finally he switched out the bloody gloves he was wearing for his heavier rappelling pair.

Before he started, Thompson used his flashlight to do a long, thorough examination of the chamber floor and where it met the walls, going over every inch with the strong cone of light and making sure none of the shadows were concealing the two agents. But there was nothing, just that one small opening to the only tunnel that could have gotten them out of there. The last thing he did was break a light stick and toss it down; the center was almost too bright to look at, but it lit the walls of the chamber with a soft green glow. He only had two of the sticks, but each had a duration of twelve hours; he'd be back long before it went out and there'd be no unseen surprises waiting for him.

One last rope check and everything was ready. No more excuses, no more procrastinating. This is going to hurt like hell, Thompson thought. His weight and swing would be controlled by his good right arm, but he would still have to manage his rate of descent and the belay with his left. There was no way around it, so he backed down the incline until he was at the edge—

Then pushed himself into space.

"Hurt like hell" didn't even begin to describe the jolt he got when the bottom of his feet hit the tunnel wall. Instead of pushing off properly, the agony that ran through his arm and shoulder almost made Thompson lose his grip; he swung out only a couple of feet, then slammed back into the rock and hung there, whimpering, barely able to suck the cool air into his lungs. It felt like he was being sliced from shoulder to wrist, like his grandfather had filleted the big catfish he used to catch in the Green River—end to end, without so much as a pause.

He hung there, right arm keeping him from simply dropping like a rock, for quite some time. He wasn't sure, but he might have even faded out for a few minutes. There was just him, the sound of his rough breathing and water dripping, and that soft, almost soothing yellow glow.

After a while, Thompson shook his head to clear it and took stock of where he was. He'd dropped about five or six feet, so not too far to go. Even if he passed out on the next drop, he probably wouldn't get hurt too badly when he fell. He inhaled deeply a couple of times, then went for it.

Maybe because he was expecting it, the second swing and impact wasn't as bad, a smaller but bearable jolt of lightning through his upper body. Thompson sucked in a lungful of air at the moment of impact, and that helped enough to push off and into the third and final swing. He landed hard on the chamber floor but in one piece, more or less. The less was the wound in his arm, which was bleeding again and now felt like someone had stuck a red-hot cattle brand against it.

But although he was down, he was not entirely broken. So it was time to get on with it.

Thompson had plenty of time to think as he went through the pain-riddled process of getting out of the harness, then changing the soaked bandage on his wounded arm and rewrapping it. He moved the steadily burning glow stick over by the ground-level opening and peered inside, but as expected, it was empty for as far as he could see with his limited resources. He had no choice but to go after them, see this through as far as they took it, and he cursed the phony FBI agents for poking their faux-governmental noses into his quiet, county business.

Shoving himself into the tunnel, dragging himself along mostly on his right arm... it was misery beyond anything he'd ever thought he would have to endure. Thompson kept himself going by thinking forward, to the pleasure he was going to get when he filled those two agents full of bullets. He wasn't a sadistic man, had never taken pleasure in another's pain. And he still wouldn't, but each push forward cemented his hatred of them, reinforced his all-encompassing desire to end them. Fast, probably not painless but as close to it as he could manage, but still...

He was absolutely going to make sure they never came out of Crystal Cave alive.

THIRTY

At first Sam and Dean didn't realize they'd come out of the tunnel that seemed never-ending. Navigating it had taken them through dry spots and wet, leaving the fronts of their jackets and jeans soaked. Dean was cold and he knew Sam was too. He had become so intent on moving forward, always forward, that he'd just been crawling along in a straight line; Sam had followed, his world narrowed down to keeping the bottom of his brother's shoes in sight. Abruptly Dean halted. "Wait," he called.

Behind him, Sam pulled himself one last foot, then paused. "What? Do you see something?"

Instead of answering, Dean looked left, right, overhead, then cautiously felt around himself...

Nothing.

Still being careful—you never knew when the space around you might play tricks—he brought up his legs until he was on all fours, then swung them around and eased himself to a sitting position. He was sure that he'd smack his helmet on rock at any second, but it didn't happen. "We're out of the tunnel."

"Seriously?"

Dean pulled out his flashlight and switched it on. "Come on up and take a look." He heard Sam's breath expel as his brother did the same movements he had, grunting in release when he could finally get his legs in a position other than straight. A second later Sam's headlamp blinked on.

"I'll be damned," he said. In another moment, he'd also pulled out his flashlight. "How long have we been out of it?"

Dean aimed his lights in the direction from which they'd come, revealing darkness between two huge slabs of rock taller than they were. "Not long," Dean said. "Ten feet maybe." He swung his lights back around until they joined Sam's. "Wow. Check out this place. Look at the colors."

The brothers turned in a slow circle, although they were apparently in an enormous chamber and couldn't see the far walls. Huge pillars of rock studded the floor, rising tens of feet overhead into utter blackness. In other places gigantic slabs of stone looked like they had been stacked haphazardly on top of each other. Even though the glow from their lights was white, nothing in here seemed black and white, as it had in other parts of the cave. Instead, portions of the huge blocks were streaked in thick bands of gray, red, and yellow. In other areas the stone looked like it was splattered with gold by a giant's paintbrush. Everywhere they turned was a brilliant new panorama limited only by what they could see in the insignificant beams from their lights.

"Well," Sam finally said, "if we have to be lost, at least we have something cool to look at."

Dean scowled at him. "We're lost?"

"Of course we are," Sam said impatiently. "I have no idea where we are or where we're going, if we're even headed in the right direction to get out. Do you?"

Dean opened his mouth, then shut it and turned away, scanning their surroundings. For a few minutes they stood there, not speaking, then Sam's head snapped to the right. "Did you hear that?"

Wisely, Dean didn't answer; instead, he froze, tilting his head and trying to pick up what his brother had. But no... the only sounds beyond their breathing was water dripping and trickling down the rocks, a noise that had ranged from faint to loud in various places during their time in this cavern, becoming familiar. He started to say no, then a different sort of noise cut through the space around them—the scratch of movement against dirt, the sound of small rocks and pebbles sliding down rock and hitting something below.

They looked at each other and Dean mouthed, The sheriff? Sam held up his hands in a gesture that made it clear he didn't know, so Dean tugged on his brother's sleeve to make him follow as he tried to move, as quietly as possible, away from the passageway they'd come through. Even working their way slowly their footfalls were picked up and echoed around the chamber.

Another noise, louder, made Dean jerk involuntarily and look to the left. Before he could comment, there was another, not quite from the same dark location. Then another, this time from somewhere behind them. Maybe from the tunnel, maybe not. Probably not.

"I don't think Thompson cloned himself," Sam said in a low voice. "I'm thinking we better try and find some place to hide."

The sounds had escalated, coming so close together that they were overlapping. Dean didn't bother answering, just grabbed Sam's arm and hauled him forward. They broke into a run, heading for a place he'd just caught sight of up and to the right, a shelf of red and gold rock that jutted out and formed an overhang. There was a small space beneath it, deep and dark, that looked protected. He had no time to consider whether it was empty or already occupied by something; they were going to find out either way.

The brothers got there and dived underneath it just as something barged into the space they'd been standing in only moments before. Dean swung his flashlight at it and got a glimpse of something human-shaped but more squat, hunched on thickened legs and with arms that hung down almost like an ape. The head was turned in the other direction but Sam yanked his flashlight away and shut it off before Dean could get a good look at it. Taking the hint, Dean slapped off his headlamp at the same time Sam extinguished everything he had, too.

"Keep quiet," Sam muttered. "We have to stay here until we figure out what we're dealing with."

"As long as they don't find us," Dean whispered back. If nothing else, the rock shelf overhead, which stuck out a good five or six feet, dampened their voices and stopped their words from carrying. They could hear the thing moving around out there, exploring the ground; worse, there were more sounds that made them realize it wasn't alone.

"Who—?" Dean began, then the darkness was wiped out. Flames—a torch—held high by another one of the figures jumping from an unseen overhead spot; it landed heavily but stayed upright, then it was joined by at least a half-dozen more, and a couple of them also carried torches.

"Crap," Sam said in a barely audible voice. With Dean next to him, he pushed himself back as far as he could, hoping the torchlight wouldn't penetrate their hiding spot. On a positive note, a bigger part of the chamber was revealed. More interesting, however, were the shapes that milled not far from them, more or less visible now in the wavering glow of the flames.

They were human... but not really. Their faces had some similarities to modern man, but other parts looked more prehistoric. Their bodies were short, under five feet tall even when they held the torches high and tried to stretch to see above them, with folds of loose, pallid skin that was streaked with dirt and heavy veins. Beneath their flesh muscles flexed in powerful-looking arms and legs; the arms reached nearly to the ground, with hands that would have looked normal except that the thumb and fingers were as thick as small tree branches and ended in substantial wickedly pointed nails that were at least two inches long. They wore no clothing, but if there were males and females, the brothers couldn't tell—they had too much skin hanging everywhere to see a difference. Their legs were jointed at the knee, but the lower part, the shin, was so short it was almost nonexistent—they had huge thighs, knees that were almost as wide, then a small bend that culminated in massive, heavy feet that were bigger than their bulbous heads. They made bizarre sounds that were a cross between grunting and bubbling breaths, as though their lungs were permanently congested from the cave's unrelenting humidity.

No hair, no clothes covering their slick skin; somewhere in the back of his mind Sam found that surprising in the cold depths of the cave. Maybe under their skin was an extra thick layer of fat for insulation, or maybe that was the purpose of all that extra skin to begin with. As one passed close to their hiding spot, Sam got enough of a look at the thing's face and neck to make him grit his teeth, especially when it leaned down and tried to see into their hiding spot.

Dean had pulled his gun but Sam put a hand on his before he could fire it. The creature—Sam could no longer think of it as human—peered into the shadow beneath the shelf of rock but didn't bother to poke the torch it was holding any farther in. Its eyes were tiny and close-set, shadowed beneath a ridge of bone that stuck out at least an inch; they could just see the dark pupils moving restlessly back and forth, but they never paused, never stopped to focus on the brothers. After a moment that felt like a half hour, it moved on.

Sam exhaled slowly and soundlessly, wishing he could get the memory of that face out of his mind; on the other hand, it would no doubt do him good—as in survival good—to remember it. He glanced at Dean and saw his brother's eyes were wide in disbelief, but at least he'd lowered the weapon.

"It's not blind, but I don't think it can see that well."

"What the hell are they?" Dean whispered.

Sam hunched his shoulders. "I don't know. They're not

cavemen—they aren't human. Or if they are, it's long evolved out."

"Morlocks, then." Dean sounded triumphant, like he'd figured out some awesome puzzle.

Sam shook his head. "Those were made up in a book—"

"They could be as real as anything else."

"They look more like troglodytes. Sound like them, too."

"Let's call them that—trogs."

"True," Sam admitted. His mouth stretched into a hard line.

That face... that head.

The top of the skull slanted straight into the creature's back, with no indentation for the neck; the same with its chin, although there had been a thick roll of extra skin rolling down from the ears to the upper chest. Small ears, really no more than shallow openings, were the only thing that broke the expanse of skin on either side of its head. Above the brow ridge were more folds of skin, almost like forehead wrinkles but much fatter. There was no nose in the triangle between the eyes and mouth, just a flat, smooth expanse above the mouth.

That was the real clincher.

Its mouth slanted down and was so wide it ran almost the width of its face. There was no upper lip, just a flat area where the nose should have been that finally curved and disappeared, but that didn't mean anything. The lower jaw jutted forward and just inside of a thick bottom lip a line of crooked, vicious-looking teeth poked upward.

"Hell of an underbite," Dean mumbled. "You think there's more teeth inside?"

"Probably." Sam stared out, trying to count. "In the top of the mouth, so it can bite down."

"Great news."

"There is, actually." Sam gestured to the tunnel where he and Dean had come into this particular part of Hell on earth. "They're way too big to fit, and the opening is in solid rock so they can't dig it out."

"You're saying we go back the way we came?"

"It might be the only escape."

"What about them?" Dean pointed out. "They had to have come from somewhere."

"True," Sam agreed. He wanted to stick his head out and see if he could spot another tunnel, passageway, anything, but he didn't dare. "But there's more of them now. There could be an entire freaking city of these creatures."

Dean's only response was a low sound of frustration. "Eventually we're going to have to do something."

"Right," Sam said. He crouched as close to the cavern as he dared. As best he could, his gaze tracked the creatures moving around in the dimly lit chamber a few feet away. "When the right time comes, we'll—"

Gunshots exploded through the cavern.

Sam instinctively jerked himself backward and landed on his rear end in the dirt, taking his brother down with him. Dean barely held back a yell of surprise. In the cavern, the creatures were bleating in fear, their formerly deep noises winding up in volume and coming almost nonstop. They were lumbering away, all moving as fast as their cumbersome bodies would allow toward a part of the wall that wound upward in a rambling natural staircase. With their concentration centered on the creatures, neither brother had noticed it before.

More shots, more panic from the troglodyte-like creatures. They were working up to total confusion in response to the racket; although they were almost falling over each other as they tried to clamber up the rocks, none of them seemed to be wounded. Several of the torches had been dropped and now sputtered on the damp ground.

"It's got to be Thompson," Dean told him. He pointed toward the tunnel they'd used. "He followed us, just like you said. It's the only thing that makes sense."

A couple more shots slammed into the edge of the rock shelf over their heads. "Damn it," Sam hissed. "He knows we're here. How can he see us when we can't see him?"

"We're going to have to run for it," Dean said.

"Where? There's no place to—"

"We'll follow the trogs."

Sam gaped at his brother. "Are you crazy? Did you see the claws on those things?"

Another volley of bullets skittered through the chamber, making them hunch down. "They're gone," Dean said. "They probably don't understand the noise and are running for their lives. We'll stay behind them so they don't see us, and maybe we can find a place where we can veer off, a secondary tunnel."

Sam ran his hands through his hair. "You realize we're just getting deeper into this cave, right? That we don't have a clue how to get out?"

Dean nodded. In the shadows under the rock shelf, Sam could see only flashes of weak firelight touching his brother's cheekbones, a glint in his eyes as he scanned the chamber.

"You ready?" Dean asked. When Sam nodded resolutely, Dean turned his body toward the stone staircase and leaned forward.

"Go!"

They ran, clawing their way out from under the overhanging ledge and sprinting toward the rock steps that led upward. More shots rang out as they made it to the bottom and began to weave upward. But none of the bullets were even close, as though Thompson was trying to herd them, force them to follow the creatures' path. The only good thing about being fired at was it ensured the troglodytes wouldn't come back in their direction.

At the top Sam and Dean ducked behind a pillar and Sam pulled out his gun, but there was no sense in firing blind. With no idea where the sheriff was, he poked his head out to try and aim, but all it got him was a boom three times as loud as anything previous; chunks of rock exploded from the pillar right above his head. He heaved himself backward. "He's got a shotgun!"

"No way," Dean protested. "There's not enough room—"

"Sawed off, mini, whatever." It was almost too dark up here to see, but around the constant, watery noise of the cave they could hear hurried footsteps from below. Sam put away his pistol, grabbed Dean's jacket and dragged him away from the column. Behind them was where the trogs had exited. There was no other place to go but the shadows. That was their only chance—again Sam had that feeling of being driven, pushed in a certain direction. "Move!"

They made it to the passageway together, but then they had

to go back to single file. Although they didn't have to crawl, neither could they stay fully upright; being wide enough so that the trogs could fit through it at least meant they weren't scraping the sides. Sam was first this time and he had no choice but to snap on his headlamp. It gave Thompson a way to track them, but they were moving fairly fast and he didn't want to run headlong into a wall or one of those beings.

"Turns to the right up here," he called back to Dean. He kept his voice quiet, barely loud enough to be heard above the sound of their shoes on the ground, which was full of chunks of stone. Although it was a natural feature of the tunnel, the turn was fairly sharp, and that was good—hopefully it would cut off the glow of his headlamp before Thompson saw it. Dean was close enough behind him so that he didn't have to raise his voice too much when he said, "Another turn, this time to the left." He wished he had a sense of direction, but it was impossible with so little light and no landmarks.

More turns, and Sam called them back to Dean as he came to each. They were still moving rapidly, still bent at the waist. Just as he was telling himself it couldn't go on forever, that his lower back wasn't going to freeze in this position, he saw something far down what was apparently a straight length of the passageway.

Light.

He and Dean slowed, working their way carefully toward the glow, moving as quietly as they could. As far as they could tell, there was no sound behind them, no indication that they were being followed. That was great, but what might be waiting for them ahead?

Finally they made it to the end of the passageway. It culminated in another chamber, this one about as wide as a basketball court but only half the length. There were pillars here as well, but they were thinner; a lot of them had been broken away and their tops were scattered around as broken chunks and points of rock. The ceiling was lost in blackness overhead, too high to make out, but smoke from two small fires at either end swirled upward; somewhere overhead was at least one opening that created a firm updraft. When the brothers scanned the room, they saw another wide opening in the center that had to lead to yet another chamber; the entrance was filled with a brighter, flickering glow—likely a bigger fire—and occasionally a shadow crossed the wavering light, then faded. Between the fires and the chamber opening were areas of darkness tinged red by the minerals in the walls.

"Regular metropolis down here," Dean said under his breath.

But Sam wasn't thinking about that. There was something on the ground at the far right end, so he motioned to his brother to follow, then began to make his way toward it. Dean followed him and the two of them crept along the wall and halted about ten feet away from the fire. There was a heavy smell in the air, not at all pleasant, but at least it was being lifted up and away by the air currents.

Dean peered to the left of the fire, trying to see beyond its glow. Then he was sorry he had. "Sam, look over there," he said in a hoarse voice. He pointed.

Sam obeyed, then froze. "Crap," he breathed.

Unable to stop themselves, the brothers worked their way stealthily past the fire, to the pile just outside its circle of light. It looked like small, separate mounds had been pushed together to form a larger, lumpy pile on the ground; the sides of it were streaked with dark lines that were mostly dry, although now and then the flames would throw light a certain way and something would glisten within the mass.

Resigned, Dean bent at the waist to see more clearly, then grimaced and pulled away. "I think it's the girls," he said, then swallowed hard when his stomach wanted to push its contents up his throat. "And," he pushed at something else on the ground with his foot, "maybe Owen."

Sam came closer. "What happened to them?"

They stared down at the bodies without speaking, then Sam crouched, breathing through his mouth. He found a small rock about an inch long and used it to prod gently here and there on the bodies. The corpses were bloody and ragged, mutilated; parts were missing—not just fingers, but pieces had been ripped out of the arms and legs that still remained; even the faces had been worked on. The torsos had been opened but not cleanly, more like clawed into, then torn apart. Among the three bodies they had only two arms, three legs, and all the throats had been split apart. They'd never seen the girls, but Sam spied the mate to the four-leafed clover earring hanging from the ear of one of the bodies; it was clotted with black, dried blood. As for Owen... they recognized him even though his eyes had been dug out of their sockets, just like those of the girls.

"They've been eaten," Sam said. His voice was stiff with revulsion, but he still managed to keep it low. "By those creatures, whatever they are. We can't even say they're cannibals because they're clearly not human."

Dean ground his teeth and turned in a slow circle. Now that they were stopped and focused on something other than running, he realized that the floor, even where they'd traversed the wall from the tunnel to get here, had bones scattered everywhere. Not the absurdly clean, white bones of horror movie props, but bones that looked more like what remained after a cooked beef dinner—dried ribbons of meat still clung to them, strings of gristle and tendon, knots of gnawed cartilage where the joints used to be.

Except they were bigger. Not like the neat pre-packaged joints of beef you'd buy in a supermarket for dinner. These were human-sized.

The nearby fire popped suddenly, shooting sparks into the air and making them both jump. "It's their clothes," Dean said. "That's what they're burning. And look back there, to the left of where we came in." He indicated a small stack of items. "Fanny packs, shoulder bags, stuff like that. It's like they leave them there. But why?"

"Maybe they don't burn well. The trogs could have learned that things inside explode, like lighters. And maybe sometimes they get picked up," Sam said bitterly. "Taken away by someone and stripped of money, anything else useful. Identification destroyed."

"Someone."

"Yeah, you know. Someone armed, able to hurt them if they got too close."

Dean's mouth compressed into a hard line. "I'm going to have a serious talk with that jerk."

Sam nodded. "Right now, though, I'd say mission accomplished. We set out to find the girls and we did, and Owen, too. Whatever those creatures are, they're freaks of evolution. They eat to survive, and that's all, plus they can't get to the surface. There's too many to kill, and the real evil is back in the tunnel where we came from."

"And maybe the town itself," Dean said softly.

"Maybe," Sam said thoughtfully. "But my guess is that only a few people really know what's going on. Otherwise someone would have plastered it all over the Internet by now—hardly anyone can keep a secret that horrible."

"So… Thompson," Dean said.

"Yeah."

"Anyone else?"

"I don't know. Let's deal with that after we take care of Thompson and get the hell out of this death trap."

"Please don't use those words."

Sam grinned at Dean, but it was strained. "I have no intention of dying down here, and neither do you. Right?"

"Right."

"Then let's—"

"You boys aren't going anywhere," said Sheriff Thompson from behind them.

THIRTY-ONE

The so-called FBI agents froze. They were only about twenty feet away and had been so focused on their conversation that Thompson had been able to catch them totally by surprise. He was close enough to see what they were doing and hear every word, but not so much they could jump him before he could blow them away.

"No, no," Thompson said quickly. "Do not move, or I will shoot you. I know you have guns. You just leave them where they are, inside your jackets, zipped up nice and tight." He stared at them without blinking. He put a little movement into the double barrel of his shotgun. "This is loaded with two 28-gauge slugs. It'll blow a hole the size of a rabbit in a man's chest. You might be able to rush me, but one of you will get shot, and at this range you'll die. Who's willing to sacrifice the other?"

The light from the fires wasn't that great but Thompson could still see by the expressions on their faces that they knew the truth of what he'd said. The one with short hair—

what was his name? Agent Taylor, that was it—in particular seemed taken aback by Thompson's shotgun, which was the sheriff's favorite.

"Now, y'all just go on and move, real slow, toward that opening over there. That's right, the big one on the opposite wall. We're going for a little walk."

The other agent, the one with long hair hanging from below the edge of his helmet, backed up a single step, then stopped. "So you're going to kill us?"

Thompson laughed low in his throat. "Me? No. I was, at first, but I've changed my mind." He tilted his head. "I'm going to give you to them."

"Like those twins," Taylor said. "And the librarian."

"And who knows how many others," the first one added. It took Thompson a moment to recall that his name was May.

Thompson nodded. "That's right."

"Why?"

The sheriff sighed. "Y'all aren't from Brownsdale so I don't see how you'd understand, but I guess you have a right to know. Those things—" he inclined his head toward the gap that led out of the chamber—"have been around for as long as this town's existed. Hell, probably way before that. But they're… hungry. As long as we feed them on a more or less regular schedule, they stay down here and don't try to get to the surface. If we slack off on that, well, they might find a way aboveground. We just can't let that happen."

The short-haired one started to fold his arms, then froze when Thompson tensed up, the end of the shotgun twitching. His hands went back to hang at his sides. "So we're what? Sacrifices?"

Thompson considered this. "Yeah, that's exactly what you are. And the rest of them, too."

Long-hair—what Thompson decided to call him in his mind, since he needed a haircut so badly—scowled. "It's horrible enough that you feed them people, but children? Thirteen-year-olds?"

Thompson's mouth turned down. "That wasn't supposed to happen. I didn't know who they were. I thought they were runaways or something, what with the backpacks they were carrying."

"But they were kids." The other agent looked at him with unconcealed loathing.

The sheriff inhaled. "Like I said, that wasn't planned. People come through all the time, working their way down from the interstate just to see the cave. It's the way it's always been. Usually about once a month or so, someone finds their way in here. A lot of the time they're given a little help with directions."

The agents stared at him, then short-hair—another easier way for Thompson to tell which was which—narrowed his eyes as two and two clicked through his brain. "You drove those girls here," he said accusingly. "We've been trying to figure out how they got to Crystal Cave, twenty-some miles, and it was you."

"I did."

"They trusted you," long-hair said. The words came out from between clenched teeth. "Because you were in uniform and in a sheriff's car."

"I didn't kill them," Thompson said. "I just dropped them off here. They were the ones who went in, by themselves, instead of going to the park service and getting a proper tour like they should have."

"But you knew what would happen," the agent with the short hair said. When Thompson said nothing, he continued. "And what about Owen Meyer? How'd you get him here?"

Thompson smiled a little, the expression of someone who was pleased about a job well done. "I told him I had a lead on the girls, that someone who didn't give their name had called in and said they saw them up here. Said I couldn't spare the manpower on an anonymous tip because we already had search parties over in Mammoth."

"And that wasn't true."

"Of course not." He lifted his chin. "No one's ever going to find out about any of this, you know. I've got all my paperwork in order, but no one's ever actually gone out to search. They all think 'someone else' was on the teams, deputies from other counties, volunteers."

Long-hair looked disgusted. "You sound pretty proud of yourself."

Thompson looked at him in surprise. "I am. You have no idea how complicated it is when there's a misstep like this, especially in this day and age of technology, where people can find out something like this." He snapped his fingers. "Nobody ever notices the usual sacrifices, all those hippies and drifters. But this…" He shook his head. "This was hard."

The barrel of the shotgun had drifted down and suddenly short-hair lunged forward. He got a hand around the end of the shotgun at the same time Thompson yanked the trigger; the resulting shot jerked the barrel out of the agent's hand at the same time the slug took a skull-sized chunk out of the wall several feet behind the two men. Short-hair swore but stopped short when Thompson swung the barrel back at him, his finger twitching and ready on the trigger. "Back the hell up," he ground out. "No—more. Now step to the side... yeah, just like that." He stared at the two younger men. "I've got one slug left, and I can get both of you in one shot. You want to try again? My nerves are wearing a bit thin."

Long-hair opened his mouth. "What about—"

"You know what?" Thompson interrupted. "Enough talking. It's time to get this over with so I can get home to supper."

Short-hair glared at him. "Glad to know you feel so guilty."

"Not a bit," Thompson said. He tried to sound cheerful but it was hard with his shoulder hurting so badly, giving him a hefty pulse of pain with every beat of his heart. Between that and the chase through the cave, he was feeling every bit of his age; the cold, aching joints, the bruises on his elbows and knees, all of it.

And no, he didn't feel guilty. Beau Pyle was too old for the job and if Thompson didn't take over, who knew what would happen to the folks in Brownsdale, to Thompson's own family, to future generations. Thompson might have done things a bit differently than they'd been done in the past, but so what. It was down to taking things into his own hands or paying the price. There hadn't even been a choice.

He fixed his cold blue gaze on the bogus FBI agents and took a step in their direction, the shotgun leading the way. Just so the boys knew he wasn't screwing around, he primed the shotgun, grinding his teeth to hide the pain it caused to hold the barrel in place while he did it. They moved back reflexively, matching him step for step. When one of them started to turn around, he said, "Nuh uh. Just keep facing me and walk backward. Don't look off to the side, just keep watching me, like I'm watching you. And remember, if one or both of you makes a run for it, I'll shoot whichever one happens to be easier.

"Now move your asses."

THIRTY-TWO

There'd been no chance to get away from Thompson, who had them maintain enough distance so neither Sam nor Dean could get to him without one of them getting killed. The entrance he guided them to hadn't been a tunnel, more the cave equivalent of a tiny foyer; he finally let them turn to see where they were going, take two steps, and that was it.

Although they could see the ceiling in this part of the cave, maybe twenty feet above, this chamber was double the size of the previous one. Trogs seemed to be everywhere, their thick bodies shuffling gracelessly from one spot to another or squatting close to the single large fire in the center. Every one of them was moving in some way or another. Even the ones crouched close to the fire were rocking on their toes, as if something—the blast of the gunshots, perhaps—had filled them with tension. The only noises they made were incomprehensible grunts and wet-sounding moans, but those were coming so frequently it seemed like every creature was adding to the din.

Even forced to move in, Sam and Dean had tried to keep their footsteps light, and at first, none of the beasts noticed they were there.

"Keep going," Thompson said in a low voice behind them. He'd closed the distance and now the barrel of the shotgun pressed painfully at the base of Dean's neck; he had no doubt the man's finger was already putting pressure on the trigger. Even so, Dean opened his mouth to tell the sheriff to stuff it, then changed his mind—he wasn't sure how good at hearing these things were, but he didn't want to test it. They didn't dare go forward and they couldn't go backward. Now what?

Knowing their gazes were locked on the creatures, Thompson took the decision out of their hands by suddenly planting his foot on Dean's backside and shoving him forward. He stumbled into Sam and they both lost their balance and fell forward, landing in a tangle but back on their feet in an instant. They spun, but the sheriff had backed into the tiny space between the two chambers so the trogs couldn't spot him. "Bad FBI men," he said in an amused voice. "This is not an exit." He had the shotgun nestled against his right shoulder and his finger was stroking the trigger.

Sam and Dean turned away from him and faced the trogs. Their weird noises had faded almost completely and they had gone from restless movement to not quite still, as if the sight of the two men had surprised them into a playing possum stance, like a fawn frozen in fear. There was a second when Dean realized the beasts had been heading toward the opening anyway, as though their memory of the gunfire had faded, then they all started making noise at once. It escalated until it sounded like a small, throaty babble, and the three creatures that were closest—too close—started for the brothers, heading toward them in a clumsy but fast shamble.

Sam and Dean leaped in different directions, moving fast, but there were so many of them there wasn't even time to yank their weapons out of their jackets. And there was no place to hide—the pillars in here just weren't large enough. The rock columns did, at least, slow the trogs down as they tried to follow the brothers' zigzagging run. Unfortunately, Sam and Dean weren't going to be able to keep up their game of trog pinball forever.

"Thompson's gone," Sam yelled.

"He might be waiting—ah!" Dean barely twisted out of the way as one of the creatures came around the other side of a rock and swiped at him, fingernails curved into the equivalent of a grizzly bear's claws.

"You okay?" Sam's voice was breathless as he dodged from one place to another.

"Yeah—Sammy, let's get out of here! I'd rather get shot than be eaten alive by these things!"

They went for the opening to the other chamber at the same time. Dean straight-armed a particularly big trog, knocking it flat on its back. At the same time, Sam jumped over it like it was a hurdle in a race, then heard the back of his jacket rip as another one of the creatures got its claws hooked in the fabric. They'd made it into the foyer, but the creature started to pull Sam back; he twisted, getting a horrifying glimpse of the beast's tooth-filled lower jaw dropping open only inches in front of his face. Then Dean had him by his shoulders, wrenching him out of bite range. Propelled by Dean's strength, Sam stumbled and went down, then fought to get back up. He looked over his shoulder just as Dean caught the trog that had almost gotten him with a full-powered side kick that pushed its knee back while the rest of its leg didn't move. It made a sound that was half growl, half gasp and toppled to the side, its writhing body creating an obstacle the others would have to climb over.

In the few seconds between Sam and Dean scrambling out of the opening and the first creature clambering over the fallen trog, both the brothers had managed to pull out their guns. More trogs were crowding into the opening, jostling each other as they tried to get through. Sam and Dean opened fire; from only ten feet away, every shot found its mark, most sinking into the pale flesh of the first creature trying to get to them. Its mouth dropped open and it roared, the sound like that of a wounded elephant somehow trapped in an outrageously small space. Then it fell forward, on top of the other one.

"That should scare them away," Dean yelled as he crouched and scanned around them; still no sign of Thompson. He must've gone back the way they'd come, certain that the creatures would finish off the brothers for him.

"No," Sam shouted from behind him. "Look!"

Dean spun back and felt his heart double-slam in his chest. Instead of running, the trogs had picked up the crying of their dying comrade, echoing it back and forth until it blasted out of the tunnel opening like the noise from a train wreck. If that wasn't bad enough, they were attacking the fallen one, tearing at it with the ferocity of starving werewolves. The trog

on the bottom was struggling to escape but it was useless—
when the blood from the dead one on top of it began to
splash on its skin, the others attacked it, too.

"We need to go," Dean said in a stage whisper that Sam
could still barely hear. He grabbed Sam's arm. "They're like
sharks in a feeding frenzy. If they remember us, we'll be next."

Keeping an eye on the mayhem behind them, they ran
across the chamber, dodging around the chewed and disfigured
remains of Owen and his cousins, stumbling over larger bones,
a pelvic bone here, a broken pile of ribs there, a skull that had
been pulled into two pieces using the eye sockets. What kind
of strength did it take to do something like that?

By the time they made it across and to the tunnel entrance,
the creatures had finished with their double feast and were
clambering over the bodies, turning back to pull their mutilated
dead out of the opening, then dragging the corpses away from
the walls. Dean started to raise his gun but Sam stopped him.
"Wait," he whispered. "They aren't thinking about us right
now. Let's not catch their attention again. Just go."

Until now, when the glow from their headlamps picked out
the wide, uneven passageway in front of them. They hadn't
realized their lights were still on. This was the tunnel that was
tall enough for the trogs but not for them; to make any kind of
speed, the brothers had to drop into a crouch and scramble like
awkward, oversized crabs. To make things worse, the braying,
wet noises they'd heard the creatures make before began to filter
through the tunnel before they even made it to the first turn.

"Already," Dean said. "What the hell does that racket
mean, anyway?"

"I think it's some kind of hunting call," Sam answered. "It's the only thing that makes sense."

"Because all of this does," Dean said sarcastically.

"Just keep going."

Another turn, and another, then Sam stopped. "Here," he said.

Dean paused, craning his head to look back at him. "What? You found an elevator?"

"It's a good spot for an ambush." Sam raised his Beretta and ejected the clip to check it; it still had rounds but he swapped it out for a full one anyway.

"Why?" Dean protested. "We should keep going—we have a good lead."

Sam shook his head, the movement making wild gray shadows in the black and white passageway. "They're like zombies. If we don't slow them down, they'll catch up, one way or another. They always do."

"And I always thought if the ditzy people just kept going, there was no way the zombies could get them."

Sam ignored him. "When the first one starts around that turn, I'm going to unload," he said. "He'll go down, hopefully block the way, and they'll go into another dinner party. If they drag the body back out like they did the others, we'll gain even more time."

Dean had to admit Sam's plans had some merit. He checked his weapon, then raised it when he heard the trogs getting closer, leading the way with that horrible, moist-sounding bawling. Closer, closer—

Blam blam blam!

Sam held his gun steady, making every shot count. The trog coming around the turn squalled and went down; before the creature behind it attacked the fallen one, Sam had a chance to register that he'd brought down a small one, not nearly big enough to block the tunnel as he'd hoped.

Without hesitation, he clawed his way back to where the trogs had stopped, keeping his gun up and aimed. He heard Dean yell behind him but kept going, and when he got to where he could see into the black eyes of the trog looming over the one on the ground, he put three rounds into its skull.

Sam started to back up, then gasped and looked down.

The creature he'd shot first wasn't dead, and it had stretched out an arm and sunk its claws into the back of Sam's leg, just above the ankle. Pain slammed up his leg—had he been hamstrung?—and he lurched backward, his gaze following the cone of his helmet's light up and to the ceiling. He fell onto his back, struggling for air as fire seemed to envelop his foot. Then Dean was next to him and firing straight into the eye of the trog that had him trapped.

The beast's hand fell away, then jerked and danced in the dirt as the trogs in the tunnel began to feed on the two downed ones blocking their path. Dean dragged Sam along the tunnel and by the time he made another turn, Sam was pushing his brother's hands aside. "Stop," he said breathlessly. "Just for a sec."

Dean let him go then crouched beside him and examined Sam's ankle. "Damn, that's nasty. We should—"

A dull-sounding rumble cut off his words.

Sam and Dean looked up, as if they could see anything

other than the jutting surfaces of the rocks that made up the tunnel's ceiling. Another rumble came from somewhere unseen, this one shaking pebbles and grit from the cracks.

"Maybe shooting inside the tunnel wasn't such a great idea," Dean said softly. "Sorry, Sammy. No time for a bandage right now." He grabbed the shoulder of Sam's jacket and hauled him forward.

Sam ground his teeth, then batted Dean's hand away and began crawling after him. He was on his knees now, the rocks making it feel like his knees were naked rather than covered by heavy denim and padding. He could favor the ankle that had been mauled but not keep weight off it entirely, and negotiating the tunnel began a true act of will as he struggled to put each fresh stab of agony out of his mind. Worse, their speed was now not much faster, if it was at all, than the hungry creatures behind them.

"Come on," Dean urged him. "I don't think it's far."

"Said nobody in a cave, ever," Sam managed. He was starting to lag behind.

"Couple more turns, I swear." Dean reached back and pulled Sam forward, towing him a few more feet.

"Stop it—that hurts!"

"Gonna hurt more if those things catch you and start chewing on your bones. Come on."

Sam sucked in air, then turned his head so he could see his lower leg. He couldn't see the wound itself, but the bottom part of his jeans looked black and wet; when he shone his headlamp down the tunnel, there were ragged splotches every few feet. The razorblade pain was making him light-headed, or was it the blood loss? He thought of dying down here, bleeding to death or being torn apart in a space so far below the earth that it would become his coffin.

No way.

Face twisted in pain, he crawled after his brother again, trying to keep his foot raised so it wouldn't hit the rocks along the way. That made his knees hurt worse, but it was that or give up. And that wasn't in his blood.

The end of the tunnel caught them by surprise. They'd been so hell-bent on just moving, a foot or two at a time, and not stopping, that they looked up and there it was. For a moment Dean thought of the drop off and how it had taken him right over the edge, but there was no such thing here. He came out, then turned and pulled Sam upright and got his shoulder under his brother's. He remembered this chamber, the small pillars that had been useless as hiding places. They hadn't worked then, and they wouldn't help now.

He and Sam were already breathing heavily, but there was a lot farther to go, and Dean began working his way through the columns of rock. If he remembered correctly, those stairs were in here somewhere, then the big chamber where Thompson had first used his gun to scare off the trogs. As long as the sheriff hadn't doubled back, they might make it. "Got to keep moving," he panted.

Every time Sam tried to put weight on his foot, that side of his body sagged, but Dean kept going, refusing to slow down.

"Dean," Sam finally gasped. "Please—stop. Just for a second. I can't keep going."

Dean shot a look back toward the tunnel they'd exited, but it was impossible to see. Too many pillars of rock in the way, too many boulders. He hoped he was going in the right direction and not just traveling in circles. Two more feet and he let his brother down so that Sam could lean his back against a rock. Sam's breath was going in and out so fast he was on the verge of hyperventilating.

"Let me see your leg," Dean said. Sam made a vague gesture in the air that made Dean realize he was in too much pain to care, so Dean gingerly lifted the blood-soaked edge of Sam's jeans. What he saw wasn't good and he had to stop himself from saying so. Instead, he unzipped his jacket, then ripped the front of his shirt open. Buttons flew everywhere and one smacked Sam in the cheek.

"What are you doing?" Sam asked. His eyes were only half open. "Strip tease?"

"Sure," Dean said as he tore a long, wide strip from the side with the buttonholes. "Thought the man-eating beasts would like it." Before Sam could reply, Dean pulled his brother's foot up and balanced it on the top of his boot. Sam hissed under his breath but didn't try to pull away. "Something to slow the bleeding," Dean said. "This is going to hurt, but it'll feel better when it's wrapped and your jeans aren't dragging across it." He threaded the fabric under Sam's ankle and crossed it.

"How bad is it?" Sam's face was shining with perspiration.

"Bad enough. One, two—" Rather than go to three and give his brother time to tense up, Dean pulled the fabric tight. Sam sucked in air, making one of those noises that was part ugly surprise, part distress. Dean wound the fabric around a couple more times, then tied a knot at the side to keep it secure. "There."

A groan was all he got in response, but Dean wasn't deterred. "Up and at 'em. Miles to go and all that crap." He leaned over and got his hands under Sam's armpits, then heaved him to a standing position. As he straightened, there was another ominous sound, barely audible, deep in the mountain's heart.

Sam swayed on one leg. "Leave me," he mumbled. "You'll never make it out unless you do."

"Screw that," Dean said.

Sam collapsed, pulling Dean to the ground.

"Dude," Dean said in astonishment. "Did you just pass out on me?"

No answer.

THIRTY-THREE

Carrying Sam over his shoulder like a fireman was no problem. Once he found them, going down the natural-cut stairs was easy and fast, and while the steps were unevenly spaced the only thing Dean had to watch out for was the edges, which sometimes wanted to crumble away. There was no sight or sound of the creatures yet and the only thing Dean could hear was the sound of his own heavy breathing, a huffing that drowned out any noise Sam made, and the occasional drip of water between his breaths. The big chamber where they'd hidden under a shelf of rock from the trogs was below, and across it, the tunnel they'd crawled out of. Dean had no clue how he was going to get Sam into that passageway unless he woke up, but there was a lot of comfort in knowing it was far too narrow for the trogs to follow them into.

But it all went south not long after he made it to the bottom of the staircase.

Dean went down the last step, then trudged to the left,

angling away from the wall and in the direction of the tunnel entrance. He could just see the set of huge, sharp-edged rocks that he was sure concealed the entrance. He'd made it about a quarter of the way over the boulder-strewn ground, steadfastly ignoring the way Sam felt like he was getting heavier, when gunfire blasted through the chamber and a bullet zinged off a pillar only a couple of inches away. Head level, too.

He yelped in surprise and backpedaled around the column of rock, trying not to slam Sam's head against the side of it. Another gunshot and chunks of rock exploded from the side of the pillar.

"Y'all go on back the way you came!" Sheriff Thompson's voice floated through the chamber.

"Not happening," Dean called back. He was torn between lowering Sam and keeping himself and his brother out of reach behind the layered stone. He wasn't sure he could manage both, but there was nothing else he could do. With Sam's weight on his back, he wouldn't be fast enough to dodge behind another column. They were trapped, and Sam's unconscious body was bearing him down more each second that passed. Thompson was using a pistol instead of the sawed-off shotgun now, and Dean wondered when he would run out of ammunition. Then he dismissed the thought as ridiculous. Like him and Sam, Thompson had probably come into this with plenty to spare.

"Then I suppose I'll just shoot you and leave you for those animals."

Thompson fired again, and this time the bullet ricocheted off the front of the pillar. "You can't go through stone," Dean yelled, then realized his headlamp, and Sam's, were still on. He twisted and had to let Sam slide off his shoulders, then snapped off the lights and pulled out his gun. The trogs' torches had fizzled out and Thompson had positioned his flashlight so that its beam washed over a good portion of the lower chamber, bleeding away to blackness at the edges. Dean wasn't sure there was enough cover in this spot, but it would have to do. The good thing was that the noise would keep the trogs scared off... at least to a point. The behavior of the creatures had changed when food had become involved, and Dean didn't exactly have a Ph.D. in troglodyte habits. Now that they had the taste of a recent meal in their mouths and a trail of Sam's blood to follow, who knew?

Dean crouched and tried to move where he could see around the other side of the pillar, closer to ground level. There was no clear line of sight to Thompson's location, but he fired anyway, a single shot aiming into the gray and black shadows surrounding the crevice formed by the rocks at the tunnel's entrance. In the short silence that followed, he heard... something, but he wasn't sure if it was the sound of the trogs, with their weird, braying calls, or something else that seemed to be coming from several directions at once. All of a sudden he wasn't feeling so confident about the creatures still being frightened by gunfire.

Thompson fired again, this time spraying a half-dozen rounds at their position. Dean couldn't be sure but his voice sounded closer. "I saw you carrying your partner, Agent. Very admirable. It won't help though." There was another shot, this one knocking a hefty chunk of rock away from the pillar. Thompson was still using a handgun, but if he was carrying his shotgun and got too close, the lawman might actually be able to blow enough of the column away to where they were revealed. Just in case, Dean dragged Sam's still unconscious form a bit farther around, away from where he thought Thompson was moving. Even though he thought the sheriff might be out of the cover of the rocks, it wouldn't help—there was no way he could get Sam anywhere else in the chamber safely, and he wasn't leaving him.

It came again but closer, that strange, soggy-sounding yowl that signaled the trogs were advancing. In their society, hunger overrode fear. He and Sam hadn't seen any torchlight back in the tunnel, but the creatures had used it before. If they did, there would be no place in this chamber to hide.

"Come on, boys. I'm getting tired of this. You—" Whatever else Thompson was going to say ended in a yelp of pain that was followed immediately by the sound of a rock falling, then another, and another. Then Dean heard someone scrabbling around in the dirt and cursing at about the same time Sam moaned and tried to sit up.

"Stay down," Dean hissed as he crouched next to him.

"What…" Sam cleared his throat as quietly as he could, then tried again. "What's going on?"

"I'm not sure." He dared a glance around the pillar. As his eyes picked out Thompson's form, he realized the man had worked his way to within forty feet of where they were. It sounded like plenty of space… but it was nothing for a bullet. Then his mouth dropped open as something came flying out of the darkness between the rocks back at the tunnel's entrance, something chunky and hard—a fist-sized rock. It bounced off Thompson's leg and he cried out again, stumbling. Whoever was throwing those things had a damned sight better aim than the sheriff did.

Thompson brought up his pistol one-handed and aimed back toward the rocks, but before he could squeeze the trigger Dean fired at him. Thompson shrieked as he dropped and rolled on the harsh, uneven chamber floor. Dean didn't waste any time; he pulled Sam up and dragged him toward the tunnel—there wasn't even time to get his brother back over his shoulder. Dodging, weaving through the shadowed spaces between the rocks and pillars, all Dean could do was keep pulling, keep breathing, and keep hoping Sheriff Thompson wouldn't blow a hole in one of their backs.

Another rock flew out of the shadows, this time coming from a few feet to the left of the rocks around the entrance. Its aim was spot on. It cracked hard into the side of Thompson's helmet and was immediately followed by three more, each one whacking into the lawman with enough force to make him howl. The last one was the best of the lot, and it slammed into Thompson's wrist hard enough to knock his pistol away.

"I'll kill you myself!" Thompson bellowed as he threw himself down, whipping his head from side to side as he searched for his lost weapon.

He didn't have time to consider where the rocks were coming from. Fighting for air, Dean just kept pulling on Sam, grateful that his brother was at least trying to help. If he didn't get to the cover of the rocks before Thompson located his gun—

"I'll get his other side."

Dean shouted in surprise and almost dropped Sam at the sound of a stranger's voice. He held on, but their headlamps were still turned off and he couldn't see anything but the wild dancing of Thompson's helmet light, which was way too close for comfort. "Who's there?"

"Beau Pyle," came the raspy answer. "Hurry now. It won't take him long to find that gun."

The name clicked in Dean's head and he exhaled in relief— the old guy from the caving store. But how strong was he? As if answering Dean's unvoiced question, Sam's weight on his arms suddenly lessened and evened out as Pyle pulled up Sam's other side, then guided them back toward the mouth of the tunnel.

Ten or fifteen yards away, they heard Thompson whoop triumphantly—he must've gotten his hands on the gun. The lawman's headlamp spun in a haphazard circle and he let out a couple of shots, clearly not aiming at anything in particular. "I'll find you," he called. "I'm done playing games."

"In here," Pyle said urgently. Dean let the older man lead the way through the tall, jagged rocks and into the tunnel. He followed, pushing Sam in front of him. Sam, for his part, hobbled as fast as he could, grunting now and then in pain.

"The creatures," Dean said. He was almost out of breath. "They'll follow—"

"They're too big to fit in here," Pyle said. He stopped and snapped on his helmet light. "But Thompson's not, and he'll be coming after us. Here's where the tunnel gets small, so we're crawling single file from here. Turn on your headlamps.

We're going to need all the light we have to move fast. It'll help you see where you're putting your hands and knees." When he fixed his gaze on Sam's face, the old man's eyes looked almost silver gray. "You gonna make it, son?"

Sam nodded, but his face was pale, his lips tight. "Sure," he managed. His breath sounded wheezy.

"All right." Pyle shone his light down the passageway. "I'll lead. I think I'm the freshest, so I'll probably be the fastest. You," he touched Sam's arm, "follow me. If you find yourself lagging, just grab onto my ankle and I'll pull you as best I can."

"I'll push," Dean said, before Pyle could tell him the obvious. "And watch the tunnel from behind to make sure Thompson doesn't surprise us."

"That'd be a damned bad thing," Pyle said. He turned and looked into the circle of darkness ahead. "Let's go."

THIRTY-FOUR

Never in his life had Beau Pyle felt less like a caver and more like an old geezer. Still, he slogged on, knowing that as awful as he might feel, it was worse for the young man behind him. He'd seen the makeshift bandage around the bottom of the agent's leg, the way the material around it was stained with blood that looked black in the helmet light. Beau didn't know if it was a gunshot wound or if one of those animals had bitten him. Either way, he'd clearly lost a lot of blood and with it, his strength. And if he'd been bitten... who knew what kind of diseases those things could transmit?

The guy behind him gave a muffled cry and Pyle paused, letting him catch up. "Grab onto me," he said urgently. "We have to keep going. It's not too far."

"Yes, it is." Sam's words were barely audible. "I remember."

"You giving up, bro?"

The other man's deep voice floated up to Pyle and he blinked as he remembered what Cinnamon had said—they weren't FBI agents at all. They were even using fake names.

"No." But the answer was a while in coming, and faint.

A distraction, Beau decided. That's what they needed. Something else to focus on besides how miserable they were. "What are your real names again? Cinnamon told me, but I can't recall except… Winchester. That was it. Like the guns."

"She told you?"

"She said you weren't FBI, but wouldn't tell me anything else."

"I'm Dean," said the one farther back. "This is my brother, Sam."

Brothers, Pyle thought. He kept pulling himself forward. Brothers fighting against the unknown. It would've sounded romantic except for the hideous reality of where they were and what they were doing. That and the fact that none of them might make it out alive.

But he couldn't think about that. He'd come down here to help, to save their lives if he could. He'd only been in this part of the cave one time. Another time he'd gone a different way, long, deep, unrelentingly narrow, and found where those animals lived; that time he'd barely escaped, had been lucky to get back into the entry tunnel in one piece. The jagged, twisting passage had been too small for them to follow. And although he'd been terrified and exhausted, he'd done his best to kick at the rocks below him and block as much of it as he could before he finally came out.

"Tell me about what you do," he said now. "Give me something to think about other than these damned rocks."

And so they did.

* * *

Although Beau didn't believe the half of it—maybe because he didn't want to believe—Dean's words, claims of battling and destroying creatures that were the stuff of nightmares and bad fairy tales, served their purpose, finally carrying the three of them out of the passageway and onto flat ground. The first thing they saw was the weak glow of the light stick that had already been there when Beau had first arrived, probably left by Thompson. When Beau brought out his flashlight and let the beam travel over the rocks beyond it, he let out his breath in relief. The sheriff's ropes were still there, firmly anchored in a crevice in the tunnel's ceiling, fifteen feet above them. The other rope, the one with knots that Beau assumed had been Owen's was also still there.

Beau pushed up, ignoring the creaks of his joints and the stabs of pain along his spine. "Old people's pangs," his grandfather had always called them, and the ten-year-old that he had been had never conceived that he would one day know exactly what that meant. "Come on," he said, pulling hard on Sam's jacket until the other man was completely free of the tunnel. Dean followed and staggered to his feet; they were all feeling the cramped position and the way the cave's cold had settled into their overused muscles. "We have to assume Thompson's not far behind. Have you got harnesses?" When the brothers looked at him with blank, dirty expressions, Beau groaned inside. What had he been thinking? Of course they hadn't. "Then we'll have to share." Panning the flashlight beam back and forth, paranoid that they might not be alone in this small chamber, the old caver led them over to where the rope lines ended in small piles on the ground. He'd come down alone but still planned on going back up with others; having Dean there would make the ascent faster.

Beau shook out the ropes, then unfastened his harness and stepped out of it. "Put this on."

"No," Dean said. "My brother—"

"Will have to be pulled up," Beau interrupted. Sam was upright and balancing against the rock, but just barely. "You go up first, then him, and I'll come up last. Then we pull out the rope."

"What about Thompson?"

"Leave him," the caver said. His voice was cold. "He'll kill us before he'll let us help him, and he'll destroy the town for the sake of feeding those things down there." He swallowed, then jutted out his chin. "It's better for everyone if he never comes out of Crystal Cave."

Dean looked at him for a long moment, then nodded. He climbed into Beau's harness, giving it a few quick adjustments so it wouldn't neuter him on the way up, then he was ready to go. Beau had picked up the light stick, and now he handed it to Dean.

"Take this up and toss it in the tunnel. Now, pull at the same time I do," Beau told him. "One, two, three."

Dean's feet were suddenly in the air. He bumped feet first against the rock and looked up, then down, obviously surprised that the ropes were holding. "Pull," Beau yelled, and he went up another couple of feet. Another six times and he was able to turn his body and get his feet on the slope below the tunnel. He pushed off then swung back and hooked one gloved hand into the rocks, balancing there.

"I'm up," Dean called down.

"Send the harness down on the rope," Beau yelled up. While he waited, the caver turned to Sam. "Come on, son. Time to put on your big boy pants."

Sam squinted up at him. "Did you just say—"

"Yep." The harness swung into his view and Pyle snagged it. "Here they are. I'll help you pull them up."

Sam scrubbed at his eyes and looked like he wanted to say something, then shook his head instead. With one hand against the rock face and the other on Beau's shoulder, he managed to get his bad leg into the harness, but that same leg wouldn't hold his weight so he could finish.

"I got you," Beau told him. He shoved a bony shoulder under Sam's armpit and straightened his body, grinding his teeth—old dentures, actually—together with the strain. "Lean toward me," he said. "And see if you can use your hands to hold yourself against the rock."

Beau wasn't sure how, but they managed, finally, to get Sam fully strapped into the harness, although the young man's face was gray and he was panting around the pain. Beau checked the ropes and gave the thumbs up signal to Dean. They both pulled and although Sam held on, he looked like a man-sized ragdoll as he rose.

They'd gotten him halfway up when Thompson came out of the tunnel.

Beau heard him first, the grunting and cursing, the scattering of rocks—Thompson must have been clawing his way through the tunnel with every bit of strength he had, trying his best to catch up with them. An instant later, Thompson started firing wildly. Gunshots and the sound of bullets ricocheting off the rocks filled the chamber. In response Beau slapped his hand on his helmet's light switch and it went out—

Leaving Sam dangling up there, barely conscious, with his helmet light gleaming like a swaying black-and-white target.

"Pull him up!" Beau screamed, throwing all of his weight onto the line. "Pull him up!"

Dean yelled something in response, then Sam was jerked upward a few more feet. Then, instead of pulling again, Dean fired into the cavern, aiming for Thompson's light. Thompson screamed something unintelligible and his helmet light winked out.

"Come on," Dean shouted down at him. Beau hauled on the rope again, and again, until Sam's light picked out Dean's gloved hands reaching out and dragging him onto the ledge.

Satisfied they were both safe, Beau whirled and peered into the darkness, trying to figure out where Thompson had gone. For a few moments, with the last of the gunshots making his ears ring and exchanging shouts with Dean, there'd been so much racket he'd lost track of the sheriff; now he had no idea in which direction he'd gone, or if he'd even moved at all.

Dean and Sam's headlamps were small wavering circles of light in the tunnel above, but Beau was sure that Dean had enough sense to stay away from the edge. Moving carefully and as quickly as he dared, Beau tried to work his way to the right. If he could get close enough, maybe he could—

Something fell from the tunnel above and thudded against the ground. Beau looked up just in time to see Dean duck out of the tunnel's mouth; an instant later, Thompson was shooting at it again, another volley of bullets that filled the chamber with echoing roars. Desperate to clap his hands over his ears, instead Beau took out his flashlight, aimed it at the ground beneath the tunnel, and flicked it on, then off. There had been just enough light to see what Dean had dropped: the harness, along with the second length of rope.

For a small, blissful moment, there was near silence. No one was shooting, no one was screaming. Just the peaceful, expected noises of water dripping and...

Rumbling.

That wasn't good, and neither was the way the rocks, most small, began cascading here and there around them. Beau darted back to where he'd been and snatched up the harness, then dodged behind the closest pillar, a spot that unfortunately put him a half-dozen feet closer to Thompson. Counting on the anxiety the mini-rockslide would cause, he jerked on the harness and haphazardly tightened the straps. So far, so good, but there was still the matter of getting back to the overhead tunnel without dying in the process.

With a start, Beau remembered that he had light sticks left, and if his present situation hadn't already been so bad, he would've slapped himself. Once you broke it, you couldn't extinguish a light stick, and he could imagine them needing to hide from Thompson, or worse, those animals. Using his old pitching skills to try and toss a light stick away somehow didn't feel as easy as just switching off a headlamp.

But right now…

Beau pulled out two of them, then tried to measure the darkness between him and where Thompson's last shots had come from. Finally, he snapped the first one and sent it flying end over end to the left of where he thought the ground-level tunnel was. Thompson squawked and fired a single shot toward the stick, not Beau. That was the panic response Beau had been hoping for, and he sent the second one whipping about the same distance to the right of the tunnel without Thompson being able to figure out where it had come from.

It wasn't a lot of light, but it was enough to feather a nice, soft glow along the side of the tunnel across from the ropes. Dean took advantage of it, and at the same time he saw Thompson crab-walking along the rocks and trying to get to one of the light sticks, Dean shot at him. He missed, but it was enough to make the sheriff turn and run back to the ground-level tunnel, where he spun and backed himself into it like a funnel spider. Beau could just see him between the two light sticks; his face was pale and streaked with dirt and his eyes seemed to blaze in the darkness, as though he had gone slightly mad.

Although he still wasn't sure how he was going to go up without being shot, Beau started to move back toward the ropes. The moment his foot hit a rock, however, Beau saw Thompson swing his pistol around. He ducked behind a pillar just before the man squeezed the trigger, flinching when a hunk of the column's side smashed apart at head level. If he'd been a half-second slower…

He was close enough to see Dean's shadow in the tunnel

above. "Go on," he yelled. "Cut the ropes and go."

"Don't you touch those ropes!" Thompson screamed. "Don't you do it!"

"Not happening, Beau," Dean yelled back. "Just hook up and we'll take it from there."

Thompson fired up at the tunnel. One of the shots was actually dead center, but the angle made it impossible for the sheriff to hit anything but the ceiling.

"You can get help and come back for me," Beau yelled.

"No!" screeched Thompson. He fired up at Dean again, then snarled something at the gun when the next trigger pull came up empty.

"Don't make me come down and get you, Beau!" Dean shook the ropes. "Move it now."

What the hell, Beau thought. Better to get shot while trying to escape than lie down and show my throat like a surrendering dog.

He ran for the ropes.

Beau wasn't very swift, but he was still pretty strong and had a body filled with hiker's muscles. He dodged left and right on purpose, even when there was nothing in front of him, if for no other reason than it was how they ran from gunfire in the movies. He could imagine Thompson taking aim, following him in the gun's sights and waiting for just the right chance—after all, he was just as faintly illuminated by the light sticks as the sheriff himself was.

Thompson's shot didn't have time to happen. Dean started firing down at Thompson, one bullet at a time but in spaced intervals that would never quite let Thompson get Beau on target. The old man skidded on the rocks by the ropes and almost lost his footing; it was Owen's rope that saved him as his hand ran down it and was halted by one of the climbing knots.

With Dean's shots still exploding through the chamber, Beau found his balance and managed to hook his harness to the right line, then gave it a hard tug. "I'm ready!" he called, There was a hard tug on the rope and Beau's feet left the ground. With the next pull, he matched it; now he was four feet up and hanging there like a human target in an old amusement park game. He never had liked it.

Another pull, two more feet up. He was trying to help but his age was playing against him—caving was difficult to begin with, but helping tow Sam and the added stress of murder and man-eating creatures kind of pushed it over the edge. Dean was alternating between pulling and shooting, pulling and shooting, and Beau was a bit over halfway there when Thompson figured out the rhythm, leaned out of his hiding place, and shot his own cam setup right out of the rock.

The old man fell, barely managing to get one hand around the knotted rope to slow himself down. He wrenched his shoulder but still held on, so when his lower body hit the first things to take the impact were his feet. His left leg was okay, but the right one turned sideways under his weight; his knee went, just like it had so long ago and put an end to his baseball days in high school. It hurt like a son of a gun and he couldn't bite back a cry of pain.

Beau hung onto the knotted rope and stayed upright on his left leg, hopping and knowing he'd never be able to get up to the tunnel now—he might have muscles but they wouldn't be enough to pull his entire weight up, and without two legs, he couldn't catch the knots with his feet. He was done for.

He heard Dean swear above him, aim at Thompson's position and let loose again, driving the sheriff back into his hole. In the back of his mind he was rather amazed at the amount of ammunition everyone had, when he had only brought—

His eyes widened.

A grenade.

Dean's head popped over the edge and took in the way Beau had been effectively hobbled. "Hook your harness to the other rope and I'll pull you up," he barked.

"But—"

"Do it!"

The only thing louder than Dean's bellow was a sudden surge of movement in the ground that came with a strange sort of low groan, as if the chambers and tunnels were its arteries and the earth itself was protesting all the damage done to its insides by these human intruders. The chamber floor steadied but more rocks slid down the walls, bigger ones than before, and Beau yelped when one that was large enough to crush him dropped from the unseen ceiling and crashed against a pillar twenty feet to his left. The vibration when it hit ran through the floor and up to his busted knee, making it feel like a small sun had exploded inside it. The agony made his hands want to shake but he willed them to be firm as he released the climbing-grade carabiner that bound him to the useless pile of ropes at his feet; one smooth move and he transferred it to the lowest knot on Owen's rope, about four feet off the ground.

Dean didn't bother asking if Beau was ready, just yanked backward on the rope as hard as he could, putting his body and legs into it. Beau's feet left the ground and when he looked up, he saw the first knot in the rope disappear over the edge of the ground that tilted down in front of the entrance; for the first time since Thompson had reappeared like a demented badger, Beau felt a bit of hope.

Another wave of rumbling erupted along with more shots from Dean. Beau's body jerked upward and he used his good leg to try and keep himself from slamming against the rock. Each movement of the line made it twist, but at least with the harness supporting him, Beau was able to put one arm out, too, and push away from the stone when it would have cracked into his already swollen knee.

From somewhere overhead he heard boulders crashing against each other, more ominous noises that preceded the disaster that was no doubt coming. He looked up and got his head jerked back as Dean hauled on the rope again, lifting Beau another three feet. He didn't feel like he was all that high; then again, it was only fifteen feet—just enough distance to be tantalizingly out of reach without climbing apparatus. Thompson fired, but not at Dean; a spot on the wall to the right of Beau's head came apart and the bullet bounced off the rock and zinged to the left, leaving a deep gouge across the outside of his arms in its wake. Blood welled from the wound and Beau yelled, more in shock than pain. At least it hadn't been his right one.

More gunshots exploded from overhead at the same time Dean towed him up another couple of feet. It had to be Sam, awake and doing whatever he could to help in the fight. Beau's body twisted again and this time it happened too fast for him to catch; his wounded arm bounced against the wall and left a bloody smear at the same time Beau sucked in air and fought not to yell out again. In spite of the pain running down his arm, he pushed against the stone with the flat of his left hand until he turned and his back bumped against the wall, trying to steady himself and pull down the zipper on his jacket at the same time. The tunnel entrance was only about four feet above him; one more pull, and Dean would drag him over the edge. Until then, he was splayed out like a man-sized target in a shooting range.

So be it.

"Wait!" he hollered up to Dean. "Don't pull yet!"

Dean's face appeared above, just long enough for Beau to see his bewildered expression. Then Beau held up the object he had taken from the inside of his jacket. The younger man's eyes widened and he disappeared back into the tunnel.

Beau hung there, gathering himself. It was only four seconds—not so long but all the time he could spare. Too many people thought throwing a baseball was all strength and aim, but in reality it was as much psychological as physical. There was an entire set of mental preparations that a pitcher went through, covering everything from confidence to the environment.

Around him, rocks and boulders were sliding to the ground and the angry earth was moving. It sounded like muffled thunder.

He blocked it out.

Above him, Dean's hands were locked around the only rope that kept Beau from being trapped in the chamber with a man who wanted to kill him.

He dismissed the thought.

There were shots coming from overhead and more from the ground, where Sam kept slipping out of his tunnel and firing. Another part of the wall shattered next to him, this time at waist level.

He paid no attention to it.

Blood and fire traveled down his left arm from the bullet wound and his knee throbbed with every rapid beat of his heart, as though someone had taken a baseball bat to it.

He ignored all of it.

There was only him and his target, the tunnel entrance across the chamber. Beau's mind went back to the last game he'd played in his senior year at high school, the sixth inning—two innings before his knee had failed him—when the other team had its power batter warmed up and ready at the plate, but Beau had already given him two strikes. He only needed the third one.

Just one more.

Beau couldn't see Thompson but it wouldn't matter if he was there or not. The tunnel height was a little smaller than the height of a strike zone and Beau's eyes narrowed as he factored in the distance and the downward angle, the reality that he couldn't cock his arm properly. It didn't matter; he still believed he could do this.

Confidence.

He pulled the pin on the grenade and threw it on the

two-second mark. In his mind's eye it went in slow motion, although he knew that in reality his pitch was quite a bit slower than it had been in the old days. Even so, Beau's aim was dead on, and an instant later the entrance to the ground tunnel was obliterated.

Beau had time to whisper, "You're out," then the concussion from the blast literally rocked his world. He bounced around like a fishing bobbin on the surface of windy water, while all around him boulders of all sizes crashed down. Dean hauled him the last few feet and Beau lost count of how many times he got pelted with falling rock; he just knew that by the time the younger man dragged him over the edge and into the tunnel, he felt like he'd been beaten up. He wiped at the dust on his face and his glove came away bloody, so he probably looked like it, too.

Dean gave Beau's arm and knee a quick inspection. "It's not going to be fun, but we need to get out of here before this place comes down on our heads." As if to punctuate his words, there was an enormous smashing sound from the chamber; when they looked in that direction, all they saw was a thick flurry of dust swirling in their headlamp lights.

"Thompson," Beau began, but Dean held up a hand, then quickly crawled back toward the edge. Beau could just see that the previous incline was all but gone; now the ground simply stopped in a straight drop off. There were more dangerous-sounding groans from the chamber.

A couple of seconds later, Dean was back. "No way is he coming out of here," he said flatly. "If the grenade didn't do the job, there's not a clear spot on the ground anymore. It's filled with slabs of rock and twenty-five-foot boulders. He's buried." Dean looked past Beau, who turned and saw Sam sitting up a few feet away. He looked like crap but at least he was conscious. "We can go together, or I can go alone and bring back help."

"And take the chance that Floyd Collins's ghost is roaming around somewhere inside this cave?" Sam shook his head. "Not happening."

"Then we're back to doing it the way we did before," Beau said. "But this time Dean goes first, then Sam, then I'll follow." The three of them looked at each other, then Beau gave them a tired but determined grin. "It's gonna take a while," he said.

"But at least we'll get out of here with our skin still attached."

EPILOGUE

The white sheets made Beau Pyle look frail and pasty, but there was no denying the expression of happiness on his face when Cinnamon Ellison knocked lightly on the hospital room door. She came in carrying a covered plate and a purple balloon with "Get Well Soon!" printed on it.

"Hi," she said. "I brought you some cookies. Chocolate chip."

Dean, standing on the other side of Beau's bed, brightened visibly. "My favorite!"

"Every cookie is your favorite," Sam said from his spot on the extra chair, a pair of crutches within reach. Although his lower leg and ankle were heavily bandaged, he looked much better; there was color in his face and his eyes were clear. The wound on his leg had been cleaned, stitched, and bandaged, and he'd been given a transfusion to make up for the blood he'd lost and a couple of painkillers. It had been no big deal until a couple of male nurses had shown up in the emergency room and held him down so the doctor could dose the wound with rabies vaccine. Since none of them could identify or even describe the kind of animal that had clawed Sam—it had seemed best to go that route at the hospital in Bowling Green—and there was no way to guarantee it didn't carry the virus, Sam wasn't getting out of this shot… or the three more he'd have to endure. He'd also gotten a tetanus shot and was starting a hefty dose of antibiotics. Better that than foaming at the mouth and ultimately dying.

"So," Cinnamon said as she set the plate on the hospital tray and tied the balloon to the bed's footboard. "Surgery on that knee?"

Beau nodded. "First thing tomorrow morning. They swear they can fix it and I'll be good as new."

"Then maybe you'll want to get both of them done." She smiled.

Beau looked at her askance, then realized she was joking. "No, thanks."

She looked over at the Winchester brothers. "And you two?"

"All good," Dean said. His gaze was still being held by the plate.

Beau looked at Dean, then snickered. "Would you like a cookie, Dean? Maybe two?"

"Absolutely," he answered happily. He was already pulling off the plastic wrap.

Sam started to say something, then realized he couldn't remember the last time either of them had eaten. "Hey," he said. "I want one."

"Here," Dean said and tossed one at Sam's head. Sam

reached up and snagged it without a problem.

Cinnamon watched them with a look of amusement, then she looked back at Beau and her expression turned serious. "So what happens now, Beau? You realize you saved this town, right? If not for you, the disappearances—the deaths—would have just kept on happening. That's a big deal. You're a hero. Maybe folks in Brownsdale ought to know about it."

The old man's mouth turned down and he glanced at Sam and Dean. "As far as I know, this is the end of it," he said. "I don't want to hear any more about it, and I damned sure don't want anyone else to know the terrible details. No more talk about Brownsdale and its disappearing phenomenon. The creatures are trapped in the cave, so it's finally over and done with." He pulled his gaze away and stared down at the sheets. "I'm ashamed that I contributed to it all these years by saying nothing, just directing folks up there and telling them it was a good place to hike and explore." When he looked up again, his eyes were rimmed in red and a tear was making a slow, crooked track down one wrinkled cheek. "I swear I thought I was doing the right thing," he said, fighting to keep his voice from cracking. "I thought the mountain was a kind of… entity. A mountain god or something, and we had no choice. Now I know different."

"What about Sheriff Thompson?" Sam asked. "And his loyal group of deputies?"

Cinnamon glanced at him, then toward the ceiling. Her eyes glazed over for a moment, taking on that hazy, distant look she always had when she was seeing something they couldn't. "They'll find his car," she said softly, "but that's all."

She blinked and seemed to come back to herself. "I don't think the county attorney's office was happy with Edwardson County's track record."

Dean's face went momentarily stormy. "So Sloane will take his place?"

The psychic shook her head. "No. He doesn't have enough experience. The county attorney will appoint someone from another county to serve until the next election, then the people will decide." She smiled slightly. "You won't believe it, but we do have some sane people in this town."

Sam's mouth tightened. "What about Marley and Fallon Dietz's bodies? And Owen's?"

"They won't find them," Beau said. "They might try going the route we did, but they'll never be able to dig down to the first chamber. Even if they somehow did, my guess is that ground-level tunnel caved in—I'm telling you, I put that grenade right into the center of that opening." He was silent for a moment. "I gave that earring to the deputy I talked to, said I found it in the part of the cave we were in before it came down. I lied and told them you hadn't seen the boy, but that I was following Owen's trail and had gotten close enough to call out before the cave-in started." He inhaled deeply. "I said he'd gone into the tunnel and died with the sheriff. I wanted to clear up any notion that Thompson had spread about Owen doing something to his cousins."

Cinnamon shuddered. "That man was truly evil."

Beau touched her hand. "Well, he's gone now." He turned his head and regarded the Winchester brothers. "And what about y'all? Are you staying around?"

Sam shook his head at the same time Dean said, "Nope."

Dean reached for another cookie from the dwindling pile on the plate, then paused when Sam cleared his throat loudly. "How about leaving some for Beau?" Sam asked pointedly. Dean's hand wavered for a second, then he dropped it and had the good grace to look embarrassed.

Cinnamon laughed and pushed the plate closer to Dean, her smile making her bright blue eyes shine. "Don't worry, I'll be making more for him. Often."

Brownsdale was sixty-some miles behind them, and they'd been driving in silence for almost an hour, heading for I-64. Dean had a Big Cave Country Breakfast Sandwich in his stomach, which tended to make him a happy man, while Sam had enjoyed a nice, reasonably sized cheeseburger and fries. Finally, though, Dean had to ask: "Comments from the peanut gallery?"

Sam shrugged, then carefully repositioned his foot. "I don't know. I guess we did the best we could given the circumstances. I never came across anything in the research that talked about anyone actually seeing one of those creatures."

"No Kentucky Bigfoot?"

"If there is, the thing's not around Brownsdale and Beau never mentioned it." Sam rubbed at his forehead. "I'm… reasonably certain the trogs are trapped in there. They weren't intelligent enough for tools. Yeah, they had big freaking nails, but I don't think that's enough for them to dig through solid rock."

Dean glanced at him. "Even when they start to starve?"

"All we can do is hope, and keep an eye on the news reports. Maybe they'll eat each other into extinction. There's just no way to be sure."

"Hope." Dean stared straight ahead. "Right."

On Dean's arm, the Mark of Cain pulsed as a reminder, just once. He looked sideways at his younger brother, then focused his eyes back on the road. That long, never-ending road.

ACKNOWLEDGMENTS

Thanks to Becky Peacock and Natalie Laverick for editing help and great suggestions. And, of course, to my husband, Weston Ochse, who never runs out of ideas and "what if" scenarios.

ALSO AVAILABLE FROM TITAN BOOKS

SUPERNATURAL
WAR OF THE SONS
BY REBECCA DESSERTINE

Sam and Dean Winchester find themselves in a small town in South Dakota, on the hunt for Lucifer. There the brothers meet Don – an angel with a proposition… How far will they go to uncover the secret Satan never wanted them to find out? A Supernatural novel that reveals unseen secrets of the Winchester brothers.

SUPERNATURAL
HEART OF THE DRAGON
BY KEITH DECANDIDO

When renegade angel Castiel alerts Sam and Dean to a series of particularly brutal killings in San Francisco's Chinatown, they realize the Heart of the Dragon is back. John Winchester faced the terrifying spirit 20 years ago, and the Campbell family fought it 40 years ago–can the boys succeed where their parents and grandparents failed?

ALSO AVAILABLE FROM TITAN BOOKS

SUPERNATURAL
COYOTE'S KISS
BY CHRISTA FAUST

A truck full of illegal Mexican immigrants slaughtered with supernatural force is found by the side of a road. Trying to find answers, Sam and Dean are plunged into the dangerous world that exists along the Mexican border. Xochi Cazadoraa, a tattooed, pistol-packing bandita on a motorcycle who seems be everywhere they go before they get there, draws them into a whole new world of monsters...

SUPERNATURAL
NIGHT TERROR
BY JOHN PASSARELLA

Alerted to strange happenings in Clayton Falls, Colorado, Bobby sends Sam and Dean to check it out. A speeding car with no driver, a homeless man pursued by a massive Gila monster, a little boy attacked by uprooted trees—it all sounds like the stuff of nightmares. The brothers fight to survive a series of terrifying nighttimes, realizing that sometimes the nightmares don't go away—even when you're awake...

For more fantastic fiction, author events,
competitions, limited editions and more

VISIT OUR WEBSITE
titanbooks.com

LIKE US ON FACEBOOK
facebook.com/titanbooks

FOLLOW US ON TWITTER
@TitanBooks

EMAIL US
readerfeedback@titanemail.com